When her employer offers the no-nonsense Shannon Nadjiwon the position of chauffeuring Séamus Daugherty, she jumps at the chance. To work for one of Toronto's most powerful families means she can make her biggest dream of owning a fleet of limos come true, something her female relations tooling away at her Ojibway community want badly for her, and she won't let them down.

His reckless need for speed cost Séamus Daugherty his license. If he doesn't marry, as demanded by his overbearing father, he will lose not only his lucrative job with the family business—the only positive aspect in Séamus' gilded cage life—but everything Daugherty.

The unpretentious and gorgeous Shannon will make the perfect bride, and Séamus is ready to strike a deal with her, one that will ensure he keeps everything he holds dear if she puts a wedding ring on her finger. However, they face three big obstacles: His family, her family, and a marriage neither truly wants, leaving both wondering if the sizzling sexual chemistry and cozy rapport they share is enough to create a happily ever after.

His Proposition
Copyright © 2022 Maggie Blackbird
ISBN: 978-1-4874-3623-0
Cover art by Martine Jardin

Published by eXtasy Books Inc

Look for us online at:
www.eXtasybooks.com

HIS PROPOSITION

BY

MAGGIE BLACKBIRD

DEDICATION

For my mother, sisters, and nieces, five Anishinaabe-kweg who miraculously balance it all — love, family, and career.

Thank you to my husband and fur babies for their love, support, understanding, and patience.

Additional thanks to Emmy, my editor, Bri, my proofer, Jay, EIC, and Martine, my cover artist.

CHAPTER ONE: I CAN'T DRIVE FIFTY-FIVE

License. Suspended.

The letter stating Séamus' demerit point interview had met with a red light lay open on Father's credenza desk. Seated in the high-back chair was the very man who'd failed to pull a few strings with the judge for Séamus' right to keep driving his three European sports cars and SUV. That came as no big surprise. Father only greased the right palm for his firstborn, his pride and joy — Cillian.

For the impending summer, Séamus' most precious possessions would collect dust in the garage.

"It's for your own good." Father removed his reading glasses. He rubbed his brow, once a rich shade of red, now fading to gray. "I'd rather see you alive than dead."

"Have I ever been in an accident?" Séamus helped himself to the coffee one of the servants had earlier set on the small table between the two chairs before he'd been called to the study.

"No. However, you can only try your luck at the well for so long before the water runs out."

"Nice analogy." Séamus sipped the strong brew served the way Father liked his joe.

The double doors drew open. Normally, Father cast a dismissive look to anyone who dared to interrupt. Instead, his green eyes the shade of the rolling hills straight out of Ireland lit up. That meant the intruder was Cillian. Nobody else

1

within the walls of Daugherty Manor had the balls to displease the patriarch.

"Called to Father's carpet again, hmm?" Cillian poured the steaming brew from the sterling silver coffee set. He added a lump of sugar and a dash of milk.

Séamus glanced down at the Persian rug, Great-great-great-grandfather's first lavish purchase after making Daugherty Enterprises a success. "I think we're both a little old to receive a tongue-lashing. We're having a discussion."

Cillian, the striking image of Father from his bright-red hair to his stocky build, sank into the opposite chair. "Did you tell him about the driver?"

Naturally, the two had conferred before informing Séamus about their plan. Maybe coming up five years short of his elder brother was the reason why the duo enjoyed planning his life behind his back. He really had to get his own place. Perhaps downtown. Enough with adhering to tradition and living as a family like a nighttime soap opera on TV.

"I was just about to." Father cast his stern stare on Séamus. "You can use the Audi. Your driver will be here at eight-thirty sharp to retrieve you for the office."

"My driver? The Audi? I see." Séamus set his cup and saucer on his lap. "What's wrong with using one of my cars? It's spring. You know this is when I like to take one of them out."

"The Audi." Father's tone matched the slant of his eyes and downward turn of his thin lips.

There was no point in arguing. Mom was right about living in a gilded cage. Séamus stood and straightened his suit jacket. "Is there anything else?"

"Yes, but we can discuss it over dinner. It'll only be your mother and me."

"Taking your wife out for some five-star dining?" Séamus looked to his brother.

Cillian raised the fine china to his lips and glanced up

under his light-brown lashes. "You know Friday night is date night for us." He sipped.

A date decided by Cillian's wife, of course.

"Then I'll see you at the office." Séamus strode from the study straight into the grand entryway.

He'd find Mom in the sunroom where she liked to take her morning meal amongst the white wicker furniture, plentiful plants, and airy setting that overlooked one of the many flower gardens out back.

When he entered, Mom peeked up from her tablet. The remnants of eggs, toast, and fruit she hadn't finished remained on her plate.

"I'm sorry." Pity filled her emerald eyes.

"Sorry about what?" Séamus plucked a napkin from the setting and sat on the white cushion of the wicker chair.

"About his never-ending insistence on how you should live your life." The sun shone down on Mom's dark-brown hair with natural red highlights. Not a wrinkle was found on her heart-shaped face, thanks to the plastic surgeon who administered her Botox treatments.

A pity Mom believed she dare not age amongst their peerage. But that was the cost of being part of high society. "I lost my license. It's only proper they took it away. One too many speeding tickets. The judge warned me—"

"Séamus . . ." She lifted the tiny silver bell beside her and rang.

The maid breezed into the sunroom. "Will that be all, Mrs. Daugherty?"

"Please get some breakfast for—"

"You don't have to, Ellen. Coffee will suffice." Séamus tilted his head up at the maid who'd been with the family since his birth. "Other than that, I'm good to go."

"As you wish, Mr. Daugherty." Ellen poured his coffee. She cast him a sassy smirk. Her teasing smile just as quickly vanished.

Heaven forbid Father caught *the help* behaving as nothing more than robots. "Thank you." Séamus couldn't resist and patted Ellen's hand before she disappeared, holding Mom's plate, back into the kitchen.

"I understand why you speed. I understand why you sky-dive. Why you put your life at—"

"Mom, you say this every time Father's displeased. Don't worry about it. He is who he is." Séamus made sure the tension in his stomach didn't spill over into his reply.

"I know." She reached for her pack of cigarettes—one thing Father couldn't take from her. "I wanted to prepare you for the discussion over dinner tonight."

"Father did mention there's something else." Séamus rolled his foot in a circular motion. The stretching of his ankle muscle also helped relieve the knots in his shoulders.

"He's going to discuss marriage." Mom set aside her lighter and blew the smoke from her mouth.

Something resembling a knuckle hit Séamus' gut. "My marriage?" He set his hand on his chest. He was only twenty-nine.

Mom nodded.

"I suppose he has a few proper ladies to introduce me to already." This time, he couldn't hide the emotion dripping on his words.

"Not that I know of, but he will insist on the . . . *right* fiancée." She stood.

"Let me guess. Irish." Séamus held up one finger. "Catholic." He held up another finger. "A wealthy family from old money." He held up a third finger. "And the proper education." He held up the fourth finger.

"Those were the prerequisites Courtney had to meet before your father gave his blessing to Cillian." The deadness in Mom's tone matched the deadness forever in her eyes.

"I knew she met all four the first time he brought her for Sunday brunch," Séamus doled out. "Otherwise, she wouldn't have gotten through the front door."

"Your father expects no less from you . . ." Mom turned her attention to the wall of windows.

"I expected it." *But I won't listen.*

"When I was growing up, times were different." She sipped her coffee. "If I didn't marry, I was to be cut off." She shook her head. "Don't think for a minute I regret the marriage. If I hadn't married your father, I wouldn't have you."

She glanced over her shoulder. "All I want is for you to be happy."

Well, that was somewhat difficult with Father's iron fist forever banging on the desk.

"You know I didn't want you to attend boarding school either." Her eyes took on the glassiness of a still pond.

"Hey, I was home for holidays and the summer." Séamus stood. The time had come to practice chin up and shoulders back. "Don't blame yourself. It's not your fault Father is the way he is."

She touched his cheek. The warmth of her palm was the same soothing caress he'd experienced as a child, when she'd defied Father by foregoing a nanny and seeing to Séamus' care with tons of love and affection before he was sent away to St. Peter's College in grade six.

"I simply wanted to prepare you for tonight and what he'll say."

"I already know what he'll say. If I don't toe the line, he'll — he'll threaten me in the way Grandpa Cassidy threatened you into marriage." *But I'll figure out a way to stop him. That money belongs to me, especially after putting up with him for the past twenty-nine years.*

"Please . . ." Her hand dropped from his cheek. She shifted her gaze to the window. "I do love your father in my own way." Her eyes remained downturned.

Growing up, Séamus hadn't witnessed any affection between his parents. At least he took after his mother's personality and beauty-pageant-winning looks.

He pecked her cheek, even though a spark of a fire burned in his chest. But he wouldn't turn his anger on Mom. "I should get going. My new driver will be here soon."

"I'll see you tonight. Have a good day at the office." Her gaze continued to reflect loneliness, the same loneliness he'd witnessed for years.

"I will." So much for moving out and getting his own place. He couldn't leave Mom in the gilded cage to suffer, but he sure wasn't going to kotow to Father's ultimatum. Before five o'clock this evening, he'd figure out a way to keep his damned money, damned job, and damned life.

Instead of making the walk to the side door that led to the garage, Séamus used the main entry and stepped outside to sunshine and a blue sky that wasn't the least bit compatible with the thunderstorm sitting over his head. Not a hint of a breeze was present.

Parked in the circular cobblestone driveway was the Audi, a car only used for out-of-town business acquaintances for its rear seat comfort package.

The stunning woman standing by the passenger door swept away the gray cloud looming over Séamus' head. Well, well, well, this was very unlike Father. Shouldn't a stern codger of old-school manners be present instead?

His new driver's sleek body possessed the same smooth lines of the metallic-blue town car. Dressed in black from head to toe with a chauffeur's hat and matching leather gloves, she exuded a perfect posture stiffer than the surfboard Séamus caught waves on in Maui.

He slyly snuck a long look at the swell of her breasts pressing on the fabric of the jacket. Full lips painted the shade of poppy never moved into a smile but remained straight and plush. Red undertones lit her bronzed skin, and hair the color of the midnight-blue sky was plaited in a thick braid.

It was too bad sunglasses tinted with the shade of a moonless night hid her eyes.

She opened the back door and used her gloved hand to motion. "Good morning, Mr. Daugherty. I'm your driver," she said in a tone smoother than a glass of single malt whisky.

"Yes, I more than assumed so." Clutching his briefcase, and one hand in his pants pocket, Séamus swaggered to the car.

"Yes, your driver." Her luscious voice, capable of melting all over his skin, was as formal as her attire.

"Do you have a name?" He extended his hand. "Séamus Daugherty."

Her black eyebrows, shaped in a perfect arc, rose slightly above her black specs. She was probably surprised he'd asked her name. Most likely when she chauffeured clients, they didn't inquire about her personal life. Since they were going to spend six months together, for sure they would get to know each other.

"Shannon Nadjiwon at your service, Mr. Daugherty." She again extended her gloved hand to the car.

He grasped her long fingers hidden beneath the leather material and clutched them in a firm but gentle grip. "Nadjiwon. That's a pretty surname."

"It's Ojibway, sir." She tilted her oval-shaped face slightly, as if bowing to him.

"Sir?" He almost clucked his tongue, although the appendage in his mouth desired to be somewhere else. Such as, what did *her* tongue feel like? Oh, it was a wicked thought since he'd only just met her, but damn, she was a fine specimen of the female persuasion.

"Let's cut with the formality. You can call me Séamus, and

I will refer to you as Shannon. How's that?"

"Whatever you wish." She gestured at his briefcase. "May I?"

"I don't allow the house servants to wait on me like a king, and I don't expect my driver to cater to my every need. I'll put my briefcase in the car. Okay?" He reached inside the black leather interior. Already the business console was down, so he set the briefcase on top.

"There." He sank into the comfortable seat. "I'm all set."

She shut the door.

Her confident stride while rounding the Audi was the same posture she'd presented from earlier—shoulders back, chin lifted, arms moving stiffly at her sides like a true marching soldier. Not a wiggle came from her slim hips or va-va-voom slender thighs.

With the grace of a princess, she slid into the driver's seat. Her sunglasses appeared in the rearview mirror. "Where are we off to Mr.—Séamus."

"Work. Bay Street." He reached inside his briefcase for his tablet. Normally, he reviewed emails before arriving at the office, but business could wait. "One sixty-one. The TD Trust Tower."

"I'm aware of where you work. You have my gratitude, though, for the address." Her sunglasses were in the rearview mirror again.

My, my she was a polite one. Someone had trained her well. "You are quite prepared. How long have you been a driver?"

"Age twenty." She guided them down the exit driveway, passing the lush trees and flower gardens.

"Do you converse much with your other clients?" He ignored the vast grounds of green they passed.

She shook her head. Her gloved hand came up on the visor, and she pressed the control to open the gate.

"We do have servants' quarters. Perhaps you could reside in one." The offer flew from Séamus' mouth before he could consider why he'd made such a suggestion. Then he shrugged. Oh well, he could argue the point with Father, stressing the lack of a license required a driver for more than work.

"If you feel this is necessary, I can take up residence at your estate."

They were on The Bridle Path. There was the same scenery of boring trees and driveway entrances for those who could not afford the real estate to set their homes deep into their property. A pity.

The speed his new chauffeur kept, not slowing to glance around, indicated she'd studied this route already. Perhaps she'd even made the drive in her own vehicle.

A few moments later, she merged them onto Post Road.

"You navigate with such flourish," he called out from the back.

"It is my job to ensure you arrive on time for your job, Mr. —Séamus." Her sunglasses once again appeared in his view.

"Ah, so you studied the route, did you?" He cocked a brow.

"Of course."

"When did you study the area?" Hmm, she had a lovely scent going on. Not the overpowering perfume he sniffed amongst his peerage, but a fresh fragrance of soothing tranquility.

"Once my boss told me I was driving for you."

"I'm assuming my father contacted your boss, because I didn't find out until this morning." He should have brought along a travel mug of joe. "Do me a favor and stop somewhere so I can get a coffee."

"Yes, sir. Do you have a preference?" She steered them past

the many stately homes.

"Any place will do. A drive-thru is fine."

"How do you take your coffee?"

"It's okay. I'll order." They were on Bayview Avenue, officially making their way to downtown Toronto. There was a coffee place at the York University Glendon Campus where they could stop.

"Yes." Her head curtly bowed for a brief moment.

Every servant within the household, if Father wasn't around, addressed Séamus as a normal person, not the youngest son of one of the wealthiest men in Canada. He had to find a way to break the formality in her voice. "I told you already, I don't expect to be treated like a king. Talk to me."

"What would you like to talk about, sir?"

"And no using *sir*, either. Don't think I didn't catch that slip from earlier." A chuckle stirred in his chest.

This time when he gazed at the sunglasses reflecting back at him, they raised slightly on her high cheekbones, indicating there was a lovely smile directed at him.

"As for what I'd like to talk about. Let's start with you. I don't know anything about you other than you are my driver, Ojibway, and your name is Shannon."

"You wish to know who I am?"

"Yes. Everything." Bedding the servants had never entered his mind in the past, probably because Father would have had a fit and fired the poor girl. But there was something special about the lovely Shannon Nadjiwon. Something very special. Now he had to unearth why he'd classed her as such.

Chapter Two: Objects in the Rear-view Mirror May Appear Closer Than They Are

Shannon hit the turning signal and guided the Audi into the parking lot of the coffee shop. Speaking on a personal level was forbidden, one thing she'd learned from her boss the very morning she'd started working for Elite Limousines. Although sociable clients existed, to engage in more than idle chitchat was a no-no.

Anything could upset a client, even favoring the wrong basketball team. Speaking about the area's history, something she'd studied up on, was a safe conversation. "I understand your community was named for equestrian bridle paths in the early planning stages."

"Yes, so I've heard. I must admit I haven't really bothered to dig any deeper. I s'pose I should."

Asking Séamus *why* was out of the question. Yet it was rather strange he wouldn't take an interest in the history of his neighborhood. She stopped at the drive-thru board so he could order.

"What would you like?" he asked.

Even a simple question coming from his mouth was a nibble to the lobe of Shannon's ear and carried a hint of *m'dear*. Such sophistication. She flexed her thigh muscles, an automatic response to tense or uncomfortable situations. "Excuse me, sir?"

"Ah, ah, ah."

She glimpsed him waggling his index finger. His wide mouth formed into a teasing grin. His emerald-green eyes, what the grass of Ireland probably looked like, crinkled at the corners. "What did I say about formality?"

"Once again, what is your order, please?" The drive-thru attendant's query came through the intercom.

"One moment. I'm in the middle of speaking to my driver." Séamus' tone was dismissive, as if used to making someone wait. He settled his delicious gaze back on her.

His discourtesy to the attendant rolled off Shannon. She'd heard the same dismissing tone from past clients. The annoyed hiss coming from the intercom didn't escape her notice, though.

"You don't need to keep repeating my name. Now, I asked you what you'd like." Séamus reached into the breast pocket of his navy-blue designer suit that hugged his athletic body.

Which sport gave him such an attractive physique? When Shannon had arrived for work at eight this morning, she'd spied a swimming pool and tennis court on the grounds. "A medium double-double is fine. And thank you."

"Not a problem." Séamus waved his hand in a casual manner. He leaned on the console and spoke at the lowered window. Once he'd ordered, he settled his delicious gaze — naughtier than a schoolboy's — back on her.

Teeth clacking, Shannon pulled up past the drive-thru window so Séamus could pay for their coffees. Her phone was off, but wait until she got home after work and told her friends she'd be moving into the guest house for the duration of her job. For sure she'd receive a more than raving reference from Padraig Harrington the fourth. Her biggest dream was at her fingertips. Mom and Kokum would squeal.

Students, no doubt from the university, strutted from the coffee house and wiggled by in front of the Audi. The girls attempted to peer through the tinted windows and into the car.

"All set." Séamus leaned forward. His smooth hand appeared, clutching the coffee.

"Thank you." Shannon gently took the cup by the lid so nothing from either of them touched. She was his driver. Of course there'd been more-than-attractive clients previously in her limo for whom she'd maintained pure professionalism, even when the men had gotten flirtatious.

She set the cup in the holder and drove off.

"Tell me . . ." Séamus began.

She glanced at his reflection holding the cup to his rose-colored lips.

"Have you driven many celebrities?"

"Yes." They were in traffic. Her job was to get him to work the quickest way possible. Already, she'd checked her phone for road conditions. The Don Valley Parkway had a stalled vehicle congesting a lane, which was why she'd taken the Bayview Avenue route.

"Oh, who?" He was in the mirror again, eyes squinted with curiosity.

She couldn't tell him her thoughts were on driving, not their conversation, lest she insult him. "Many."

"Ah, you don't kiss and tell, so to speak?" He arched one elegant black brow.

"I would elaborate, but I'm endeavoring to get you to work safely and quickly." She used her most respectful tone.

"Training, hmm? They taught you both hands on the wheel and no distractions?"

Thank goodness the business console was in the middle of the back seat, or he might have scooted forward to lean in and talk. The last thing Shannon needed was his breath on her ear. "Yes. Your safety is my first order of business, along with your time."

"You do know why I require a driver, right?"

She nodded. "Your father informed my boss."

"Why didn't you tell me, then?" The curiosity she'd spied earlier in his eyes echoed in his question.

"It's not my place. Why I'm driving someone is their business. My job is to simply drive."

"I see. Is this something you always wanted to do?"

She refused to inform him about her former love for stock car racing and how she'd participated every weekend back home until her move to Toronto. "Let's say I enjoy being behind the wheel."

"Something tells me you're not giving me your full answer." His droll comment seemed more to himself. He tapped his index finger just below his diamond-cutting cheekbone. "Do you golf?"

"Golf?" She almost sputtered. A good swallow allowed her to maintain a formal composure. "No."

"Tennis?"

"No."

"Then what do you do in your spare time?"

Work? What else. Whenever the boss needed her, she was off to her limo. Living downtown wasn't cheap, which was why she shared a house with her two best friends. "The movies. Coffee. Shopping."

"Do you play any sports?"

Unless go-carting counted, no. "I haven't had the time."

"You're under contract with us for six months. And I do enjoy a round of golf. I'll set you up with quality clubs and your first lesson. The season is upon us."

"Oh, uh . . ." Was he serious? If not for her training, she would've craned her neck and gaped at him. "Lessons?"

"Yes, lessons while I golf. It beats sitting in the car waiting for me, doesn't it?"

"True." She'd become so used to waiting on clients, she kept her e-reader on hand, along with a ton of songs on her iPod that she refused to trade in for streaming music.

"What do you do while waiting on clients?"

Funny how they'd been thinking the same thing. "I read or listen to music."

"Read? Really? Which do you prefer — non-fiction or fiction?"

"I enjoy both."

"What are you reading right now?"

"Moon of the Crusted Snow."

"Oh? What's that about?"

"It's about a post-apocalyptic future when the power goes out at a northern *Anishinaabe* community and the impact it has on the people."

"What is *Anishinaabe*? I must confess I've never heard of that tribe before."

"*Anishinaabe* is what I am. Ojibway. It means First People."

"Ah, I see. Then what does Ojibway mean?"

"It's French for puckered moccasin people. The Indigenous People use different stitching to make moccasins. Our stitch allows for a puckered toe."

"Really?"

Again, she expected him to strain to lean over in the front seat.

"It's delightful to know you're well versed in your culture. The most I know about Ireland is that my great-great-great grandparents emigrated to Canada during the late nineteenth century, and he built Daugherty Enterprises."

That was strange. She flicked her gaze at the mirror. He was sipping his coffee and staring at the traffic. "You've never been to your motherland?"

"My motherland?" His laugh was on the dry side. "I consider Canada my motherland. It's my grandparents and father who consider themselves Irish. As for visiting, yes, I've been there. Trips are compulsory in the household." There

15

was a sneer in his answer. "Every two years we must visit the small community where they came from. As for the cottage, it fell to the elements before I was born."

How weird he didn't take pride in his roots. He was also rather an open book, tossing offhand personal information about himself.

"What about you? Do you know much about your culture?" His tone implied he was arching his slightly thick brow.

"Of course. It's a big part of who I am."

"You attend powwows then?"

"Yes."

"Do you dance at them?"

"No, but my friend does."

"Which friend? Does she reside here?"

"She's my roommate."

"You don't elaborate much, hmm? Such brusque answers. What does it take to get you to open your mouth more often? Torture?"

She'd best be honest. "If I'm driving, I'm used to the smallest of chitchat. My boss encourages us to maintain our distance. He said this is what makes a driver successful. Friendly, but not too friendly. And always professional."

"He's not your boss right now, is he?"

"Technically, yes. Your father contracted our services. My boss picked me. And your father approved of me to become your driver."

"Yes, my driver. You mentioned music. What do you listen to? Drake? Rhianna?"

Not a hint of embarrassment smothered Shannon as she proudly announced, "Gordon Lightfoot. Neil Diamond. Barry Manilow. Tom Jones."

"Uh . . . wh-who?"

The laugh sat in her throat and tickled her belly. Goodness,

16

for once Séamus was shocked and had lost his amused pretense. "You never heard of them? C'mon, you must've." Their conversation was reminiscent of sitting in the living room at her townhouse, poking fun at her friends. "They're singers. And quite good. My kokum listens to them. My mom worked full-time when I was a child, so I went to Kokum's after school. I'd dance to the music she played, well, after I ate my homemade blueberry jam sandwich."

"Kokum?" His question had an eye squint to it.

"Grandmother. But I call her Kokum."

"Ah, I see." A smile was in his voice. "I got you to finally break your formality. Blueberry jam, hmm?"

"I did lots with my kokum and mishoomis. Mishoomis is what I call my grandfather. Back home when I was growing up, berry season meant a lot to my grandparents. I went with them all the time. Same for tapping the maple trees."

"Really?" People still tap the trees?"

"They have to if they want maple sugar or syrup." She almost guffawed. "That's where your bottle comes from when you put it on your pancakes."

"Yes, but I assumed companies had people who did the harvesting."

"There are, but lots of Indigenous people prefer the traditional method of going into our tree stands in the bush and tapping the trees."

"Really?"

"The same for ricing. Where I come from, we're all about wild rice."

"Ah, I've had wild rice before. Rather delicious."

"But you've never had traditionally made rice. That is the only kind any girl from the rez eats. We'd never be caught eating the stuff sold in grocery stores. That crap's for soups and casseroles."

"Crap? There's a difference? Pray tell what it is."

"If you smelled a bag of traditionally made rice, I guarantee you'd never eat the stuff bought in stores, ever." Pride swelled in her chest.

"And what is the scent like?" His curiosity never stopped. He truly wasn't humoring her.

"The woods."

"Do you have any? Perhaps you could cook me a bowl to sample." This time, she knew he was teasing her.

"A bowl served with maple sugar? That's how my ancestors ate it, and how we still eat it." Shannon couldn't help her grin.

"What do you say, then?" This time he wasn't teasing. The flirtatious question coming from his mouth was something Shannon had heard in the past from other clients who'd propositioned her.

"I don't have any and won't until the fall. Ricing season, or *Manoominike-giizis*, as we call it, isn't until late August."

"A pity. I would have really loved to sample traditionally made rice.".

His disappointment was enticing enough to dare Shannon to offer a flirty rebuttal, but she swallowed the temptation on her tongue. At twenty-eight, she was pushing thirty, the deadline she'd given herself to finally own at least one limo. Plus, being a trust-fund baby who'd been given the position of Director of Marketing by his rich father, Séamus was no doubt like the other wealthy clients who enjoyed a *taste* of the help, but only a taste.

No roll in the hay was worth her dream. And there was something that sat wrong in her stomach at the thought of an office romance. Too unprofessional. She needed to earn the utmost praise from Séamus' father to secure future clients if her own private business was to succeed.

Shannon guided them off Bayview Avenue and merged them onto the Don Valley Parkway. Traffic was up to speed here, having avoided the single-lane jam. They'd be down-town in no time.

"Where do you reside, exactly?"

Shannon stiffened. She never gave out her place of resi-dence to clients. "Downtown."'

"Yes, but where exactly? Downtown's a big place."

Séamus didn't seem like the stalker or serial killer type. "King West Village."

"How do you manage? Living downtown isn't cheap."

Heat flooded Shannon's face. What a personal question. "I own a townhouse with two friends."

"A townhouse?" His eyebrows arched in the mirror. "You've done well for yourself. You and your friends. What do they do exactly?"

"One is an electrician, and the other is a tow truck driver."

"An electrician? A tow truck driver? Such interesting pro-fessions you and your friends have."

"The pay could be better. It's why we bought a house to-gether last year. We were tired of handing over cash for rent. And we wanted a pet."

"A pet. How quaint. What kind of pet?"

"Pets. We each have a cat."

"I see. Hmm . . . I guess you'll have to bring your cat to your new residence."

"I'd like to. Keemooch is aptly named, though. He's around five or six, the shelter told me. He still hasn't out-grown his kittenish behavior."

"What an interesting name. Is it Ojibway, too?"

"Yes. Keemooch means sly, full of trickery."

"Ah, I see. I look forward to meeting him."

Shannon stiffened. "You want to meet my cat?"

"Of course. We're going to spend a lot of time together. It's best we get to know one another. I have a very active business and social life. We'll be in this car an awful lot. I must say, you are a true pro."

She stole a peek at him glancing at his watch, no doubt worth ten grand.

"Excellent timing, Shannon."

She had turned off onto Bay Street, where a mecca of sky-scrapers welcomed them to the downtown core of business and prestige.

"You got me here faster than I normally do."

She pulled over in front of the TD Trust Tower. Just as she was about to throw the car into park and vacate the vehicle, his words stopped her.

"No need to attend me. I'm perfectly capable of opening my own door. You can fetch me at five o'clock sharp. While I'm here, you can spend the day moving your belongings to the guest house. I'll call ahead and tell Ellen to expect you. She's our housekeeper." With that, he bounded out of the vehicle, designer sunglasses on and all. His briefcase swung in rhythm with his confident stride.

Shannon had been given orders. She would return to the townhouse, call her friends at their workplaces to let them know of her new accommodations for the next six months, and then begin packing.

Chapter Three: Turn the Page

Since nobody was home, and although it wasn't Shannon's turn to park inside the one and only garage stall until next week—for easier loading of her belongings—she pulled the Audi into the bare parking space. By the time Ronnie and Pashney returned from work, Shannon would be gone. But she'd call tonight and inform them of the great news.

She vacated the car and entered the ground floor, where the washer and dryer, upright freezer, and other items they stored were kept. Her luggage was in the main closet. If she was staying for six months, she'd need all her clothes.

Townhouses were convenient, but the caveat was the numerous stairs she had to climb. At least the suitcases fit within one another, so all she had to do was lug the big one up three flights, which didn't prove too shabby, since the wheels on the bottom helped. She huffed past the main level.

They took turns once a week cleaning. Hopefully she wasn't expected to play maid on her scheduled time to tackle the kitchen, dining area, and living room, plus the bathroom she shared with Pashney. Ronnie had won the coin toss and had claimed the master suite.

Lungs almost bursting from the mighty jaunt, and to still her breathing, having reached the top floor, Shannon pressed her hand on the doorframe to her bedroom.

Footsteps pounded below her.

"Shan, I know you parked in the garage. That's your Fifth Avenue ride, isn't it?" Pashney called out in her voice grittier than dirt and stronger than Mike Tyson. "Move it or I'm gonna hook it to my truck and leave it in the street."

Shannon's shoulders slumped. Didn't Pashney have some-one else to tow? "I'm only gonna be an hour. I need to pack. That's why I'm home already."

"Pack? Pack for what?" Running shoes squeaked on the stairs. From the quick pounding of Pashney's rubber soles on every step, she was racing up each flight, probably to bite off Shannon's head.

"Mr. Daugherty asked me to stay in the guest house while I'm driving him." Shannon unzipped the big suitcase. She withdrew the other luggage and placed them on the floor.

Pashney stomped into the small hallway. She set her hands on her hips. Baseball cap turned backward to hide her buzz cut, not a stitch of makeup on her bronzed face, taut muscles flexing beneath her snug, black t-shirt, and her square jawline set tight, she was a burglar ready to pounce.

Keemooch watched from the bed. He flicked his gray tail.

"What do you mean *move in?*" Pashney's dark eyes nar-rowed.

"I'm his driver for six months. He expects me to be at his disposal. How can I do that when I'm downtown and he's in North York?" Shannon blinked. For crying out loud, Pashney was forever making a big deal out of anything.

"What about the mortgage payment? What about the cleaning schedule?" Pashney folded her arms. The stern look she cast was a prelude to an argument.

Shannon shut her suitcase. "I'll keep making my share of the payment, but I can't clean if I'm not here."

"We make decisions as a threesome." Pashney held up three fingers. "You can't up and break the rules because Mr. Rich and Snotty says so."

"I'm gonna be doing more than driving him to work." Shannon couldn't divulge that Séamus' license was sus-pended. That went against client and driver privilege. "I'm gonna be on call twenty-four hours a day, seven days a week."

Pashney unfolded her arms and leaned on the doorframe.

The tension in Shannon's chest relaxed. This meant her dear friend wasn't going to lace up her boxing gloves. Instead, she'd throw upper cuts at some sorry partner at the gym. "I don't like leaving you guys high and dry, but this is my big chance. If I can get the elder Mr. Daugherty as a reference, I am *this close* to buying my own town car." She held up her hand, index finger and thumb almost pressed together.

"I get it. I do." Pashney's permanent scowl vanished. Her upper lip bordered on turning upward into a rare smile.

"His father's one of the richest men in the country. His stamp of approval is going to help me . . ." Shannon reflipped open the suitcase. "I might finally reach my dream if I ace this job."

Pashney shoved her finger in Shannon's direction.

Shannon took a step back. Everything was supposed to be cool between them, and finger-pointing in the world of the *Anishinaabe* was considered rude, so everyone used their lips to point.

"I'll let it pass because we're talking about your dream. I'll tell Ronnie when she gets home." Pashney lowered her finger and swiveled on her heel. She marched from the room.

A film of delight spread across Shannon's chest. Her friends were going to let her renege on her cleaning responsibilities, which meant double the work for the girls. She almost high-fived herself because her besties were going to support her on this venture.

She scooped Keemooch off the bed and lifted him high in the air. He yowled, all four legs stiffening harder than cement. "We're going. We're going, and soon your momma's gonna have her own biz."

She spun in a circle, giggling.

Keemooch yowled, producing his claws.

She stopped cold. "Easy. Easy." She petted his soft fur. "I'm happy. Don't you wanna be happy with your momma?"

The look Keemooch cast was a cat welcoming the neighborhood's peskiest dog.

She kissed him on the top of his furry head. "You'll understand in due time." She returned him to the bed.

Wait until she told Mom and Kokum. The two most important women in her life would be proud. She was living their dream, doing what they'd only wished on a star about.

"I never let you down," she whispered, as if Mom could hear her in the bedroom. "Tell Kokum this dream is for all three of us."

Keemooch yowled.

Shannon swiveled. If her two dearest friends were handing her their blessing, she wasn't going to let anything screw it up—especially Séamus Daugherty, no matter if he had the most gorgeous emerald-green eyes flecked with ultra-long black lashes and the most perfect arch to his black eyebrows, or the most dazzling smile that could charm the panties off a woman.

Oh hell, his physique alone could coerce a girl to unzip the back of her dress. Strong shoulders, not big and broad, but the right touch for a woman to lay her head on. Firm thighs, not pumped like at a gym, but the right amount of muscle for a girl to stroke. He probably had some nice leg hair going on, too. Silky, even. Enticing enough to trace with her finger.

Shit, she was in trouble, big trouble. Putting him from her thoughts was her top priority, but that was impossible if she was going to live at his place and drive Mr. Chatty around for six months.

"Are you going to disclose the vital stats on the hottie who dropped you off this morning?" Holding a cup of coffee, Ethan swaggered into the office, sandy-blond hair slicked back and ultra-white veneers on display.

Leave it to Séamus' best friend and co-worker to always bring statistics into the conversation. Being the business analyst for Daugherty Enterprises, of course Ethan spoke and thought in terms of acquired or soon-to-be acquired data to assess.

"She's my driver, nothing more." Séamus shoved away his laptop.

"Hey, if you don't sample the domestics, you can't analyze whether they'll be effective at their duties or not." Ethan threw back his head and chuckled. He plopped in the chair opposite the desk in front of the big window.

"I'm aware what you do each time you hire a new cleaner for your place." Séamus picked the mug off the desk and sipped the hot brew. Naturally, Ethan's father didn't care if his son had been enjoying bedroom romps with the staff ever since he'd turned eighteen. Ethan's father did the same thing and wasn't an overbearing ass.

"Talk to me, bud." Ethan set his Italian leather shoes on the desk and crossed his legs at the ankles. "You passed on clubbing tonight, and I caught you staring at your laptop instead of working. What's piloting around your head? What'd your ol' man do this time?"

Séamus might as well fess up the truth. Ethan wouldn't relent until he got the scoop. "Father's requesting a special dinner tonight."

"Ah, how lovely. Just what you enjoy — another order from the tyrant." Ethan glanced beyond Séamus' shoulder. "I think it's time you —"

"And have him cut me off?" Séamus snorted. He'd be renting a room at the local Motel Six.

"He's been threatening to disinherit you since elementary

school." Ethan moved his mug back and forth in a *cheers* sort of manner. "I'd say it's time you called his bluff."

Séamus set aside his coffee that no longer smelled of fresh roasted beans but resembled day-old garbage. "And lose my job?"

"You can always find another." Ethan sipped.

"You know what this job means to me. And if I leave, he'll have me blacklisted. He'll smear my name."

"Oh, c'mon. Disinheriting is one thing. But outright sabotaging his own flesh and blood's career?"

"Maybe I'm not his flesh and blood and that's why he's always had it out for me?"

Ethan's blue eyes widened. "Don't talk nonsense. You're his flesh and blood. I can hardly see your mother stepping out on your ol' man. She's too classy a lady."

True, if anything, Mom's upbringing demanded the ultimate elegance and refinement. She'd never have an affair on Father, no matter how miserable he'd made her life. "I s'pose I'm not the product of the gardener. Mind you, Sam does a fine job." Séamus winked.

"There we go. Chin up." Ethan's eyes brightened. "There's always a way out of a hopeless situation. If he orders you to marry, go ahead and marry. Marry someone before the dinner takes place." The roar of his chuckle said he was simply jesting.

A lightbulb went off inside Séamus' brain, almost blinding his li'l thinker. He tapped his finger on his mouth. As the director of marketing, he should've devised such a scheme. If he married before the dinner happened, Father could not expound the requirements for a potential bride, because once the dinner occurred, his future fiancée would have to meet the same prerequisites that Cillian's wife had met.

First, he had to buy some time—such as jetting off in the private plane to a destination far from Toronto, and then convince . . . yes, convince the stunning Shannon Nadjiwon to marry him. She'd be a perfect bride. A woman with her own job, goals, and life. A woman not impressed by wealth.

He'd bring her with him, put forth his proposition, and see if she'd buy. His game was marketing, after all, and he knew how to sell anything with his persuasive tongue.

Shannon zipped the last suitcase shut. She was almost set. "Okay, time to pack you up." She scratched Keemooch under his furry chin. "Let me get your stuff." That meant another trip to the ground floor.

Her cell phone rang. Not her personal one, but her work phone. Either the boss was calling, or her new client. She quickly hit the green button. "Shannon Nadjiwon speaking."

"There's been a change of plans," Séamus said in his dry tone of rich boredom that was becoming familiar to Shannon's ear.

Changes in plans were par for the course. This wasn't the first time Shannon had to act fast. "Where do you need me, Mr. — I mean, Séamus?"

"First, have you packed your belongings?"

"I finished up. I'm seeing to my cat now. Once I have his possessions ready, I'll be on my way to your home." Shannon ensured to keep her words formal.

"Good. Good. Once you've settled your suitcases at the guest house, I'll have Ellen unpack everything and see to your cat, because I'll need you to retrieve me at the office. I'm going away for the weekend."

"As you wish . . ." Shannon brightened. This would give her time to make herself at home in the guest house, but his order of having the maid unpack her stuff and care for Keemooch was on the strange side.

"I'll need you to accompany me, since I'll require a driver."

"Oh . . ." Keemooch would be left alone, frightened in his new home without her to help him adjust. But she couldn't tell Séamus no. This was her job. "As you wish."

"Ta ta for now."

The line went dead.

Shannon shoved the cell phone back into her jacket pocket.

Pashney lounged in the doorway again. "What's up?"

"He wants me to drop everything off at the guest house and then go and get him at the office. I guess we're going away for the weekend." A tinge of discomfort settled in Shannon's chest. She wasn't sure if the tightening around her breasts came from abandoning Keemooch during his hour of need or spending forty-eight hours glued to Séamus' side.

Shannon pulled the Audi into the garage. From the back seat, Keemooch meowed in protest.

"I'm sorry, but I have no choice. This job keeps you in food, litter, and toys." She switched off the car.

Keemooch meowed again.

Her heart shriveled to the size of Keemooch's favorite treat that required her to merely shake the can and the cat was running for his snack. "I'm sorry."

She got out and rounded the car. Keemooch withdrew to the back of his carrier. "You're a smart guy. Of course you know something's up." She grabbed the handle.

With Keemooch still protesting, she left the garage where the fleet of cars were kept. She couldn't help giving the Porsche a quick once-over. Nice ride. No doubt her sexy client was the owner of the powerful sports car.

The brick path led to the back entrance, where a lanai offered respite from the sun on a hot day. The area was set up formally, inviting one to sit in the plush outdoor chairs and fan themselves beneath the table umbrella.

A woman with salt-and-pepper hair opened and shut the

back door. "Good morning. I have your accommodations ready. Mr. Daugherty asked me to show you to your quarters and get you unpacked."

"Thank you. My suitcases are in the—"

"No need to retrieve them. I'll have Rollins see to your luggage. He's Mrs. Daugherty's driver. Come." The woman beckoned with her hand, indicating for Shannon to follow her on the path past the pool area to where three cottages were located.

"This is where some of the servants stay. Rollins lives above the garage, and the butler lives inside the manor. You have cottage number two." The woman held a key.

"I'm Shannon Nadjiwon." Shannon cleared her throat.

"I'm already aware of your name. Ellen Mayberry. It's good to meet you." Ellen waddled to a home that matched the other two cottages with real brickwork and shuttered windows straight from the tale of *Little Red Riding Hood*.

"The lodgings aren't large, but more than adequate." Ellen opened the door.

Shannon followed her inside to the scent of fine linen hanging on a laundry line, reminiscent of Kokum and Mishoomis' backyard aroma.

She was in the small living area done up in comfortable wicker furniture and an adjoining eat-in kitchen.

"You have the basics here. A kitchen, front room, bedroom, and bathroom. Your laundry is done inside the main house. As for cleaning, Missy will see to it." Ellen motioned at the bedroom. "My objective is to have you ready for Mr. Daugherty. He doesn't approve of tardiness and loathes waiting."

"I won't give him a reason to wait." Shannon straightened her shoulders. "I am his driver, and his needs come first."

Delight shone in the older women's gray eyes. "Now I see why the elder Mr. Daugherty chose you."

Shannon wouldn't correct the housekeeper that her boss

had chosen her, not Séamus' father, but the elder Daugherty did have the final say in her boss' recommendation and approved of her for some strange reason. Why, she wasn't sure. If anything, she'd assumed Charlie would've gotten this luxurious position because he'd been with the fleet for over twenty-five years and embodied everything people assumed a personal driver should be.

Maybe in due time she'd find out, or she could cough up the courage at the end of her contract, since she already planned on pleading for the elder Daugherty's reference once he witnessed the fabulous and professional job she'd done driving his son around.

CHAPTER FOUR: THIS FLIGHT TONIGHT

A flight attendant waited on one side of the open plane door. Four steps led up into the interior of the private jet, capable of accommodating nine passengers. They were at Billy Bishop Airport, where the Daugherty's craft was stored. During their drive to the island, Séamus had been unusually quiet for such a chatty man, other than supplying Shannon with information about the plane. Furthermore, his silence had aroused her suspicion, and it prickled at the back of her neck.

As the driver, she should be overseeing the luggage, but a man had come out from the hangar and had begun rifling through the Audi's trunk.

"This way." Séamus extended his hand. "Have you flown before?"

Shannon nodded. "Yes . . . but not on a private plane."

"Jet, not plane." Séamus indicated for Shannon to go first.

Here went nothing. She edged her way to the four stairs and put her foot on the first step. The scent of fresh leather wafted from the interior. When she entered, pure luxury enveloped her. No wonder she'd smelled leather, because the fabric was everywhere. A rich beige color invited her to sink into the lavish seats, but she stood at attention, not daring to sit.

Séamus popped in behind her. "I allowed you in before me so you could have first choice. Take your pick." The *droll* was back in his voice.

"My apologies, but I'm used to taking orders. This'll be a

hard habit to break." A tinge of heat flecked Shannon's ears.

"I see . . ." Séamus plopped in the first seat hidden behind the partition. He swiveled the chair back and forth. "Join me." He pointed at the chair opposite him.

Shannon sank into the fine material. The fabric swallowed her, reminiscent of being wrapped tight as a baby in a cotton blanket.

"The seat suits you." Séamus' elbow rested on the wide armrest. His index finger was set on his slightly broad chin. He possessed the same look Keemooch did when the cat was about to purr. "This is the first time I've witnessed you content."

"Maybe because I feel like I did as a child."

"Really?" He crossed one leg over the other, still wearing the same suit from this morning. "Tell me."

"In the old days, we used cradleboards, but Mom, being from a newer generation, didn't. She kept with tradition, though, and wrapped us tight in our blankets."

"Our? You have siblings then?" He arched his brow, something he did quite often if curious, Shannon noted.

"A brother and sister."

"Older? Younger?" He bared his gleaming white teeth, a smile Shannon hadn't caught a peek at this morning because he'd kept his lips sealed.

This man's curiosity never ceased. She'd better get used to playing twenty questions all weekend. "Older. My sister. Brother. Then me."

"May I ask something else?"

He'd been asking all day. "Sure."

The redheaded flight attendant approached them. "Everything's ready. After take-off, I'll see to getting you your drink."

"My driver, too." Séamus rested his attention on Shannon. "What would you like?"

Shannon shook her head. "I'll be behind the wheel once we land. No alcohol for me."

"A soda, perhaps?"

"A cola. Please." She gazed at the attendant.

"Of course." The attendant's tone was a smidgen cooler. She pivoted and strode to the back of the plane.

Shannon wasn't surprised she'd received the nose-in-the-air treatment. She was a minion just like the attendant, nothing more than a duffel bag accompanying the five-star luggage.

"Were your accommodations adequate?" Séamus kept the chair swiveled.

Thank goodness the aisle allowed enough room so their knees didn't touch. "Very adequate." Shannon glanced toward the cockpit, where noise came from. Perhaps the pilot or pilots had come on board, or maybe they'd always been present. She wasn't sure because of the partition.

The intercom dinged. A male voice announced their departure.

"I guess we'd best buckle up." Séamus' long fingers grasped each end of his seatbelt. There was grace to the way he secured himself in the chair, an easy movement likened to running a feather up and down Shannon's skin.

Chill-filled tingles spread across her flesh. She fumbled for the buckles. The engine had started. She'd best fasten her seatbelt, because they'd be taxiing quickly. Of course, it was improper to ask where they were going. As for appropriate clothing, she'd passed and had only packed casual wear for inside the hotel room and a spare uniform for taking Séamus to his social destinations.

From beneath her lashes, she stole a peek at him carefully watching her with the same scrutiny as Mishoomis when he was hunting and had sighted a deer in the scope of his rifle. Right about now she could use a cola, because her mouth was beginning to morph into a desert.

"So tell me, who was your most famous client?" He kept his legs crossed and rolled his ankle in a circular movement.

A trickle of warmth spread across Shannon's ears. "I can't disclose who our clients are."

"I see . . . can I at least ask if the person was a *he* or a *she?*" He possessed boyish dimples that contrasted with his full-of-amusement attitude.

She should have noticed those sexy indents on his face before. Then again, she'd been intent on proving her worthiness this morning. "A *he.*"

"Oh?" He cocked one black brow. His elbow remained on the armrest. "I'm presuming your beauty didn't escape his notice."

Beauty? If her ears got any hotter, she might as well sit in the sweat lodge in the backyard of Mishoomis and Kokum's house. She didn't mean to clear her throat, either, but the bothersome little niggle hovering in her windpipe had appeared out of nowhere.

Even worse, a clearing of the throat informed him she was not at ease. Nor was she about to admit to him or herself that his lazy gaze skimming her legs, stroking her thighs, breezing up her stomach, walking slowly past her breasts, and then settling on her face, was enough to make anyone reach for a strong drink.

Her nerves were wide awake, poking her on the shoulder while loudly screaming at her that his curiosity stemmed from more than mere nosiness — rather, pure physical attraction. The undercurrent between them was his throbbing, hard cock readying to fuck her wet and willing pussy.

The humming of the plane's engine taxiing down the runway was the right kind of distraction she needed. Instead of holding Séamus' steady gaze, she focused beyond his kissable strong shoulder to the outside full of nothing but pavement.

Well, they were at an airport. What had she expected?

This was when she'd kill to have Godzilla and King Kong slugging it out on the runway, anything to interrupt her racing thoughts.

Séamus turned his head ever so slightly and glanced over his shoulder. "Yes. Hmm . . . very interesting." He rested his attention back on her like he was laying his palm on her knee. "I do admire the color black, too."

Okay, not only were Shannon's ears hot, but her face had also caught fire. She was an accelerant ready to ignite the plane's fuel tanks and burn up the damned private jet before they even hit the air.

His laugh was more of an elegant chortle. He kept annoyingly rolling his ankle in a circle. "You never did answer my previous question."

"Qu-question?" She dug her nails into the armrests and straightened her back.

" . . . if this famous *he* took note of your beauty."

The urge to lick her lips surfaced, but she pretty much stomped it down with the heel of her boot.

"Mmmhmm." Séamus set the tip of his index finger where his dimple should be. "He propositioned you, didn't he?"

She dug her nails farther into the upholstery. If this was some sort of loyalty test, he was dead wrong in assuming she'd fail. "It doesn't matter if a client propositions me or not. The fact is, I remain professional with everyone who contracts the services of Elite Limousines. It's why your father approved of me, did he not?"

At the mention of his dad's name, Séamus' black brows furrowed. He clucked his tongue. "I'm not sure why he approved of you. Honestly, I was expecting . . ." he moved his hand up and down. " . . . someone of the male persuasion, and much older."

It was her turn for curiosity to pique her interest. First,

Séamus had shown no interest in his lineage or history. Now, the mention of his father had produced a black cloud above his head. She'd assumed wrong about his life being one of extreme boredom or extreme excitement. Maybe there was more to him than his cushy job, cushy life, and cushy trust fund.

Wait, she was treading into dangerous territory if she looked beyond her first assumption of a spoiled rich man who had nothing better to do but quiz *the help* to satisfy his morbid curiosity.

Bright blue appeared in the window behind him, reaffirming they were high in the sky, heading for a place he'd yet to inform her about.

Again, Séamus glanced over his shoulder. "Interesting view? All blue this time instead of black?"

Fine, she'd fire out the question burning her tongue. "Are you always this chatty with *the help*?"

The amusement died in his eyes. He uncrossed his legs, pushed back his shoulders, and set both feet on the floor. The stare he pinned on her was Mishoomis readying to spank her bottom for daring to break into his storage room where he kept the furs he trapped with a *No-no. That's Mishoomis' money.*

Dammit, never in her life had she'd pissed off anyone she'd driven.

"You are not *the help*. Understood?" Séamus lifted his hand to take the offered drink the flight attendant held. He tilted the glass and sipped. "One of my closest friends is a woman I completely respect, and she *helped* my mother raise me."

Shannon had to stifle the gasp sitting at the back of her throat. "I see . . ."

The flight attendant had perfect timing, because her arrival with the soda gave Shannon something to do. She grasped the cola and used both hands to clutch the glass. "Thank you."

Séamus' eyes moved to the side. The signal was clear. He was asking the attendant to take her place at the back of the plane. At least he hadn't given the woman a cold look. From the quick retreat of the attendant, this wasn't her first rodeo of becoming invisible. So how many women had Séamus charmed on his daddy's fancy jet?

"What's your favorite drink?" There he was with his questions again.

"I don't drink often." Shannon continued to grip the cola.

"Really?" He studied her.

"I do a lot of driving. I need all my senses working."

"Ah, here we go. Those short, sweet answers." He chuckled. "Humor me and elaborate."

"I told you. I need all my senses. I'm responsible for driving people. I can't afford to be . . . well . . ." Her cheeks burned from having to use slang in the company of a client. "Hungover."

He threw back his head. His laugh was delicious and unleashed the same fizzle on her throat as the drink she held.

"There's nothing wrong with saying hungover." His elegant chuckle died. He resumed rolling his ankle. "You won't offend me."

Her mind stumbled for a reply, but she'd hit a kink in the sidewalk and tripped. "Err . . . thank you."

"Ah, Shannon, what am I going to do with you?" He tilted the glass and sipped but continued to gaze at her beneath his lashes.

"I don't understand."

"I keep asking you to relax. You may be my driver, but I don't see you as a servant. Or *the help*. I don't see anyone who works for my father in that light." Now it seemed he was chiding her. "Since you don't have many opportunities to indulge, I insist you have a drink. Orders from your boss, since you perceive me that way."

"I can't. When the plane lands—"

"I'll have a limo retrieve us," he finished. The sternness in his order said there'd be no further discussion on the matter.

"A limo?" She stifled her sputter. As his driver, she couldn't argue. But the sinking of her stomach reaffirmed she'd done something wrong if he didn't require her services. If his father learned Séamus had put her on standby, she probably wouldn't get a recommendation from Padraig Daugherty if his son was dissatisfied.

"Don't look so alarmed." He angled his head slightly to the left. "I simply want to give you an evening off to enjoy yourself."

"Oh . . ." Immediately, the knots in her stomach uncoiled, and her shattered future became a reality she could reach for once again. Nobody who'd contracted her services had gone out of their way to take her feelings into consideration before. "Well . . . thank you."

"Now what would you like from the bar?" He gestured toward the back of the plane.

"Some rum for my cola?" She held up the glass.

"Ask and you shall receive." His dimples appeared. "A rum and cola for Shannon, if you please, Tonya."

Although danger didn't ooze from Séamus, and his handsome looks didn't lean toward daringly devilish, he was somehow capable of producing a red siren of warning in Shannon's head. Maybe it was his charm and natural affability that made him a true competitor to peel off the panties protecting what lay between her thighs from such succulent fingers.

The smile on the attendant's lips never reached her hazel eyes.

"Thank you." As Shannon touched the glass, her hand shook. She silently cursed her pathetic body for betraying her nervousness.

"What are your plans after you finish driving me everywhere?"

Shannon wasn't about to tell Séamus her plan. "I'm sure my boss will have something lined up for me."

"You sure are full of mystery . . ." His words were a murmur. He swirled the contents in his glass.

"There's nothing mysterious about me. I'm simply a girl from the rez trying to build a life for myself." The rum on Shannon's tongue was pure silk and delicious. She could only imagine how much the liquor had cost. Someone of Padraig Harrington's caliber wouldn't send the servants to purchase a bottle off the shelf at the local LCBO.

"This is very good." She raised her drink.

"Nothing but the best for my father." Séamus' ankle continued to roll in a circle, which should have indicated he was relaxed, but the narrowing of his brows said otherwise.

Shannon wasn't about to ask if dad and son were close, or if the two were at war. Séamus' family life wasn't any of her business.

"Talk to me." His smile resembled a mischievous boy up to no good.

She could almost see the horns sprouting from his head.

"I was hoping the rum might relax you some," he added.

His constant request of asking her to loosen her tongue rattled Shannon's nerves. She set the drink on her lap. "I'm your driver. What would you like me to say?"

"Say anything . . ." He drank the last of the liquor in his glass. "I'm serious. Off the record. Whatever you say shall stay between the two of us."

She couldn't resist teasing him. "You hope to get me intoxicated so I'll loosen my tongue?"

"Why not? I'm betting you know everything about me. Fair is fair. If you're as good as I think you are, I have a hunch you studied up on my family. You did study my work route, did you not?"

Wow, talk about perceptive. She shifted. "I'll be honest.

Okay?"

He nodded.

"The driver-and-client bond is one of respect. This is what helps my boss and me succeed in our field. Aren't you the same way with people who work under you?"

"Work *under* me?" There was a slight chuckle to his reply.

Oh God, she hadn't meant to slide in a sexual innuendo that of course he'd caught right away. Why couldn't the weekend be over already? By Sunday, he might end up sneaking her life story from her bit by bit with his constant persistence, blowing every ounce of professionalism that was slowly leaking through her grasp.

CHAPTER FIVE: DRIVE MY CAR

They would land in fifteen minutes, so Séamus refastened his seatbelt. He had to admit Shannon Nadjiwon was an expert at playing possum. So evasive. But they'd shared two drinks. By the time they got into the limo, the rum should kick in. Maybe he was the one who needed more booze, since he was about to ask a stranger to marry him.

Leave it to Father to have control over his life from almost four thousand kilometers away, but this time the old man had no say in whom Séamus wedded. Not that he had much choice. Evading the family dinner before being given the strict rules for which single lady he should put a ring on did unclench his stomach muscles, because satisfaction was patting his smugness.

Oh, Father, you'll never know what you brought upon yourself. He almost laughed but did his best to keep a straight face. And he'd better get down to business by initiating phase one. "Have you ever thought of marrying?"

His question must've shocked Shannon. She spit out the drink in a very unladylike manner.

Tonya raced over, napkin on hand.

Shannon waved the attendant away, using her finger to motion at the drink while shaking her head back and forth. Her mouth was clamped shut, but remnants of the drink dribbled down the front of her driver's uniform. "I'm fine," she sputtered.

Tonya glanced to Séamus. He used his eyes to motion to the back. She turned on her heel and left.

"Everything okay?"

"Oh, uh, yes." Shannon set the drink on the table beside her. "Uh, well, your question took me off guard."

"It did? Why?" There was something rather amusing about peeling away the layers of professionalism wrapped tight around Shannon's lovely lithe body.

"I never had anyone ask me such a personal question before." A hint of red colored her strong cheekbones. Cheekbones reflecting her heritage. Truly, she was a beauty.

Of course, he must inquire about her personal side to unearth her Achilles heel, because that would clinch marriage for him. Women of this era didn't need to wed like Mom had. They only committed if they desired to claim a life partner for themselves, whether it be for love, sex, or money. For Shannon, being so devoted to her career, he had to dig deep for her true goals.

"It was a simple question. Nothing more."

"And you? Do you wish to marry?" Her head was tilted, which meant she wasn't being coy by answering a question with a question. No doubt she found the topic baffling.

He flicked a piece of lint from his trousers. *I have no choice now unless I wish to become blackballed and lose my inheritance.* "It's expected of me."

She squinted. He'd witnessed her giving him the *something's up* look a couple of times. Maybe she was catching on to the dislike he held for Father, and the predicament he found himself in now.

As a driver, she was most likely perceptive if she had to anticipate her clients' needs to succeed in her career. And she was successful if her boss had chosen Shannon to drive for Father, which was why she'd refused to let down her guard no matter how much cajoling he'd used.

They'd be in Banff soon, the perfect place to isolate himself from stress whenever he needed to get Father off his back. How predictable she'd never asked or hinted at finding out where they were going.

"Marriage, then? In the cards?" He set aside his glass so Tonya could retrieve it for safety purposes.

"Honestly, I've never thought about marriage." Shannon crossed and uncrossed her legs. Her lovely earlobes were growing a tad red, visible because her hair remained braided.

"Too intent on your career?" Yes, this independent lady was up to something big for herself. And why not? Ambition was a good trait to possess.

She nodded.

I'm going to get you to unseal your lips, sooner than later. Over dinner tonight, I am sure you will divulge what I'm seeking. That was a promise.

Shannon did her best not to gape out the black-tinted window. To do so, even though she wasn't on the clock, was highly unprofessional while accompanying her employer. Her attention must remain focused on him. Still, she'd never witnessed the mountains before. Her eyes kept begging for a peek at the majestic view.

Her peripheral vision had caught only a glimpse of the quaint town they'd already been driven through, set with a mountain in the backdrop. Now they were on the Trans Canada, traveling to Lake Louise, surrounded by rows and rows of spruce on each side of the double-lane highway with a mountain straight ahead of them.

Her navigational skills also wanted to kick in, mark land masses or signs for emergency purposes.

"Relax . . ." Séamus poured them some champagne. "You are wound up tighter than the cork I just popped."

"Is Tonya staying in Banff?" Shannon took the glass. She stiffened at her error. It wasn't her job to ask questions about the other staff. Maybe she should refrain from drinking another drop of alcohol, because her tongue was speaking on its own.

Séamus' dimples appeared. The coy smile was truly a panty-removing device. "Now that is what I want to hear."

Simultaneously, Shannon noted the speed sign of ninety kilometers an hour and the wired fence to keep the wildlife from wandering onto the busiest highway in Canada. "What did you want to hear?" She also couldn't help realizing they were driving on maybe the side of a mountain from the way the land sloped upward to her left and downward to her right.

"Questions. What else?" Séamus' sensual chuckle was caressing her ears. "Please, by all means, enjoy the view. Or are you in work mode—taking in the quickest route to Lake Louise?"

"No. I'm simply admiring the view." She gripped the glass and sipped.

"There we go. Silence again." Séamus wagged his finger. "You're not working. You are my guest accompanying me to the hotel."

"I thought I was supposed to be your driver?" Never had Shannon encountered a client wishing for her company, other than driving. Unless . . . She shivered. "That's why I'm here, aren't I?"

"Perhaps I desired a chance for us to become better acquainted? No worries, I am a gentleman. We have two rooms to my suite."

"Suite?" Why hadn't she assumed he'd acquire them the best room possible?

"Yes, I always stay in a suite. The master bedroom is upstairs. Your lodgings are downstairs. You'll have ample privacy."

"Thank you." And she meant it. His parents had raised Séamus as a gentleman. He was the opposite of the egotistical rock stars, sports stars, and movie stars she chauffeured around, who believed that because she was a woman, she wanted to sleep with them.

"Your eyes just narrowed. Pray tell why?" His dimples vanished, and he knitted his black brows.

"Nothing." Shannon shook her head and sipped more champagne. "You're . . . well, different, that's all."

"Different?" His scrunched brows rose upward.

"Yes. Different. You really want to talk." *Which is so weird. Why do you want to talk to me?*

"I enjoy chatting. I find people interesting. Don't you?"

"Well, yes, but I don't have time to talk, or they don't have time to talk, and it's all for the best that we don't talk, because I'm simply their driver."

"You are forever stressing you are simply a driver. And I have told you that you are more than my driver. I shared with you about Ellen. She raised me. So why wouldn't I see everyone associated with Daugherty Manor and Enterprises as more than servants?" He sipped. "My best friend works for my father."

True. The longer they were together, the more he kept presenting himself as an ordinary man, instead of the offspring of one of the wealthiest men in Canada. No, he wouldn't pass for a guy back on the rez, or a white-collar hottie in one of the bars she patronized with her friends, but he wasn't a self-proclaimed pedestal-sitting king like the celebrities she met on the job. He was somewhere in the middle.

She rubbed the stem of her glass. If he'd hired them a limo, it was clear he didn't require a driver. So why had he requested she accompany him? Yes, he'd gotten them a suite, and she had ample space since she was downstairs, but still . . .

Fear slick with perspiration inched down her spine. Once they reached the hotel, she'd find out.

"This is the main sitting room." The valet extended his hand toward the walls of windows offering a gorgeous view of the emerald lake hugging the Victoria Glacier that matched the hue of Séamus' eyes.

"In the winter, they skate." Séamus shoved his chin at the massive wall of windows toward the aptly named lake before them.

"It's beautiful . . ." Shannon had only seen such color in pictures. She couldn't believe water could be this pure and green.

"The hot springs in Banff are to die for." Séamus stuffed his hands in his pockets. "Come. We'll get you settled. There's plenty of time to check out the grounds and admire the view."

"And you said this is where you ski? You mentioned skiing." Shannon followed Séamus and the valet across the hardwood floor to a room.

"Your lavatory . . ." The valet pointed out the bathroom.

They were in the platinum suite, probably the most luxurious room of them all. They had two private balconies, a spiral staircase leading to the second floor, their own dining room, living room, and a mini kitchen for a light breakfast or midnight snack.

The mahogany wainscotting and rich hardwood everywhere was reminiscent of old Victorian houses Shannon watched on her favorite British TV channel. Yet, contemporary furnishings blended seamlessly with the updated interior design.

Her gaze wouldn't stop moving about. Ever since they'd landed, she couldn't cease drinking in the beauty of the Banff area. Too bad they didn't visit the hot springs Séamus had spoken about. Imagine bathing in water straight from the mountain.

"You said they have another hotel in Banff and Jasper?" Shannon whispered. How strange to speak into the warm ear of her employer, something she'd never done before, or would have considered doing.

The rich scent of Séamus' cologne she'd inhaled on the plane and in the limo was stronger under her nose now. Even the warmth coming from his athletic body was tickling the goosebumps on her skin.

He turned his head and flashed his dimples. His lips were close enough to taste, daring her to find out if they were as plush as they looked. The aroma of the champagne he'd drunk in the limo lingered between them. "Yes, they do. Are you interested in seeing Jasper? Spending some time in Banff?"

Shannon could not hold back the sputter flying from her mouth. "Wh-what? Well, no. This is your vacation."

"And you are my guest." Séamus set his hand on the wall. When he leaned in, the alcohol scent became more powerful. Only a hint of air separated them. "I always acquiesce to my guests."

"G-guest. I'm your driver." Knees jittering, she frantically searched for her confidence, even her professionalism that had buggered off to Lord knew where. The alcohol wasn't intoxicating her. It was Séamus' smell. Cleanliness she hadn't sniffed before, even though he most likely hadn't showered after work.

He was the finest linen sheets, daring her to slide beneath them and revel in the lushness.

"I . . . I . . ." She held up her hand.

From behind his firm shoulder, the valet appeared from the bathroom, discreetly glancing at the bedroom door, because as a servant, she would've done the same thing, and had, when one of her clients was attempting to seduce a woman in the back of the limo.

She wasn't some starstruck girl, turned on by prestige, power, and money. It was best she square her shoulders and lift her chin. "If you don't mind, I have some unpacking to do. Is it okay if I leave your presence?"

"You don't need to ask." Séamus bared his white teeth. "Whatever you desire is what I will grant you."

"Okay, genie. Unpacking is what I desire." She firmed her tone.

"As you wish." He snapped his fingers, then motioned at the valet. "Please show me my quarters."

Shannon scampered into her room and closed the door behind her while letting out a big breath that her lungs thanked her for doing.

There was something going on. This *break* of Séamus' made no sense. Her gut feeling said she'd find out tonight.

The valet, for an additional tip, continued to unpack the suitcases.

Séamus stood in the master bathroom. Once he'd bathed, he'd order up sparkling cider to sip on. His goal was to loosen the work-mode strings wrapping Shannon's tiny waist, not inebriate her. And his plan was working. The woman she kept hidden was beginning to surface.

"Everything has been laid out for you, Mr. Daugherty. Is there anything else you require?" The valet stood outside the bathroom door.

"Yes, there is." Séamus lifted his bathrobe off the hook. "I'll require a full dinner for eight-thirty." They were on mountain time. They'd gained two hours, which left him an hour to shower and dress.

"May I ask what you would like served?"

"The prime rib. Medium well for her, and medium rare for me. Two gourmet potatoes." There was no use elaborating on the trimmings that came with the meal, or the salad and soup.

The waiter nodded.

"For drinks, send up a bottle of sparkling cider."

"As you wish, sir."

Séamus worked on unknotting his tie. If all went as planned, Shannon would accept his marriage proposal over dinner. By the time they returned to Toronto, he'd have a new bride.

He couldn't help his smirk that was a sardonic grin in the mirror's reflection. Bastard. Leaving him no choice but to marry. And there wasn't anything Father could do about it once he'd dropped the news in the tyrant's lap.

Chapter Six: Life is a Highway

Séamus rose from the oodles of water swishing around him in the jetted tub. The froth of bubbles lapped at his knees. He'd best dry himself off and slide into his tux hanging on the door hook before he turned into a raisin. Shannon might find dressing for dinner rather formal, but formality was required at home, starting from the age of ten when he'd been allowed to sit at the table in the main dining hall with the adults, instead of the family's private dining room.

He should've asked the driver to stop in Banff so he could purchase Shannon appropriate clothing. If she'd assumed she was driving him everywhere, no doubt she'd packed, besides the uniform she'd been wearing, whatever she required for a stroll outside and something to curl up in once her duties were complete.

He drummed his fingers on his wet thigh. What was done was done. He could phone downstairs and have someone retrieve her a beautiful dress in the gift shop. By her slim form, he could guess her size.

As for an engagement ring, a jaunt into Banff would suffice. There were many fine jewelers on the main drag.

Just as Shannon was about to slip on the jeans and t-shirt she'd laid out for dinner, a knock came at the door. She swiveled on her heel. Weird. Séamus had said he'd meet her in the dining area.

"Yes?" She tightened the belt of her bathrobe.

"Hello. I'm Melinda from the clothing boutique down-stairs. I have something for you, as requested by Mr. Daugh-erty."

"Oh . . ." Shannon clamped her mouth shut because she'd been about to tell the attendant she hadn't ordered anything, but whatever the salesperson was bringing came from Séa-mus. "Please. Come in."

The door opened. A woman who could've been a fashion model with her ballerina body, sharp cheekbones, and blonde hair pulled back into a chignon held a white box with a red bow on top. "For you. Compliments of Mr. Daugherty." A hint of envy had snuck into her singsong voice.

"I . . . uh . . ." Shannon reached for the box. She set it on the queen-size bed. "I wasn't expecting anything."

A hint of a sneer crinkled the woman's red lips.

Irritation spread across the back of Shannon's neck. "Thank you." Was she supposed to tip the lady?

"Please, can you try it on? Mr. Daugherty wants to make sure it fits properly." The woman clacked her nails that re-sembled talons on her sleek hip.

"Try it . . . on?" Shannon quickly opened the box to the color black and tons of sequins. When she slid her fingers into the fabric, pure elegance gathered against her skin. Heart skipping a beat, she held up the evening gown. Her mouth fell open.

It was a dress fit for clients she'd driven to gala events, all smartly outfitted in designer labels—the color black set off by glittering sequins, a heart-shaped neckline, fitted, long sleeves, and a mermaid hem, intended to mold as one with a woman's body.

"I . . . uh . . ." Yes, she had plain black pumps to wear, but she couldn't accept the gift. The dress must have cost a for-tune. "I . . . uh . . ."

"Please, try it on." The attendant left the bedroom and

closed the door.

A fire was about to erupt on Shannon's face. What was Séamus doing giving her gifts? This was absurd. She couldn't accept the dress, much less try the thing on.

Clutching the elaborate material, she marched from the bedroom, right past the attendant, and straight up the spiral staircase to her client's quarters. The double doors were closed, and she gave a quick three raps on the heavy oak doors.

Her skin prickled.

"Enter . . ." Bemusement was in Séamus' greeting.

The man really did only have two speeds — droll or bored.

Shannon opened one of the doors and darted inside to Séamus standing at a full-length mirror fixing the cuffs of his white shirt that must've been bleached in the sun, almost blinding. The rich fabric hugged his strong shoulders. He'd yet to tuck in the hem, and the shirt hid his lean hips. His eyes twinkled in the mirror's reflection.

"Do you like your gift?"

He was beaming, of all things, proud of what he'd done. Shannon held the dress closer to her chest. Didn't he understand the etiquette between an employer and employee? Of course he did. He was the director of marketing for his father's company. He probably had many people working under him.

"I . . . well, yes, I do." When had it become easy to forget the *sir* she'd previously glued to her tongue? "But . . . I can't . . . this is too much."

"Never mind the cost." He fastened the cuff link. From the way the jewel caught the light, the gold was real and had cost major dough — besides the dress.

"I can't accept this. I really can't." She held out the dress.

He pivoted on his polished black shoe. His dimples seemed to dare her to touch them. "It is a gift, a gift I am asking you to accept, if you please."

His sophisticated yet beseeching tone hit her with tiny tingles of shock on her spine. Such gentleness swathed each spoken word.

"Well . . . if you insist." Shannon swallowed.

His lazy gaze gentlemanly feathered her skin from her toes to her head.

Oh hell, where was her discretion? She'd entered her client's room wearing nothing but her bathrobe. She skittered backward. "I'll . . . I'll finish dressing." She held up the dress. "I'll see you . . . see you downstairs."

She whipped on her heel and almost kissed the one closed door, fumbled her way out through the open door, and dashed downstairs. Her wet hair slapping her back reaffirmed she'd truly entered his room while highly indecent. The cool hardwood on her bare feet also chastised her for not having the modesty to at least don slippers.

How could one man cause her to make so many mistakes—after eight years of adhering to every single rule her boss had drilled into her?

Shannon inched from her room. She'd never gotten this dressed up for dinner before. Sure, she'd dined at fine restaurants, but her outfits couldn't compare to the expensive material melting against her skin.

Séamus sat at the table beneath the dim lighting. His skin glowed, and his dimples appeared. He rose, holding out his hand. "You look stunning. I didn't realize you had bangs." The surprised delight in his voice said he approved.

She'd styled her hair just like the sales attendant from the boutique but had let her bangs sweep to the side. As for her fringes, she'd left them loose and had curled them with an iron to frame her face. A necklace and earrings would've complemented the gown, but those were at the guest house in

53

Toronto, since she'd never expected to need jewelry.

"I wear it back for work all the time." The familiar heat filled her cheeks. She'd better get used to a hot face when around this man. "It's more professional."

"True." Séamus rounded the table and pulled out the chair. "Please. Sit." Delight and surprise remained rooted in his sparkling eyes.

Her walk was stiffer than an unoiled engine. The ambience of the room screamed romance. But if Séamus was her client, why this elaborate dinner? "Thank you." She sat.

He assisted her with pushing in the chair. His rich, familiar scent was too close, almost caressing the back of her ear.

"You strike me as a meat and potatoes lady. I ordered prime rib. I hope you don't mind." He rounded the table and took his seat.

"Guilty." A giggle tickled the back of Shannon's throat. It'd been ages when she'd actually laughed with a client. Sure, there was the odd chuckle and smile, but nothing too friendly. Oh, screw it. She let the giggle escape.

"Why did I have a hunch your laugh would be as classy as you?" Séamus raised his wine glass.

An attendant appeared from wherever he'd been hiding, holding a bottle.

"Oh, I don't think I should have any more wine." A trickle of fear replaced the giggle. If Shannon drank one more drop, the booze would swallow any professionalism she had left.

"It's not wine. Sparkling cider. It's a drink I enjoy when I want something flavorful and dry, minus the alcohol. Try it."

If the drink allowed Shannon to keep what was left of her faculties, she was all for a taste. She nodded at the attendant, who poured.

"To my new driver." Séamus lifted his glass.

Was he serious or joking? Shannon followed his lead, but she couldn't help her nervous smile. "I never had anyone toast me before."

"And why not? You are most deserving of a toast." His grin said he was bordering on casting a flirty wink.

Face still flaming, Shannon sipped. The attendant had magically vanished again.

"Please, relax. You're off the clock." His tone wasn't flirtatious anymore but leaned toward a friendly gesture.

Well, they were here, and she might as well enjoy the dinner. But the nagging at the back of her head kept whispering she teetered on ruining her chance to buy her first car if she dared to get too close.

Think of your own town car. Your own business. Your dream. Mom and Kokum rooting for you getting to do something they could only dream about.

"So, tell me . . . ." Séamus set aside his glass. "Do you plan on working for Elite Limousines for the long term?"

This man never stopped and was determined to know her on an intimate level. She also set aside her glass. "No. Like anyone else, I have plans for the future." Silently, she patted herself on the back for skirting his question.

"May I ask what plans?" he asked while motioning at the attendant.

The man laid out fine china filled with salads before them.

How could she answer? What if he was insulted that she wanted his father as a reference? "Can I ask if you could share your plans?"

Séamus waggled his finger. "I asked first." His reply was on the chiding side, with a hint of teasing. "And once you share yours, I'll share mine."

"Really?" Hmm, okay, she'd bite. If he had some big important future, it would be interesting to find out what he was cooking up. "I want to start my own business."

"Your own business?" He cocked his brow. "What kind of business."

She added a hint of Italian dressing to her salad. Thank

goodness her hands never shook while pouring from the glass bottle. "My own limo business."

His features remained smooth, so obviously she hadn't shocked him. Maybe he suspected she'd stay in the field.

"That's an ambitious plan." He pressed his lips together. "I have a hunch you'll succeed, even with the fierce competition."

"The competition is more than fierce. Dog eat dog."

"When do you see yourself purchasing a fleet?"

"Not a fleet." She slipped some salad between her lips. The greens and bell pepper were almost dancing on her tongue. Fresh and crisp. "For now, one car. But it's going to be finer than Fifth Avenue."

"Like the Audi?"

"Plusher than the Audi. As you said, the competition is fierce. I want to make sure everything a client needs is available to them, even a sound sleep from the airport."

"I take it you're doing your research."

Shannon nodded. "I have." And the cost was enormous.

"You do know what custom European vehicles run for?"

She could build a house back on the rez for what she'd shell out for one of those babies. "Yes." She set aside her fork. "Now that I told you my plan, what about yours?"

He again waggled his finger. "I still have a few more questions, if you don't mind. Then I'll tell you mine."

"Fair enough." Something weird was going on. If she didn't know better, she'd swear he was filing everything she'd said in his brain for future use, or even present use.

Marketing was his game. No doubt he was capable of unearthing what people desired and how to grant them what they needed—with a price. Men like him always had a price of some sort.

"Did you give yourself a deadline to meet your goal?" He'd yet to touch his salad and kept his searching gaze pinned on her.

Shannon set down her fork. It was impossible to eat being under his stare. "I hoped to do this by the time I was thirty."

"How old are you now?"

"Twenty-eight."

His lips spread into a wide smile, not the flashy smile he'd been tossing her way from the moment they'd met. Cunning. Even sardonic. A cat eating a canary.

She stiffened. How stupid to have lowered her guard and allowed him to glimpse inside her dreams. Maybe this was a game. He was super-rich and due to inherit a Fortune 500 company from Daddy. The guy had no clue what it was like to grow up poor on an Indian Reserve full of dirt roads and houses all built the same, purchased as packages by the band council with a good six to ten people stuffed into each one.

"I'm twenty-nine. We're a year apart."

"We may be a year apart, but that's about all we have in common." The stiffness in Shannon's back had transferred to her words.

"I think we have a lot more in common than what you're presuming." Séamus finally lifted his fork and dug into his salad. He munched on the greens first, wiped his mouth, and then reached for his cider. Once he'd sipped, he kept hold of the glass. "We both have goals. And we'll do anything to reach them."

"Not . . . anything." Shannon fisted her fingers beneath the table. "My parents raised me to abide by the Seven Grandfathers' teachings. I have my limits."

"The—what?" He blinked.

"In our culture, we have seven teachings we follow that come from our ancestral grandfathers. They were given to us so we could survive as a community. We are governed by the circle. Everyone has their place and what they contribute so we can flourish."

He clasped his hands together. "How interesting and true. It's how we function as a society, is it not? Someone to market, and someone who drives the person to work so he can do his job. As I said, we have more in common than you'll admit."

"True. My role is your driver. Your job is to market the business to potential customers." The stupid heat was back on her face. Why had he answered the way he had? It was as if he understood.

He moved his finger in a circle. "My best friend is our data analyst. His duties are to ensure our performance as a company meets the objectives of the board."

"So he analyzes your marketing plan?"

"My plan is based on the objectives of the board, who base their objectives on our bottom line. We always want to be in the black."

"Everything you do is based on how much money you can make?"

"Of course. Isn't this why your boss is in business? To make money? Isn't this why you want to own your own business? To make money?"

Shannon kept squeezing her fingers. "It's more than making money."

"You're referring to the circle again. Hmm." He tapped his finger against his U-shaped chin.

"Finding employment on the rez isn't easy." Shannon pushed her plate away. So much for eating. "We had to come here if we wanted good jobs. My mother didn't want me growing up the way she did. She wanted me to reach my dreams."

"Is this more about your mother then?" His voice had dropped to almost a whisper.

"She always encouraged me to make something of myself. Maybe she didn't want me to end up like her."

"And how did she end up?"

"Cooking at the local restaurant. Raising kids. Playing bingo in the evening." Shannon shrugged. "She said there's a big world out there, and she told me to see it before I thought of settling down."

"What if I could help you then? See this world? Reach your dreams? Everything your mother wants for you?" He sat back and folded his arms, but his gaze remained assessing.

"How could you help me?" And did she want his help?

"By marrying me." His words were evenly spoken in a hushed tone, as if his shoulders were bunched over, although he remained straight in his seat.

Chapter Seven: Get Out of My Dreams, Get into My Car

Thank goodness Shannon wasn't holding her fork or wine glass, or she would've dropped them. since her stomach had hit the top of her head. This was the reason for the special dinner? Her gown? The trip to Lake Louise? He'd done all this to ask her to marry him? But they'd only met this morning.

"I don't . . ." She blanched. "Is this some kind of joke?"

"Do I look like I'm joking?" His tone remained hushed. His gaze was as quiet as his voice.

Holy motherfucker, he wasn't joking. The man was serious with a capital S.

"Uh . . ." What could she say? If she told him *no*, he might run to his father, exclaiming she'd thrown her glass of sparkling cider in his face. But if she said *yes*, she'd be marrying a perfect stranger, a big *no thanks* to that nutty idea. "Why? You said if I answered your questions, you'd answer mine."

"Ask away. I'm an open book with nothing to hide." He parted the folds of his jacket to reveal his whiter-than-snow shirt.

"Was this all planned . . ." She did her best to keep the annoyance from her question now that her heart had resumed pattering at a normal pace. No need to call in the paramedics. " . . . to ask me to marry you? And why do you want to marry me?"

He never blinked or widened his eyes. Instead, he picked up his glass and sipped, as if he was out on the deck at his exclusive country club, talking about how well he'd played his round of golf. "My father's a tyrant. Plain and simple." He swirled the contents in the glass. "I'm supposed to be having dinner with him tonight, but I'm with you."

Shannon blinked. He was terrified of his father and couldn't face the man at dinner? "Seriously?"

Séamus frowned. He set down the glass and leaned in. "I know what conclusion you've drawn. I'm a coward. I was born without a spine." His brows narrowed. "Let me share something. You have yet to meet my father. He may run my older brother's life, but he doesn't run mine. If I'd attended the dinner, I would've received news I've been anticipating since the day I was born."

Shannon hadn't meant to upset him. Nor did she mean to judge him unfairly. They barely knew each other. He was her client, a client who'd asked her to freaking marry him. "I'm sorry. I wasn't—"

"You weren't?" He lifted the glass. Again, he swirled the contents. He was probably also moving his ankle in a circle.

Her ears heated. "Please, do go on. I didn't mean to interrupt."

"Thank you." He drained the contents in the glass.

Right away the attendant appeared, holding the bottle. "Another?"

"Yes, please." Séamus pushed his glass at the man. "My mother warned me in advance this morning what our conversation would entail over dinner."

"Your father's going to tell you to marry someone?"

"No. He was going to *order* me to marry, and just like Cillian, my elder brother, I would have been given four prerequisites my bride has to meet." He sipped. "However, since I'm not at the dinner, I haven't heard his prerequisites."

No, he wasn't. He was in Lake Louise with . . . her. She licked her dry lips.

"There's nothing he can do if I'm already married."

"Can do?" She shivered. What kind of father did Séamus have?

"Yes, like disinherit me. Or fire me. Or blacklist me if I try to find another position in my field."

Shannon gasped. "Blacklist?" Only a heartless bastard blacklisted his own flesh and blood.

"I told you already. He's a tyrant."

"I wasn't—"

"Yes, you were. Don't feel sorry for me. While I was growing up, I rarely saw him unless I was called to his study. Plus, I spent most of my time at boarding school."

Boarding school? Shannon shuddered. Her grandparents had been forced to move far from home as children and attend the Indian Residential School by order of the government. "Why? Why did he send you away?"

"It's a tradition in my family. All children must attend an elite boarding school demanded by my great-great-great-grandfather once he'd made his fortune." He traced the rim of the glass, gazing at the sparkling cider.

"In those days, the Irish were looked down upon. Racism was rampant in Toronto. If you weren't an Orangeman, you were out." He snapped his fingers. "My great-great-great-grandfather built Daugherty Enterprises on his back. From what I'm told, he was a brittle old man when he passed away. The laborious work he'd put himself through to achieve success left him crippled because he was determined to prove Irishmen could succeed."

She'd learned in history class about the racism in nineteenth century Toronto. How not only the Irish had been looked down upon, but also Jews, Chinese, Italians . . . anyone who wasn't a white Anglo-Saxon protestant.

"Canada likes to believe it's a fair and equal country, but it's not. In the past lies a very ugly, dark history." Séamus' upper lip curled into a sneer. "Now I must pay for what my ancestors experienced."

"By keeping the tradition alive . . ." Shannon finished, more to herself.

"Yes."

"I see . . ." He sounded screwed, no matter what he did. If he thumbed his nose at his father and didn't marry, he'd be blacklisted. "Where did you attend university?"

"U of T. Tradition . . . again." He continued to sneer. "Heaven forbid I select a school of my choice."

"You had to do everything according to his wishes?" Un-fucking-believable.

"Wishes?" Séamus snorted, the first snort she'd heard. "More like demands."

"I see . . ." Well, what was she supposed to do? She couldn't throw her life down the toilet because she felt sorry for a client. "Look, I feel bad about the predicament you're in, but I'm your driver —"

"A driver whom I asked to marry me." His gaze had turned to steel. Even his brows slanted inward.

"I can't . . ." She coughed. "I can't marry you. We don't even know each other."

"That's because you won't allow me the chance to know you." He settled both hands on the table. "Allow me to get to know you. I can provide you with what you truly desire — your own town car for clients. Your own business."

"Where are we going to get married? This place is a tourist resort." Okay, what she'd said was dumb, but that was about all she was capable of uttering right now.

"Banff. I can procure a ring for you at a local jewelry pro-prietor. It's simply a matter of visiting the town hall to obtain a marriage license."

He was truly and utterly serious. She sagged in her chair and set both palms on her temples.

"Goodness, Shannon." He chortled. "You look as if I asked you to rob a bank with me when I simply asked for your hand in marriage."

Hearing her name on his lips again left a velvet-like tingling sensation on her skin. She glanced up. He continued to sit with both hands on the table, simply staring.

"Marriage is a serious commitment—"

"I think I know how serious of a commitment marriage is." He finally lifted his filled glass and sat back. From the way he moved, he must have crossed his legs. His elbow rested on the arm of the chair. "There has never been divorce in my family, otherwise I think my mother would have left my father ages ago."

"Is this why your father is strict about who you'll marry?"

He grinned while sipping from his glass. "No. He prefers to keep with tradition. Every son and daughter of a Daugherty marries into another family from old money."

"Then I think he'd have our marriage annulled," Shannon pointed out—anything to stop this crazy conversation from going a step further.

"Never." Séamus' grin vanished. "He wouldn't do anything to smear the Daugherty name. As I said—there has never been divorce in our family. Annulment isn't an option, either. We are Irish Catholic."

"You have a strong faith?" This took Shannon by surprise.

Séamus flicked his hand. "I attend Mass when I'm obliged."

Well, his beliefs weren't any of her business. No doubt his father ordered Séamus to attend service for special holidays and such. He was correct in one respect, though—his family's outlook was from over a century ago.

"Now . . . I offered you your own business. What do you say? Yes?" He took another sip from his glass.

He was so nonchalant about everything. Maybe it came

64

from being stinking wealthy and having whatever he wanted at his fingertips.

"Your father wouldn't approve. I'm not Irish. I'm not Catholic. I'm not from this old money you speak about. I never even attended university. I'm Ojibway and from the rez. I follow the teachings of the Seven Grandfathers."

"No, he wouldn't approve, but I think you are perfect."

"Perfect?" She shifted in the chair. "How?"

"You're everything I would want to marry." He motioned at the attendant. "Let's eat first. We can discuss this further on the balcony."

Shannon wasn't sure if she'd have the appetite to swallow the prime rib, even though the scent of the beef was permeating the room.

She was thinking, of this Séamus was sure. Dinner had been quiet, but Shannon had eaten her full meal of salad, the main entrée, and dessert.

He motioned at the balcony. "Would you care to sit outside?"

She stood. "Sure."

His eyes had a will of their own and stroked every inch of her sleek arms, legs to her neck, and tiny waist poured into the gown. Striking. Exquisite. No, he didn't wish to marry, but with his hand forced, he'd easily pick Shannon. She was far removed from the pretentious life of his family and friends. Reputation meant nothing to her.

Although he'd yet to see her in streetwear, instinct told him she didn't covet designer labels. As for plastic surgery, a scalpel would never touch her body or face. She'd probably never heard of cool sculpting, either, something Cillian's model-slim wife had undergone to ensure she had the perfect thigh gap in her bikini.

He opened one of the French doors to the slightest hint of a breeze. The nights were cooler here than in Toronto, so he set his glass on the outdoor table to remove his jacket.

Shannon hugged herself while still clutching her glass of sparkling cider. No doubt she was already experiencing the nip of mountain air.

"Here." He held out his jacket.

"Oh, I couldn't . . ."

"Please. I don't have a shawl for you, and I'm unsure if you packed one."

"Just a hoodie," she weakly replied.

"I don't think a hoodie would complement your gown, but a man's jacket will." He continued to hold out his coat.

She nodded.

He draped the garment around shoulders a mannequin would envy. A hint of something floral invaded his nostrils. He inhaled her lovely essence. The jacket slipped around her, too big, obviously, but looking oh-so-perfect on her body.

"I'm guessing this isn't the first time you offered your jacket." There was a twinkle in her gaze. Her short nails were perfect for her slim fingers clutching the wine glass.

"I was raised a gentleman." He scooped his glass from the table behind him but remained a breath away. The warmth coming from Shannon was an invitation to stretch out and relax, even lay his head in her lap.

"I'm sorry." She craned her neck. Their lips were now a breath apart.

"Sorry for what?" His mouth yearned to lean in and taste whether she was as succulent as she looked. Sure, dating would've been a great way to slowly work his way into something with her, but thanks to Father, he'd have to get to know Shannon as his wife.

"For your father putting you in the position of having to ask a complete stranger to marry you." She then stared out at the lake.

The sun disappeared fast in the mountains. All that was left was the azure sky and the lights from the hotel reflecting off the black water that would return to a crisp emerald come morning.

"There's nothing to be sorry for. I knew this day was coming."

"Is that why you lost your license?" She turned her head. Again, her lips were a breath away. "Do you intentionally drive fast to upset him?"

"I do what I do because I enjoy it." He shrugged.

"Skiing? Snowboarding?"

"No to snowboarding. I much prefer to ski, and surf."

"Do you race on the amateur circuit?"

"No."

She fiddled with her wine glass. "I used to drive in the stock car races back home."

"Really?" Curiosity and amusement raced up his spine. "Tell me more."

"There isn't much to tell. We have a track up in the north end area. I raced on Saturday nights in the women's division. My brother got me into it. He was really good."

"A tomboy?"

Her chuckle was a throaty purr. "No. But I loved being a part of the pit crew. I did want to do more than change tires, though. I begged him to teach me."

"Are you an expert mechanic then?"

"No." She blushed. "I can change the oil, the coolant, replace the air filter, the fuses, spark plugs . . . maintenance everyone should be able to do on their own."

On their own? He had no clue how to even change a tire. That was what roadside assistance was for. Oil? He took the vehicle into the garage for repair.

"And what would you think of me if I admitted I don't

know how to perform those tasks?" He couldn't help teasing, but he also held his breath for her answer.

"I'm your driver," she reminded him. "It's my job to get out and change the tire if we, God forbid, have a flat. But we'd never have a flat. Not on my watch. Unless we ran over a nail or something."

"Oh?" He couldn't help his grin.

"I thoroughly check the vehicle every morning. The cardinal rule is to never ever make a client late."

"I wouldn't mind if you made me late." Her soothing reply of reassurance was creating the most wonderful sensations on his back, as if she was rubbing her palms along his skin.

"I would." Her grin was cheeky. "It would mean I'm not doing my job properly."

"I'd never hold it against you. I'm also great at keeping secrets." He placed his finger over his lips. "It'd be our secret."

"But I'd know." She was still smiling, a damned good sign of being relaxed in his company. "And I'd feel as if I'd failed you."

"I don't think there's a thing you could do that would fail me." He hadn't meant for his words to come out like silk, since he'd meant to tease her, but they had.

Her smile vanished. Her mouth moved into a straight line, and her mischievous gaze became searching.

He couldn't help himself and broke the barrier of air separating them. His lips brushed hers that were purer and plusher than the finest Egyptian cotton. Her scent was upon him, a lovely hint of whatever soap and shampoo she'd used.

When she didn't back away, he deepened the kiss and tasted her sweet lips.

CHAPTER EIGHT: I'D RATHER RIDE AROUND WITH YOU

Hit the brakes. The thought kept screaming through Shannon's brain. As much as her mind hollered the warning like a flashing amber up ahead on the road, her body refused to cooperate. Her lips had turned traitor and continued to taste Séamus' mouth that was a blending of cider and a hint of mint from the candies they'd sampled after dinner.

She had her friends to think about, the pact they'd made, and their townhouse.

But gosh, his kiss was finer than the champagne they'd drunk this afternoon.

She had her dream to think about.

But geez, he'd offered to help her purchase a town car.

She was an independent woman doing what her mother and kokum had yearned for. How disappointed they'd be if she didn't see it through.

But cripes, his mouth sliding over hers was a seamless fit. Perfect.

His arm snaked around her waist. He drew her in closer until her breasts melted against his chest—pectorals that weren't overly muscular and gym-made, but firm and athletic from skiing, surfing, and golfing.

He even smelled wealthy and powerful, a fine scent of expensive cologne and a hint of a plushness from his tuxedo.

The deciding factor? Séamus wasn't a snob who thought he was better than her, another horny client on the make, expecting her to be grateful for a taste of his dick.

His fingers brushed at her waist, gliding in a tiny movement back and forth. His touch was magical, and her skin responded with shivers and goosebumps. The soft puckers he offered became firmer, deeper.

When his tongue traced her closed lips, the warning bell rang again in her head. She had to stop him before one thing led to another. But darn, the temptation was so great.

Since the wine glass sat in her one hand, she settled her free palm on his chest for a gentle shove. Touching his crisp silk-like shirt and what hid beneath was pure electrifying excitement between her legs. What she didn't want to throb with anticipation was pulsating, much to her vexation.

Of all the predicaments to find herself in.

"Séamus . . ." Where she found the strength to break the kiss, she had no clue.

"Hmm?" His eyes were closed. Not tight, either. Sleepily shut, as if he was in dreamland enjoying a very . . . erotic fantasy.

"I . . . I'm getting cold." Lying was stupid. She was perfectly capable of dealing with a man honestly.

"My jacket isn't helping?" His lips, only a mere kiss away, broadened into a grin. He ran his finger along her cheekbone. "Do you require something warmer?"

The shivering she was undergoing was far from the nip in the air. She knew he'd have a magnetic touch, besides magnetic words. It was best to get away from him. Far away. She took a step back. His hand on her waist slid off, but not before lazily caressing her hip.

Having him stroke such a taboo spot was an explosion of stars firing in her heart. She set her hand over her breasts that heaved from her quick breaths. "I think . . . I think we should go inside."

"A great idea." His coy smile said he was accepting an

invitation to her bedroom.

"I mean . . . inside. Just inside."

His lips formed into a straight line. Not of anger, but acceptance. He nodded. "Okay. We can do that." He motioned at the door.

Shannon scampered across the concrete floor of the balcony and dashed to the warmth of the suite. She continued to clutch the glass. The fireplace lacked a fire, since it was spring. She stood in front of the marble mantel anyway. There was a picture above of a soaring eagle with the mountain in the backdrop.

"Shannon?"

She glanced over her shoulder. Why did his voice always have to caress her skin like a silk blanket? "Yes?"

"It was drummed into me from birth to always be a gentleman. My father lives by this code. So does my brother. My maid, Ellen, never let me forget who I am and how I'm to conduct myself." He shut the door and stepped forward. His shoulders were back, and determination glinted in his eyes. "But with you, I want to drop the pretense."

"Pretense?" She shivered. "You're not really a gentleman?"

"Perhaps I am. Perhaps I'm not. There's a side to me Father couldn't breach." He moved in closer.

"The need for speed? For adventure?" His jacket still draped her, but even that couldn't stop the shivers and cold on her skin. The material carrying his scent reaffirmed he already had a grip on her, and she was swathed in what he owned.

Séamus had that same look going on — the one wanting to take her to his bedroom.

"I should . . . I should get some sleep." She shoved her chin in the direction of her quarters. "I'm sure you have a lot planned for tomorrow."

"I told you already," he reminded her, "you're off for the

weekend. And I also proposed marriage."

"But we don't know each other." How many times did she have to repeat herself?

"We'll get to know each other." Reassurance filled his confident tone. "Your wedding present is your own town car. Price is not relevant. Pick whatever you wish. I am a helluva marketer. I can help you get that business established."

But when she'd moved to Toronto, she was supposed to work her way to the top independently. "Marketing is right. You're doing a great job selling yourself."

His cocky smile said she should've kept her mouth shut. "I want you to think good and hard about my offer. Get a wonderful night's rest. We can discuss my proposal over breakfast in the morning."

With that, he turned on his heel and sauntered to the spiral staircase. She couldn't stop staring at him as he ascended the stairs, taking each step with a lazy but confident gait. At the top, he vanished from her view.

Shannon scampered to her bedroom and slammed the door shut. Thank goodness she had her cell phone on hand that she'd yet to turn on. Conferring with her two besties was necessary, because, dammit, the offer he presented was too darn tempting. *He* was too darn tempting.

No, she didn't want to get married, but he could help her start the business sooner than she'd expected. Once she hung her gown, scrubbed her face, and made herself some tea, she sat on the bed cross-legged and video called her friends. She sent up a silent prayer to Creator, begging the girls would be home.

Ronnie and her big glasses appeared on the screen. "Hey, I was going to call you. Pash told me you gotta live at the fancy mansion for the duration of the contract." Her black hair was damp. The patterned flowers on her collared shirt said she'd already changed into her pajamas and had removed her contact lenses.

"You're never gonna believe this." To emphasize her point, Shannon drew a straight line using her hand.

"What? Is he hot? Is he gonna make you break your personal rule?" Ronnie giggled.

Just then, Pashney's face appeared behind Ronnie. "What's up?"

"Give us a tour of your place. I bet it's as royal as the main house." Again, Ronnie giggled.

"I'm not at the guest quarters." Shannon drew in a big breath. "I'm in Lake Louise."

"Lake Louise?" the girls exclaimed at the same time.

"What's he like? Is he a jerk?" This came from Pashney, which wasn't surprising.

Shannon stiffened. She should give herself a smack for letting her defenses rise on Séamus' behalf. "No. He's very . . . polite. Very nice." *He asked me to marry him.*

"So where did you take him?" Ronnie asked.

Shannon had called to tell them about her dilemma, but the words wouldn't leave her mouth, even though she had the perfect opening. "He was tired after the flight and wanted to dine in once we got to the hotel."

"Spill. Now." Of course, Pashney got straight to the point. "You never called about a client before."

"I wanted to let you know I'm in Lake Louise," Shannon blurted out. Her friends always said her ears turned pink when she was lying. Thank goodness she'd brushed out her hair and the strands covered the tell-tale sign of her fib.

Pashney folded her arms. Her stern look screamed *bullshit*.

There went Shannon's chance of discussing the biggest decision of her life. Why couldn't Pashney have gone somewhere for the night, leaving Ronnie alone? "Oh, I hear him. Maybe he changed his mind and needs me. I gotta go. I'll talk to you guys later."

Before Pashney could cast another stern glare or open her no-nonsense mouth, Shannon hit the *end call* button and also made sure to turn off her phone. Her heart was flipping and flopping. She pushed back her hair and banged her fists on the mattress.

She fell back on the bed. The lavish comforter was what she needed, because the rich material seemed to wrap her in a much-needed hug.

Come morning, she would have to give Séamus her answer. There went a good night's sleep, and hello to tossing and turning.

Too much tossing and turning. The kink in the right side of Shannon's neck, that also slid into her upper back, was a burning pain ibuprofen wouldn't cure, but she'd take two anyway. This was not the way she'd hoped to meet with Séamus over breakfast.

She closed the door to her bedroom, having dressed in comfortable cotton pants, a t-shirt, and her indoor shoes. When she approached the table, she found Séamus done up in a crisp white shirt, dress pants, and polished shoes. No doubt he ate breakfast formally, too.

If she said yes to his proposal, her life would become one of gowns and designer dresses. She plopped in the same chair where she'd sat last night.

"Good morning." His cheerful smile said his sleep had rivaled Rip Van Winkle's.

"Good morning. I didn't realize you dressed for breakfast, too."

A different attendant approached the table with a coffee carafe.

"Dress however you wish." Séamus plucked his napkin from its spot. "As for me, old habits die hard." His attention centered on the attendant pouring the coffee into the china cup in front of him. "And how was your sleep?"

The sincerity in his question urged Shannon to cough up the truth. "Not very well."

"Ah, I should've guessed." He plunked two cubes of sugar in his cup just as the attendant rounded the table to Shannon's spot. "I did leave you with much to think about." As he set aside the coffee, the cup lightly clattered against the saucer.

Shannon's cup was also filled.

"Ask and you shall receive."

She stole a peek at him and then at the attendant, whose expression said he might as well be sitting in the bathroom reading the morning paper. No doubt the attendant had signed a non-disclosure agreement.

"Ask what?"

"Whatever you wish so you will agree to marry me," Séamus simply replied.

"I have a car payment. A mortgage payment. Bills split three ways. I'm obliged to clean every third week." She didn't have servants to see to everything, or a trust fund, or a six-figure job. With Séamus, it was probably seven figures.

"Done." He added a dash of milk to his cup. "Consider your portion of the mortgage paid for, and your car paid off. As for cleaning, it's no problem to hire someone to care for your share of the upkeep until they can acquire a new room-mate."

His nonchalance was a punch to her stomach. "Uh . . . wh-what?" How blasé could a person be? She dropped the spoon she'd picked up. "Th-this is my life we're talking about. I had plans. Big plans."

"You told me you wanted to reach your goal before you turned thirty. Now you will." His tone implied *tut, tut*.

"Well, yes." She came close to shaking her head. "But . . . but not as your wife."

"Am I that ugly?" He made a ghoulish face while grinning,

baring his devastating dimples.

"You are far from ugly. But . . . I'm supposed to be your driver. Your parents will never approve of me. I have a life. You have a life."

"I won't have a life unless I get married, and I refuse to marry someone from my social circle." His gaze became thoughtful. "I need your help, Shannon."

Dammit, why did he have to say her name like she was the most beautiful woman in the world? "Séamus, I'll admit you really piqued my interest, but we're talking about a life I created for myself. I don't want to see you disinherited or lose your job, but there must be another way."

"There are no other options. Once I arrive home, I will be called to Father's study and given a timeframe to marry, and the prerequisites my future bride must meet." He glanced away. The glare he positioned on the potted plant matched the disgust in his words. "If I come home married, he will not have anything to say."

"Oh, from the sounds of him, I think he'll have a lot to say." Shannon sighed. "What about . . ." Wait, what if they only said they'd gotten married? "Will he want proof?"

"You mean my marriage certificate?"

"Yes."

"If I know my father as well as I do, he'll want details right down to the cost of your engagement ring and wedding band." Séamus flicked his hand.

"You mean he'll want to see the actual certificate?"

"As I said, he has to control everything."

Shannon bowed her head. Yes, she wanted to help him. Her upbringing dictated she assist those in need, but at her own expense? Her own dream? She pressed her lips together. Séamus continued to thoughtfully gaze at her. The heat coming from the coffee cup matched the warmth growing on her cheeks.

His offer was too tempting. She'd have her debt erased and the chance to start her own business. But the price was higher than the CN Tower.

This was why she'd refrained from disclosing the truth to her friends last night, because Pashney would've called her insane for even considering the offer. As for always sympathetic Ronnie, if in the same predicament, her dear friend would have seriously considered Séamus' proposition. So naturally, Shannon had kept her mouth shut when Pashney had appeared on the screen.

"You said I could start my business."

Séamus nodded. A gleam was surfacing in his eyes.

Great. He knew he could market everything, even his very own self. Shannon grimaced. "You said you'd pay for my portion of the mortgage on the townhouse."

Again, Séamus nodded.

"You said you'd take care of cleaning services until my friends get a new roommate."

A third nod from him.

"There's my job. I'd have to give a minimum of two weeks' notice before I leave."

"I will contact your employer and tell him we wish to contract your services on a permanent basis."

Shannon blanched. Not giving two weeks' notice was irresponsible. "It's very important that I give him notice. He'll need a driver to—"

"I will see to it that your employer has a driver right away to replace you," Séamus assured her.

With that kind of promise, there was nothing else for Shannon to say other than, "Where will we live . . . if I say yes?"

"For now, at Daugherty Manor."

Shannon almost fell off the chair. She didn't wish to live with some tyrant who was forcing his son into marriage. "We have to have our own place."

"It's tradition to live at home until a child is born. That's how it's always worked."

"Ch-child?" Oh geez, they'd have sex. Well, yes, they'd have sex. They'd be married. And married people had sex. "Umm . . ." She licked her lips. "About the . . . umm . . . wedding night . . . I think we need time to get to know each other first, if we do marry."

"I will leave that up to you," he smoothly replied. "Well?"

Shannon drew in a big breath. "Yes, I'll marry you."

Chapter Nine: Honeymoon Avenue

Séamus knew Shannon would agree to his proposition. So sitting at the Chippendale table inside the jewelry store in Banff wasn't a shock to his system. Maybe Father's threat was a blessing, because nobody could market and sell like Séamus could. And this was his greatest triumph of all—beating Father at his own game.

"Pick whatever you wish." Because of his soon-to-be bride's natural practicality, he'd ensured to tell the clerk to show them something under two hundred grand. He was a Daugherty. The ring had to be of good expensive taste, but not selfish good taste, because his hunch told him Shannon would view a million-dollar ring as a waste of money.

Her focus was on the five rings the clerk had laid out in front of them.

Séamus already had a good idea which one he wanted sliding on her finger. The ring in platinum with two round diamonds framing a round center stone. He'd be forking out one hundred and fifty thousand, something she'd approve of.

"What do you think?" He held up the ring. The design allowed a continuous stream of light to pass through the diamonds from the warm yellow lamp above their table.

"It's beautiful." She held out her hand that shook slightly.

He plopped the diamond in her palm.

Her mouth formed into an O. She held the ring between her index finger and thumb. "I guess I'm not supposed to ask how much it costs."

The clerk chuckled. "That is only for the ears of Mr.

Daugherty. Rest assured, he asked me to select those you'd find beautiful but practical."

"Practical?" She kept staring at the ring. "I'm assuming you took into consideration my — "

"Of course. I will be your husband by the afternoon, won't I?" He set his arm on the back of her chair. The warmth coming from her slim physique was pure relaxation to his once tight shoulders.

She licked her lips and glanced at him. "Your proposition is very enticing, but . . ."

"Add the matching band," Séamus informed the clerk. He glanced back at Shannon. "Come." He stood. "We have an appointment at the town's administration center for our license."

With a gorgeous mountain behind them providing a stunning backdrop of the town, the driver pulled over in front of a contemporary-style building across the street from what looked to be a hotel or restaurant from its lodge-style façade.

"I didn't realize they'd be open on a Saturday," Shannon murmured, since a big part of her had silently crossed her fingers and truly hoped they'd arrive to a closed sign. But the universe was working against her.

Three steps wide in width, followed by a landing, and four more steps led up to an ample outdoor lobby that should've been inviting but merely reaffirmed she'd seal her own fate in minutes. The two bright-red doors, screaming like sirens in the night, punched Shannon in the heart and made her already tense organ beat too fast.

"Everything is open for a Daugherty." Séamus stepped from the car. "The clerk is waiting for us. Already, we interrupted his morning game of golf. Let's not be responsible for interrupting his rescheduled afternoon tee time."

On a Saturday, the parking lot to the left of the gray building with red trim was empty.

Shannon set her fingers on the door handle. Before she could step from the vehicle, the driver was present, hand out, ready to assist her. She should've known the man would be quick on the draw, since she was of the same philosophy to always anticipate each move of her clients.

They were on Bear Street. Perhaps the name derived from the local grizzlies. She forced herself from the safety of the car with the driver's assistance to blue sky and the odd puffs of clouds. Maybe the warm, sunny day was a good omen.

Her parents would freak. Her roommates would flip. So why had she agreed to this crazy proposition? What was compelling her to take each step up to the building where the clerk waited to provide them with a marriage license?

It was more than obtaining her own town car and starting a limo business. Séamus was so kind, so thoughtful, and his bastard of a father had left the poor man with no choice but to either marry her or marry a more suitable woman from his circle of high class, old money friends, something he'd made quite clear he did not desire.

Séamus' warm palm rested on her lower back as he guided her up the remainder of the concrete stairs.

"Are you ready?" He opened one of the double doors.

No, but Shannon swallowed and nodded. Never had she'd done anything this daring and rash in her life. Not even stock car racing and the roar of the engine could produce the crazy zooming of her heart rate.

They entered to a cool interior as contemporary as the façade of the building.

The door closing behind them was the clank of a jail cell door being slammed shut on a prisoner serving a life sentence behind bars.

Not only had Séamus laid out his plastic for Shannon's wedding ring set, but he'd also whisked her off to a boutique to purchase her a dress for their ceremony. She was in the change room while he waited in a chair, glancing through a magazine. From the rack, she'd selected three to try on.

The judge would be by their suite tonight to officiate their vows. He'd asked the hotel if two staff persons could be on hand as witnesses. Once they were married, they'd go out for dinner. He'd stay true to his word and retire to his own room until Shannon was comfortable enough to embrace him as her husband.

The door to the changing room opened. He almost dropped the magazine. She modeled the dress he favored, the one with the high-waisted A-line skirting and plunging V-neckline, giving him a great view of her décolletage. The lace sleeves hugged three-quarters of her slim arms and lay flat on her elegant collarbone. Silk swathed her breasts and flat stomach, the fabric appearing so light that it swung freely as she pivoted in front of the three-way mirror. The hem dropped just below her knees, elongating her legs.

"Lucky on the first try." Séamus stood. He set aside the magazine.

"You like?" Shannon did a little twirl on her bare feet.

"Very much so. It's you." Her body was made to capture the ethereal elegance of the dreamy-style dress. Séamus' feet had a mind of their own and stepped forward, closing the gap between them.

"I have the perfect shoes for that dress, Mr. Daugherty." The salesperson beamed. "Give me one second." She dashed off.

Shannon laced her fingers together. One foot turned inward, as if she were a shy schoolgirl being asked to dance her first dance. "Thank you."

"It really is you. If you wish to try on the other two, please do, but I think this dress is perfect."

"I think it is, too." Shannon turned back to the mirror.

The urge to slip his hands on her shoulders was a buzzing sensation on the tips of Séamus' fingers. *Do it,* the naughty appendages seemed to say. But he willed them to remain attached to his just as eager palms. They were in a boutique, and Shannon might be embarrassed about public displays of affection. Then there was the whole matrimonial ceremony happening tonight to consider. Didn't all brides experience the jitters? Especially one who'd only known her groom for a full day?

The salesperson returned, holding up a pair of golden high heels, carrying them by the ankle straps. He could well imagine what those would look like on Shannon, who had the loveliest calves. So slim and sexy.

Shannon bent down, slipped her slim feet into the shoes, and fastened the straps. When she stood, Séamus could've used another magazine to drop from the radiance of her beauty in the silk and lace dress and high heels. All she needed was a bouquet and veil.

He'd called the florist while she'd been in change room, slipping from her sweatpants and hoodie she'd worn for the day, having admitted to him she'd packed casually because she'd assumed she'd be in her driver's uniform all weekend.

Well, it was time to take her back to the hotel and get married.

At the suite, hidden in the bedroom she was occupying for the weekend, Shannon smoothed her dress in front of the full-length mirror.

She'd done her makeup, pulled her hair into a loose bun, and was ready—or was she ready?—to marry a perfect stranger. The natural rapport that had developed between them didn't make tying the knot any easier, nor did it untie the knots in her stomach.

Mom and Kokum would call her irresponsible. Pashney would call her an idiot. Everyone would find what she'd done more reckless than taking the final turn at the stock car race at an outrageous speed to win the women's finals that one Saturday night.

Her own limo business danced in front of her. Wasn't this why they'd come to Toronto? Wasn't this what Kokum and Mom had urged her to do? Be a success instead of toiling at a dead-end job back on the reserve? And Séamus needed her help. Yes, she'd keep telling herself that.

A knock came at the door. She dashed over, still having to slip on her shoes. "Yes?"

"For you, Miss Nadjiwon."

The attendant held out a small bouquet of bunched roses. The scent coming from the pink petals hit her square in the nose. "Thank you."

He simply nodded. "The judge will be here in fifteen minutes." He closed the door.

Rather strange how blasé the man was being. Then again, she'd been just as blasé when witnessing the antics of some of her clients. And she had fifteen more minutes of freedom before becoming Séamus' wife.

She set the bouquet on the bed and sat to slip on her shoes. Trying to buckle the ankle straps proved vexing, because her hands wouldn't stop shaking. Was she doing this for her dream, or because she really wanted to help Séamus, who proved to be nothing but a gentleman caught in a horrible web spun by his tyrannical father?

She let out a breath and glanced at the clock on the nightstand.

A door opened and closed. Séamus' voice carried into the

bedroom. He was greeting someone, most likely the judge.

Shannon shook her head. Truly, a Daugherty could do anything—like plan a wedding in under twenty-four hours on a weekend.

With another big breath and squeezing the bouquet of flowers, Shannon inched from her bedroom and into the small hallway. Her heels clicking on the floor gave away her presence as she approached the living area.

Séamus was in the middle of clutching the judge's hand—a white-haired older man in a suit instead of his robe—but stopped shaking. His gaze wandered from Shannon's shoes, danced up her legs, caressed her belly, skimmed her breasts, and then rested on her face.

"You look absolutely lovely." Séamus' voice was sweeter than cotton candy.

The compliment heated Shannon's earlobes. She gulped. "Thank you."

"So this is the bride, hmm?" the judge inquired in a tone he must've used to upbraid a criminal in front of the bench. His faded blue eyes squinted, and the wrinkling of his thick brows matched the crow's feet under his scrutinizing peepers.

Shannon glanced back to Séamus. He was too handsome in a light-gray three-piece suit that hugged and accentuated each muscle on his athletic body. No doubt it'd been custom made by some famous designer.

The engagement ring he'd bought was nestled perfectly on her ring finger. She didn't have the matching band, but that would happen in a matter of minutes.

"What does your father say?" the judge mused. "I'm rather surprised he didn't throw you a shindig like he did for your brother. How is Cillian?"

"He's fine." Séamus never looked at the judge but kept staring at Shannon. His penetrating gaze was almost burning a hole through her dress.

"Are you ready . . . miss?" Given the judge's continued narrowed brows, he did not approve.

Shannon stiffened and nodded.

The old codger fastened his judgmental stare back on Séamus. "Is your father aware?"

"He will be once I return home," Séamus nonchalantly replied. "And I do thank you very much for coming here on such short notice."

"Anything for your father." The judge clucked his tongue. "Is there anything you have planned?"

"No. You may simply marry us." Séamus held out his hand.

Seeing his offered palm squelched the hint of perspiration that had gathered at the back of Shannon's neck. She edged forward.

Evening was upon them. The last of the sunlight was streaming in through the many windows flooding the living area, allowing a perfect view of the mountain.

She took Séamus' hand that was warm, even reassuring. His thumb caressed her skin. Tiny jolts of heat and electricity shot through Shannon's veins and straight up her arm. She was guided in front of the mammoth array of windows.

The attendant stepped forward, along with a redheaded woman Shannon hadn't seen before, no doubt another staff person from the hotel.

"I imagine you are using discretion." The judge removed his reading glasses from his breast pocket and opened a small book.

"I am a Daugherty. Discretion is what we do best. And not showing emotion." The *droll* had returned to Séamus' voice.

"Obviously." The judge slid on his reading glasses. "Are you two ready to marry?"

Ready? Never in her life had Shannon been so unprepared. Somehow, a *yes* managed to eke out from between her lips while Séamus merely gave an "of course."

This was it. There was no turning back. Or was there?

CHAPTER TEN: WHIPLASH

The cold gold band with the row of encrusted diamonds almost blinded Shannon like the sun in the winter out on the ice, reminding her she wasn't single but married. Somehow, she'd said *yes* during the simple five-minute ceremony. The judge had already left, pronouncing them husband and wife. Also discreetly unseen were the two witnesses.

As a young girl, Shannon hadn't given her own wedding much thought, because taking the plunge hadn't entered her mind back on the reserve — only success.

She stole a peek at Séamus. He was now officially her husband. She was a Daugherty, in-law to one of the wealthiest families in Canada. Marrying billionaires didn't happen to girls from the rez.

"A toast to us?" Séamus' voice remained casual, as if wedding a stranger was something he did every weekend when he jetted off from Toronto.

"I guess the deed is done." Shannon attempted to swallow, but nothing went down her parched throat. "You'll have your job and inheritance. Your father can't blackball you."

"No, he can't." Séamus reached for the champagne chilling in the bucket. "I didn't think you'd want to dine out tonight —"

"No." Shannon shook her head. The last thing she needed was to parade around in her just-bought wedding dress and have everyone who knew Séamus congratulating them on their marriage, because there was nothing to celebrate. They had a deal. Nothing more.

"The first thing I will do once we return is commence working on your business. I am a man of my word." Séamus popped the cork. He remained in his suit and tie. His gaze again caressed every inch of Shannon's skin, as if he was trailing his fingers along her flesh.

She shivered and hugged the bouquet closer to her chest.

"I must admit you are lovelier than spring itself. A true breath of fresh air in my cold, formal world of winter." He set aside the cork and poured them each a glass.

His words were poetic, something she hadn't expected from him. Then again, he was a perfect stranger. They'd be dating during the first year of their marriage. "Thank you." She took the offered glass.

"To us." He held up his champagne flute. There was a twinkle in his eye.

"To us," she murmured.

Their glasses clinked.

This moment was more awkward than having spinach stuck between her teeth. Since she had no words, she sipped the delicious flavor of the drink. Smoking might be a good habit to start, because it'd give her something else to do. She clutched the stem of the glass.

"Dinner will be served pretty quick." Séamus motioned at the sofa. "Have a seat while we wait."

Perhaps he had the right idea. It'd give them time to talk. There was a lot she did not know about him. She slid on the sofa, still clutching her drink. Instead of taking a seat on the opposite side, Séamus plunked down on the middle cushion.

A slither of heat climbed up Shannon's inner thighs. She pressed her legs together. "So . . . uh . . . why don't you start by telling me about your home?"

"My home . . ." Séamus chortled. He tipped back his head. His arm rested on the back of the couch, his fingers close enough to touch Shannon's arm where goosepimples had sprung to life. "It's a home like any other."

"It seems rather large to me." Shannon glanced to the dining area.

"Can you please look at me?" His question wasn't a command but a soft plea.

She forced herself to obey.

His gaze searched her face. "I'm good on my promise. As soon as we return, I will begin helping you secure your own business."

"I know you will." She wet her lips. Suddenly, her lap became quite interesting.

"If you wish, you can spend your first day when we get back acquainting yourself with the house and staff."

"I have to drive you to work." Her ears, for the umpteenth time, heated from her stammering.

"You're my wife now, not an employee. I'll have your former employer acquire me a new driver."

A buzzing sounded in her ears. She'd always worked, starting from her paper route at age ten. Now she wasn't an employee of Elite Limousines. "Okay."

"I'm sure my mom will host a dinner to formally introduce you to the family." His tone had become sharper. He folded his lip over the other and glanced to a Chippendale side table.

"We'll live at the house?" Throat burning, she gulped back a mouthful of champagne.

"For now."

The attendant appeared from wherever he'd been hiding. "Dinner is ready."

Séamus set down his silverware and wiped his mouth. Now that they'd eaten their first meal as a married couple, they should retire to bed together. But they weren't typical newlyweds. He'd get to bid his wife goodnight and sojourn upstairs . . . alone.

Maybe maintaining his job, escaping a blacklisting, and keeping his inheritance might have been a better option. After all, what kind of life did he have now?

The beautiful woman sitting across from him was untouchable, until she said otherwise. Maybe she'd never give him the go-ahead. What if he ended up with a marriage like his parents'?

His collar was tightening like a noose around his neck, and he tugged at it.

Everything grew more restrictive — from his hand-crafted shoes squeezing hard against his feet and his belt strangling his waist, to his tailor-made linen shirt constricting.

"We do have our honeymoon to plan." The words seemed to tumble from his mouth. Perhaps his ears needed to hear his bride speak after such a silent meal.

"Honeymoon?" Pink flecked Shannon's sharp cheekbones. She glanced up.

"Yes. Wherever you wish to go. Let me know, and I'll get my assistant to make the arrangements." Strange, at one time he'd had his eye on his assistant at the office but had pinned his gaze elsewhere because he did not believe in taking advantage of those under him. Why was his new wife the exception? He had to unearth what it was about her that had caused him to break his personal rule.

"Mom and Kokum did want me to see the world." She wiped her mouth and set aside her napkin.

"Europe? Asia?" He leaned into the table.

"Europe sounds nice. I've never been there."

"Then Europe it'll be. Where exactly in Europe? We can do a tour of the western part of the continent." *The only trip I wish to take you on is to my bedroom.*

She pushed at a stray strand of hair that had slipped from her updo. "I'll let you be the tour guide."

He'd give anything to release the rest of her hair. If the heat on his skin kept up, and his itchy fingers didn't behave themselves, he'd be forced to sit on his hand. "Then I'll start planning one for us as soon as we get back."

She nodded.

The uncomfortable silence hanging in the air was comparable to the stillness of nature before a tornado arrived to wreak havoc. "I guess . . . well . . . I guess it's time to retire. We have a long trip ahead of us tomorrow."

"Yes. Tomorrow." She glanced down. "I'm sure . . ." She glanced up. There was a hint of fear in her dark eyes. "I'll get to meet your family."

"Have no worry. I'll install you in our quarters and deal with Father. Is that okay?"

"Sure. I have phone calls to make, so it'll give me time to . . . speak to my parents and friends."

He straightened his shoulders. Only rebellious schoolchildren feared the repercussions of decisions made in haste, but they were two adults. He was not going to let Father keep controlling his life. "Then allow me to walk you to your room." He stood.

She stole a peek at the wall of windows and rose. The dress swirled around her hips, accentuating her slim calves delicious enough to lick.

Although he'd eaten, hunger unfurled in him. He extended his hand. God, why did he have to be raised a gentleman? Silently, he cursed Ellen, who'd done too good of a job and should've allowed him to grow up to be a seducing shmuck like Ethan.

After Shannon had spent the night tossing and turning, the sun seeping in through the curtains she'd left opened hit her face. Sunday. They'd fly home today as a married couple. She rubbed the soft sheet covering her. Any other bride retired to sleep in her husband's arms on her wedding night, but she'd woken alone.

Coming from somewhere inside the suite were sounds of plates being set, dishes rattling, and another noise she couldn't distinguish. It was time to rise and face the world as a married woman.

The first thing she'd do upon arriving in Toronto was find a time to tell her friends what she'd done. Her eardrums already hurt at the words Pashney would spit out.

Tonight, she'd have to call Mom and Dad.

Then she'd probably have to meet Séamus' parents.

Oh boy, this was not how she'd anticipated starting her first day as a new bride. No, she hadn't spent countless hours planning her wedding as a girl, but she'd expected to marry a man she loved and wanted to grow old with, just like her parents and grandparents.

Well, the deed was done. Now she had to find her courage and face reality. First, she'd shower and dress. Before she could hide under the covers and continue to let her thoughts reprimand her, she rose and had a quick shower. Once finished, she made her way to the main area to find Séamus absent.

Her peripheral vision caught movement outside. He was on the balcony. She'd join him. Maybe he was also having regrets, which was why he wasn't present to greet her. She poured herself a cup of coffee and headed outside.

The door clicked behind her.

Séamus pivoted, smartly outfitted in a sweater and chinos. Didn't this man ever dress down? Yet, the attire he'd selected was smart, rather preppy, what she'd expect of an Englishman at his country club.

"Good morning." His gaze was brighter than the sun. "How'd you sleep?"

"Fine." There was no point in concerning him about her

tossing and turning. "How about you?" *I'm talking to my husband. He's my husband. This is unbelievable.*

"I won't lie. I could've slept better." He sipped his coffee.

If he was being honest, so could she. "Same here."

"You didn't sleep well?"

"No. I just . . . I didn't want to alarm you or anything."

"You admitted so the other morning."

"That was expected, considering I had a big decision to make." She needed something to do with her hands, so she also sipped her coffee.

"Shannon . . ." Concern deepened in his gaze. "I want you to understand one thing, okay?"

"What is it?" God, whenever he spoke her name, he produced ripples down her spine. She could only imagine how her name would sound coming from his lush mouth when they were finally between the sheets.

"My parents never communicate. Ever. Father simply gives Mom orders. Or informs her if he thinks she requires to know something. Let's be honest with each other. And open. Deal?"

She winced. He probably didn't want a marriage anything close to resembling his parents'. "Deal." She nodded.

The knitting of his brows disappeared. "Thank you." He kept studying her. "If you like, we can spend the day shopping before we leave. I thought you might want to select a new wardrobe."

"New . . . wardrobe?" But he had to tell his parents about their marriage, and she had people to talk to. "You didn't want to go home right away?"

"There's nothing to hurry for. I'll tell my parents, and that's that." He shrugged. "Mom will plan a dinner party to introduce you to our family and friends, most likely the following weekend or the next, considering the last-minute notification I'm giving her."

"I need to tell my parents. I also need to speak to my

roommates. Sunday's their day off."

"You can't meet with them in the evening over dinner?" He held up his hand. "I'm not trying to dictate your schedule. I want that understood. I simply wish to spend more time with you before we leave, that's all. You are my wife. I thought a day in Banff would be perfect."

He was right. And his concern about wanting to know her better . . . Warmth grew in her belly. He was communicating with her. Being honest. He truly did not desire a marriage like his parents'. "We can do that."

His lips stretched into a wide smile. "Let's have breakfast, pack, and then we'll be on our way."

"On our way . . ." To her new life as the wife to one of the richest men in Canada.

Séamus wasn't much for shopping. From the day he'd been born, everything had been tailor-made for him, so purchasing a new outfit was a matter of heading for Armando's to select the fabric he wanted. But watching his new wife try on gowns, dresses, sweaters, pants, skirts, and shoes wasn't boring but fun.

Her modesty always won out when she looked at the price tag, but he'd tell her to buy it anyway. She had a new spring wardrobe fitting for a woman married to a man due to inherit half his father's empire.

He sat in another boutique, thumbing through a magazine while Shannon changed in the dressing room. The attire they were seeking was on the casual side for Sunday brunch at home, or simply lounging around the house. He still hadn't turned on his cell phone. Every message was going to voicemail, and he could imagine how the messages were piling up.

The dressing room door opened. He set aside his

magazine. Shannon emerged. Or should he say *his wife*? She didn't glance his way but moved toward the three-way mirror. She brushed at her thighs covered in wide-legged, yellow linen pants. The white knit short-sleeved top with the V-shaped neckline and tiny pearl buttons enhanced her bronzed skin.

The outfit was made for brunch at his favorite restaurant back in Toronto after Sunday Mass. Dressy, yet not too dressy.

On a Sunday afternoon, they were the only customers. The sales lady was up front at Shannon's request, who'd wanted to shop in peace. She'd explained to him she wasn't used to being fussed over while browsing and deciding to purchase something.

Séamus stood. He'd meant to remain seated, but his body had a mind of its own as he traveled across the hardwood floor to stand behind Shannon. The mirror captured their reflections.

He couldn't help but stare at them. At around five-nine, she was the perfect height for his six feet and two inches. Of their own accord, his hands slid over her shoulders. "This outfit was made for you."

"You like it?" Again, she smoothed the pants. Her gaze was directed on him in the mirror.

Without her hair secured in a braid, the fringes at her sides brushed her high cheekbones and feathered the delicate material of the shirt. Her bangs were swept to the left, giving her a coyness to her usual serious or business-like face.

"The outfit can be as beautiful as it wants, but it all depends on who's wearing it," he whispered while leaning into her ear. The heat from her lobe touched his lips.

She turned her head slightly. Her gaze was directly on his.

He molded his mouth over hers. The kiss was gentle, just enough to tell her how beautiful she was. When her lips moved in motion with his slow rhythm, warmth filled his heart. She was responding to him, instead of feeding him the obligatory kiss as she'd done during their wedding ceremony.

No, he hadn't wanted to marry, and the same for Shannon. But the chemistry almost melting his flesh said she more than wanted him. And successful marriages had begun with even less of a chance.

Chapter Eleven: Car Wheels on a Gravel Road

This was it. Show time.

Their ride in the jet had been quiet, both tired after such a long and surprising weekend. Séamus had read while Shannon slept. When they'd landed at the airport, there'd been a hint of tension coming from Shannon while gathering up the mounds of luggage and shopping boxes, since there was nobody to oversee the transporting of the goods to the trunk. He had married the chauffeur, after all.

If Shannon was tense, Séamus should drive. Once they arrived at the manor, he wanted her relaxed. Too bad he'd lost his license and couldn't take the wheel. He opened the Audi's passenger door to the front seat.

Where he now sat was a reminder of what he'd taken away from his new wife and what had first drawn him to Shannon from the beginning—a woman with ambition and goals. An independent female who didn't mind packing a trunk, retrieving luggage, or setting mounds of boxes and bags inside the vehicle. The back seat was a hoarder's wet dream come true from their shopping expedition in Banff.

Shannon's outfit was as smart as her. White dress pants to enhance her sexy legs and tiny waist. The yellow button-down top gave a peek at the swell of her breasts that would fit perfectly in the palm of his hand. And chunky-heeled white sandals to show off feet more elegant than his home. She'd braided her hair on the jet and left her bangs sweeping to the side, allowing a full look at her high cheekbones, lips that weren't too plump or too thin, and eyes with a hint of a slant.

She shifted the gear. Her left hand rested on the steering wheel. The engagement ring and wedding band glittered under the outside lights of the hangar. "I'll have to call my parents in the morning, and maybe set up dinner with my friends for tomorrow night. They really have to know."

"Of course." Arriving late was a blessing, because there was much to address, the biggest hurdle being Father. "Drive away . . . driver."

Her lips parted into a half smile. With the way she tapped her nail, an edge of nervousness was no doubt growing in her.

There wasn't a chance Séamus would allow Father to demean his bride. He should've packed some boxing gloves, because he'd need them once they arrived home.

With the staff overseeing the car, Shannon was led by the hand not to the guest cottage, but to the side entrance of the manor. Her heels clicked against the cobblestone pavement. The scent of flowers wafted under her nose.

Even though it was dark, and the garden-like setting to the house was supposed to provide soothing tranquility, her stomach became more than butterflies, more like buzzing bees having their nest disturbed.

She'd never met the tyrannical Padraig Harrington, but the monster Séamus spoke about during their weekend was a *Wi-indigo* hiding in the closet, ready to jump out and tear off her flesh for consumption.

The house was lit, even the side entrance. They hadn't left Banff until six o'clock. Since the mountain city was two hours behind eastern time, and the flight had taken well over three hours, it was now midnight. She'd expected total darkness to greet them.

The side door swung open. A gray-haired man in a stiff, formal suit and just as stiff, formal frown greeted them. "Your father wishes to see you in his study. As for the lady, I shall take her to her accommodations."

"Accommodations?" Séamus stopped, and Shannon almost bumped into him.

"Yes, accommodations." The man motioned at the door. "Sir?"

Séamus squeezed Shannon's fingers. "I shouldn't be long. Called to Father's Persian rug again for daring to leave without informing anyone of my whereabouts, and for failing to answer my cell. I'll be up right away."

Shannon nodded, but being taken to Séamus' bedroom before they could talk about their sleeping arrangements ramped up her pulse points to a speed faster than the jet that had returned them to Toronto.

"We can use the family staircase," the butler informed her in a rigid, low voice. "Right this way, Miss Nadjiwon."

Shannon almost blanched. He knew her name? The only staff she'd met the other morning was Ellen. As for when she'd picked up the town car to first drive Séamus, a different man had been present to hand her the keys to the Audi. Maybe it was true about butlers knowing everything about the manor they served.

As expected, the staircase wasn't grand and winding, but a flight up with a landing to the family floor.

"This is the guest wing." The butler continued to stride down the hall. "I have readied the Pearl Room for you."

Shannon should be thankful her sleeping arrangements were decided on for the night, but as Séamus' wife, why wasn't she shown to his suite?

Speak up, a little voice ordered her.

But she was in chauffeur mode, a lowly servant meant to

take orders and obey. She clutched her purse tighter against her stomach.

The butler swung open the single door to a room reminiscent of pearls with its ivory walls, butterscotch wainscotting, and off-white tray ceiling. Dainty and feminine. The butler presumed she'd desire a four-poster bed done up in snow white with matching sheer curtains, a teak writing desk, and chaise lounge.

He should see her bedroom at home — well, the townhouse. Messy and mismatched furniture bought at garage sales. She was from the rez, not the majestic hills of countryside Ireland.

"Rollins is seeing to your luggage. He shall be up soon." The butler, about as robotic and stiff as Lurch from the *Addams Family*, moved toward the door. "Is there anything I can get you, Miss Nadjiwon?"

Her voice had returned. She cleared her throat. A smidgen of courage crawled up her spine. "That's Mrs. Daugherty. And yes, I'd like some lemon tea."

Fine, Séamus had wanted to tell his father about their marriage, but she wasn't going to stand for a single second more of being talked down to and addressed as a nobody. She'd given up her single life and individual dream for Séamus, and by God, his family and servants would treat her as a true daughter-in-law.

The butler didn't even raise a brow. "As you wish, Mrs. Daugherty."

"One more thing. My cat's in the guest house. I'd like him brought up here."

The butler's face remained impassive. "Of course." With that, he turned on his heel and closed the door.

All Shannon could do was wait. She'd keep an ear out for footsteps. Since she knew Séamus' gait by now, once his feet padded on the floor, she'd open her door and find out why the butler had installed her in a guest room. The decision of where she'd stay was Séamus' to make.

Séamus sat in his usual spot in front of Father's desk. There was no tea served. Not even a glass of water.

Instead of planting his butt on his throne, Father stared out the window at nothing available to view but what the outside lamps had lit. His hands were clasped behind his back. This was a first, which tipped off Séamus to a foreboding nightmare about to appear in the dead of night.

Father kept clasping and unclasping his fingers. In the window, his reflection was drawn brows and drawn-in cheeks. "Why?" was all he said in a hushed yet stern voice.

"Why what?" Séamus moved his foot in a circle. He picked at nothing on his pants. At midnight, his weary body yearned to retire upstairs and find out where his wife desired to sleep tonight. Hopefully, she hadn't been alarmed when Johnson had shown her to his suite.

"Why else would I ask you in here? I heard from Judge Morson yesterday evening. He said he performed your marriage."

Way to go, Mr. Judge. Séamus should've have expected no less from a man in the old boys' club. Being a friend of Father's, it was no big surprise the judge had picked up the phone and broken the news before Séamus had slid the wedding band on Shannon's finger.

"He said you married Shannon Nadjiwon. The very woman I approved to be your driver." Father's calmness meant a storm was brewing.

Séamus didn't brace himself. He'd done as instructed and married. "Isn't this what you wanted?"

"W-wanted?" The natural pinkish-red undertone of Father's face became the color of a ripe tomato. He thrust his finger. "You know damn well what I wanted."

"Yes, what you wanted, Father." Séamus remained in the chair. But he couldn't help sitting straighter. "Did you think to ask me what I wanted?"

"I know exactly what you want. A night with the ladies. Surfing. Skiing. Golfing. Tennis. Vacations. When are you going to grow up?"

"I think I more than earned those holidays. I give my blood, sweat, and tears to Daugherty Enterprises." *I gave my blood, sweat, and tears to you, too, but you couldn't have cared less to notice.*

"You knew exactly what I wanted to discuss on Friday night." Father's brows narrowed even further.

"You simply told me you wanted to speak to me. But I decided to—"

"... thwart me by marrying a woman I'd never approve of." Father adjusted his suit. Even at midnight, the tyrant had to play dress-up.

"What's wrong with Shannon?" Séamus did a quick blink to feign innocence. "She's an industrious woman with ambitions."

"She does not fit the criteria each woman must meet ever since your great-great-great-grandfather immigrated to Canada."

"I see. Not Catholic. Not from old money. Not educated. And not Irish."

Father nodded. "I am going to have this marriage annulled—"

"Or what? You do know the scandal this will cause. Isn't that what you wish to avoid at all costs?"

"You little bastard." Rage pounded in Father's eyes, a hurricane ready to touch down on Séamus and obliterate him. "You may think you've won this battle, but I did not keep this empire successful by allowing anyone to get the better of me."

"This isn't about ..." Séamus clamped his mouth shut. If he denied the accusation, he'd be lying, because he had married Shannon to thwart his father. "Why is it so bad that I made a decision on my own without consulting you first? Did you ever think that maybe I wanted to choose my own wife?"

"I planned on allowing you to choose your wife, as I did for Cillian."

"Yes, from a small pool of women. How many fit the mold in this city?"

"For goodness sake, she didn't have to be from Toronto. There are plenty of women in this country who are Irish. There's the States, Ireland . . . all over the world. Need I go on?" Father's legs purposely moved one in front of the other as he bore down on the desk. Ah yes, it was time for the tyrant to unpack his walk of intimidation.

"And was I supposed to go on a tour seeking a wife?" Tension scraped the back of Séamus' neck. Always having to be taller, standing above people, was just like Father, a great tactic to proclaim himself as alpha. So Seamus also stood.

At his height, he looked down on Father, who was a mere five feet and ten inches.

"Sit." Father thrust out his finger. He rounded the desk, once again finding a way to make himself king of the castle as he sat upon his leather throne behind his desk of dictatorship.

Séamus did sit. There was no point in standing, especially since his tired legs and aching back demanded he crawl into bed and sleep. But his brain wasn't tired and demanded to fight.

"Since you have solidified a position in this private battle you have going on between us by marrying against my wishes . . ." Father put his hands together and gave a loud, slow clap. "Bravo, Séamus. Bravo. Maybe you do have it in you to truly be a Daugherty as your brother is."

A cold wave of suspicion from the insult hit Séamus across the face like a loud backhanded slap. "What's that supposed to mean? I am every inch a Daugherty as Cillian."

"I didn't think you were, but considering your tactic to sink my battleship, shall we say, you have proven to be quite unscrupulous. Anything to win, hmm?"

Séamus stiffened.

"Tell me, did she jump at the opportunity when you proposed marriage? A girl from an Indian Reservation?"

The air drained from Séamus' lungs. He blinked. Shannon was innocent in this battle, and he'd let his pride and ego interfere in her dreams. She'd come to the city to make something of herself, and he hadn't relented until she'd said yes. Shit, he'd become what he'd sworn to never be — as manipulative, domineering, and dubious as Father.

"It's Indian Reserve. Shannon would say only white people use the term reservation. In Canada it's Indian Reserve. But as you and I both know, the Indigenous People prefer to use First Nations community. And . . ." Dammit, he couldn't out Shannon by confessing she'd only said yes because of the deal he'd proposed. That would for sure smear her name.

"She was . . . hesitant, but being the director of marketing, I'd say you would've been quite proud of how I sold myself." Séamus held his father's narrow-eyed stare.

"And what did you offer her exactly? Judge Morson said there wasn't even a prenup. Do you realize what you've done?"

"She doesn't want my money or your money." Séamus couldn't help the bite to his words. Shannon wasn't a gold digger. "As a matter of fact, I had to persuade her to undertake a shopping expedition."

"Shopping?"

"Yes, I can't have my bride sitting down to dinner with us in her casual attire, can I? And because she works so hard, she doesn't have a proper wardrobe required for this . . . house." Séamus moved his hand around. "She hardly takes a day off."

After having spent his entire life surrounded by wealth, for some reason the Persian rug, crystal chandelier, great-great-great-grandfather's refurbished desk, and every other damn thing in this room costing a fortune was the scent of a skunk having sprayed Séamus' nose.

"I hired her for her credentials. Her employer told me she is the best he has next to Mr. Richardson."

"Then why not Mr. Richardson?"

"Because he's set to retire next year, so I selected . . . well, I guess I can't call her Miss Nadjiwon anymore, can I? So much for her professionalism that Mr. Bouchard assured me of when he recommended her."

"Shannon is highly professional. It was I who pursued her, not vice versa." Séamus also set his hands on the desk.

They hovered above Great-great-great Grandfather's most prized possession. Eye to eye. Close to mouth to mouth. The light from the lamp cast shadows across Father's face, reminiscent of an ominous figure in a horror movie.

"I guess then we'll see if she is up to becoming a Daugherty." Father maintained his stance. His glare was a serial killer ready to abduct his victim. "If she fails, the marriage will be annulled, scandal or not. And then you will find a proper wife, or . . ."

The threat lingered in the air like the calm before an avalanche ready to smother skiers in mounds of heavy snow.

"She won't fail. Ever." But becoming a full-fledged Daugherty wasn't the deal Séamus had made with Shannon.

His inheritance and livelihood were still on the line.

Chapter Twelve: Pull Up to the Bumper

Séamus stormed up the family staircase. Only the hall light was on, creating dim shadows across the many paintings hanging on the walls. From beneath the Pearl Room door, illumination lit the crack between the floor and the door's bottom.

His heart stopped for a moment. There was only one reason why a guest room would be occupied. He came to a full halt and tapped his knuckles against the hard, heavy wood.

"Yes?" Shannon called out.

His heart not only had stopped but sank to his feet. "Is everything all right?" He shouldn't be upset she'd chosen to stay in another room that wasn't his when he'd told her they could move at her pace.

The door opened. Shannon stood before him in jogging pants and a t-shirt. Her unbound hair swirling around her shoulders and almost brushing her waist dared him to taste the succulent midnight-black strands with his fingers, even his lips.

"Everything's fine." She motioned at her accommodations. "Your butler showed me here when you went to your father's study."

"He showed you here?" Séamus' heart returned to its normal spot. A flame erupted in his chest. Such liberties Johnson had taken with his bride. Then again, the family butler had probably been following Father's orders.

"Yes. Someone named Rollins brought up my luggage. The man I met on Friday morning. He also fetched Keemooch." She pointed at the gray cat kneading the plush comforter.

"You could've selected any room you wished to sleep in." The thudding of Séamus' heart was loud enough to wake the cranky butler.

"He didn't give me an option, but I did set him straight once I . . ." Shannon raised her chin. "I won't be treated as a guest."

"No, you shouldn't be. If you wish to sleep in my room . . ." *Where the hell is this courage coming from?* Under her dark, scrutinizing eyes, she'd reduced him to a schoolboy trying to sneak his first kiss. "Well, that is entirely up to you. The family suites are situated in the west wing."

"I'm not a guest. Tell Rollins to move my luggage." Shannon drew back her shoulders. "Let me get Keemooch. He goes wherever I go."

"Not a problem. He's welcome in my suite." Séamus wasn't sure if Shannon's decision stemmed from mere pride at being shown to a room beneath her position in the house, or if she really wanted to stay with him.

Neither reason mattered, other than the fact she was moving to his room.

Séamus' suite shouldn't have surprised Shannon. He came from a first-class family and would have first-class accommodations. She stood in what she assumed was his sitting room where he could relax and listen to music or watch TV. There was even a desk and two bookshelves, but she had a hunch he wasn't a *work at home* person. More of a *stay late at the office* instead.

"This is really nice." And it was. The sitting room alone was the size of her bedroom and Pashney's combined back at the townhouse.

Already, Keemooch was sniffing about, exploring his new home.

There was a knock at the door.

"That's probably Rollins with your luggage. Enter," Séamus called out.

Rollins strolled by them, hauling the luggage toward two double doors.

The bedroom—that was where the man was heading. Shannon shivered. Her pride had brought her to Séamus' suite, or was her pride fully responsible? No, she hadn't enjoyed being treated as a guest, and she'd sealed her fate by putting her foot down. But as his wife, she did belong in this room. If she was to establish herself firmly in this family, she couldn't afford a cent of meekness or apprehension. They were Daughertys and had built an empire. People didn't become billionaires by playing fair.

Her culture was a million miles away from Séamus' lifestyle. Yes, they spoke about the circle, but the Daughertys viewed what was sacred to the Ojibway through a different lens. Somehow, she had to find her footing without sacrificing her principles.

"I'd better show him where to store what I brought." Shannon entered the bedroom to a massive four-poster bed that looked bigger than king-size. There was even a dais to step up to where Séamus slept.

Rollins ignored the two armoires and continued to a door leading to another room. Shannon followed.

She stood in a room that could have been one of the boutiques in Banff with lines of racks on each wall, filled with Séamus' clothes, from pants and suits to tuxedos and outerwear. In the middle was a bureau island with drawers on every side. There was even a chair and a three-way mirror.

Rollins opened another door to the bathroom. "I'm

assuming Mr. Daugherty will move the two of you to a more appropriate suite that can host two people. This is a single suite."

"Single?"

"Yes, his brother and wife have a suite that obliges a husband and wife." Rollins set the carry-on beside the vanity. "I'm sure you would like a dressing table for your toiletries and makeup."

Her own station to do makeup? Of course. Shannon nodded.

"Consider the suite temporary." Rollins bowed his head slightly. "If there is anything else you require, just ring. I will be sure to move the cat litter, as well."

"Thank you."

Rollins left the closet. Or, well, the room.

Séamus passed Rollins on his way out. "This is only temporary."

"That's what Rollins told me." Shannon couldn't help gawking at her husband's magnificent wardrobe before her. There was even a shoe rack and every designer label possible.

"I know it's late and you have a lot you wish to tackle tomorrow . . ." Séamus motioned his hand at the entranceway.

"Yes, I do." *Like call my parents and drop the bomb. Bring over takeout so Ronnie can congratulate me and Pashney can read me the riot act. Or maybe they'll both box my ears.*

"We can discuss everything in the morning over breakfast. I know you want me to get started on your business plan right away. And I need your banking information so I can pay off your portion on the townhouse."

"There'll be a prepayment penalty. When we applied for the mortgage, the bank told us about it."

"We can discuss that in the morning. Come. I know you're tired. You had a lot to digest this weekend."

His fingers snaked around hers. Warmth not only spread across Shannon's belly but also between her legs. He was her husband and had every right to take her hand. She let him lead her from the closet and into the bathroom.

"If you need to use the lavatory in the middle of the night," he said.

The bathroom was whiter than white and held not only a soaking tub but a glass shower big enough to fit three people. There was only one sink.

"We'll be moved to our new suite in the morning while we're out. Ellen will take care of everything." Reassurance was in his tender voice. "I know you'll want to unpack your toiletries before we retire. Perhaps a bath or shower?"

"A quick shower sounds nice." After the amount of traveling, her skin demanded she wash off the grime. "Thanks."

"I'll leave you to your bathing." His expression of a straight line to his lips and blank stare left his countenance hard to read. He closed the door.

With shaky hands, she set to readying the bathroom for the night, removing her toiletries from the overnight bag Rollins had left by the vanity. Once she was in the shower, scrubbing herself left her trembling, because she couldn't stop imagining Séamus gliding his fingers over her wet skin.

Ten minutes later, she left the bathroom wrapped in a silk robe and a matching nightgown. She'd rolled up her wet hair to not dampen her sleeping attire or pillow. The bedroom was empty except for Keemooch, who'd claimed the chaise lounge as his bed. Perhaps Séamus was in the massive closet readying to sleep.

As she climbed up the dais, the bed became a monster, ready to swallow her whole. She'd lay her head down where her new husband slept every night. Butterflies peppered her stomach. Already, the sheets had been turned down, inviting her to rest in their posh confines.

She removed the robe and set the silk garment at the foot. With still no sign of Séamus, Shannon crawled under the covers to pure plushness wrapping her like a cocoon of coziness. Although her lids begged to close, the sound of running water coming from the bathroom made dozing off impossible, no matter if her body screamed for rest.

Séamus was in the shower cleaning his athletic body and washing his thick brown hair.

Shannon shivered. She rested on her side, hands tucked between her knees. The beating of her heart boomed in her ears. Goosepimples spread across her body. No matter the season was spring and the night air was not too hot or too cold, and the scent of the flower garden was wafting in through the open window, her joints had become stiffer than a board.

When the running water stopped, she tensed and flicked open one eye.

Footsteps padded across the floor. Bare feet. He was undressed, most likely.

She coiled even tighter.

The scent of his soap was in the air, telling Shannon he was growing closer. There was a hint of a squeak, indicating he had ascended the dais. Rustling happened. Perhaps he was removing his robe. Then what did he sleep in? She couldn't imagine Séamus in pajamas.

The bedside light dimmed to blackness.

Shannon snaked her hand out from her knees and squeezed her pillow.

The mattress heaved slightly, and the covers were drawn back on his side. A smidgen of air snuck beneath the blankets, caressing Shannon's backside. Then the tiny bit of air vanished. She bit down on her lower lip. Her breath automatically held on its own.

More movement came from Séamus. He was turning onto his stomach. Shannon continued to keep her back to him. The blankets rustled some more, followed by the puffing sound of his head sinking into the pillow.

She squeezed her toes.

"Goodnight, Shannon."

Dammit, why did her name on his lips always resemble his fingers gliding up her thighs? She managed to choke out a "Goodnight, Séamus," through the frog stuck in her throat.

Sleeping would be impossible, no matter how big the bed was. No, she couldn't feel his heat because he was too far away, like two people living on opposite ends of the city, but his presence was suffocating her like an anvil sitting on her chest. He'd said they'd consummate their marriage when she was ready, which meant he wouldn't try seducing her into succumbing to his tasty lips and wet tongue.

All she had to do was roll over, but no matter how much her mind willed her to do the deed, her body wouldn't cooperate and continued to lie on its useless side. What did she have to do to get some teamwork around here? Yell at her hips and legs to roll the hell over?

This wasn't the nineteenth century. She had every damn right to ask for sex. He was her husband, but also a stranger she'd met on Friday morning.

"Shannon?"

His whispered word shot her flagging spirits from her feet up to her chest where warmth grew. "Yes?"

"I know we need to spend time together. You mentioned seeing your friends tomorrow. How about the following night then? I'd love to take you out. We could go to a play? Dinner?"

"I'd love that." This time her body cooperated, and she rolled over. As she propped on the pillow, the words easily flew from her mouth, "I'm glad you want to spend an evening together."

"You are?" Surprise was in his reply, as if he couldn't believe she wanted anything to do with him.

Strange. Because she wanted everything to do with him.

"Yes, I am. I'd even like to go out tomorrow night, but I really need to talk to them."

"Great." He also propped himself up. "It must feel strange to be in a different bed."

"A little."

"Would you mind if I held you then? Would that make you feel better?" There was hope in his words.

"I don't mind." *But I'm not sure how my body will react being so close to you.* She scooted across the massive mattress.

He shifted onto his back and spread out his arm. The closer she got to him, the more heat from his flesh reached her. She settled into the pit of his arm and rested her head on his chest. The warmth of his skin enveloped her in a reassuring embrace. No, he wasn't naked but wore some type of light cotton pants, something she suspected he did for her benefit.

"Is this always how you sleep?" She couldn't help the teasing. His chest was hard but also inviting, the perfect place to lay her head. The scent from his shower clung to his flesh, an aroma of what she suspected was an Irish spring day after a light rain.

"You mean alone? With the light off?" He was probably smiling, given the tone he'd used.

"In pajama bottoms." Her fingers itched to draw a circle on his flat stomach, but she didn't dare move and kept her palm at rest.

"These aren't pajama bottoms. I don't own any." This time, she knew he was teasing

"Oh? Then why did you buy me this beautiful night-gown?"

"Are you saying you also don't sleep with anything on?" He might as well have slapped her, because his question was as cheeky as hers.

"I have my fave t-shirt." Her breath was reflecting off his nipple that was almost touching her lips. The temptation was great to kiss the erect, hard nub. "What about you?"

"Nothing. The raw." His chuckle was as sassy and mischievous as the dimples he'd flashed her way this weekend.

"So you put on your jammies for my benefit?" A giggle easily slid from her throat. The tightness in her belly unwound. And she did draw a circle around his naval.

His abs contracted beneath her touch. His breathing grew heavier, moving his chest up and down, along with her head resting on his glorious pecs.

"I told you—I was raised a gentleman." Even though he murmured, there was a scratchiness in his reply. Was this how he sounded when aroused?

Her leg ached to draw itself over his thigh. "You didn't have to do it for my benefit. I'm your wife. I want you to be comfortable."

"Comfortable?" Something resembling a snort came from his mouth.

"Aren't you comfy?"

"It depends on your definition of comfy." This time a touch of hoarseness was in his reply.

"What do you mean by that?" She came close to peeking up at him, but his firm chest was too tempting to dare lift her head.

"Comfortable, as in, am I content lying in bed with you? Very much so. Comfortable, as in, am I content merely lying with you? I won't lie. I'd love to do more than hold you close to me, but I told you already we will proceed at your pace. A gentleman always lets the lady take the lead." His silken whisper was reassuring her that how she felt meant everything to him.

The ball was in her court. She had to respond—and make up her mind on how she'd reply.

CHAPTER THIRTEEN: RIDE THE JACK

"So I'm leading?" Shannon silently slapped her stupid vocal cords for daring to shake and embarrass her. This was her first time with her husband, for nutty's sake. At twenty-eight, she was far from a virgin and even farther from being a high school teenager.

"You're the driver, aren't you?" Gone was the quiet hesitation in Séamus' tone. "Make that *my* driver."

"Yes, I'm *your* driver." She kept speaking into his nipple that remained hard and waiting for a tasting. "I'll admit I wish you would've worn your usual attire to bed."

"You mean skin?" There was a bite to his reply, as if he was nibbling at her nipples that were as hard as his.

"I don't want you to feel obliged —"

"Perhaps I don't. Maybe it's called consideration, hmm?" His *droll* was back, the teasing one when they'd first met.

If they were going to get their marriage off on the right track, it was time to put their sexual chemistry to the test that had sizzled between them from their first meeting. Shannon lifted her head to peek at him.

His lips crushed hers.

A jolt of shock and electricity shimmied up her spine. She hadn't expected to be drawn into a deep kiss reeking of hunger. His mouth was puckering, lavishing hers with sensual caresses. She returned his silky strokes, tasting his lips that had tempted her from day one.

Just as she'd suspected, he was an excellent kisser, taking the time to explore her mouth, but also allowing her to draw a breath. His tongue flicked at her closed lips, and she parted them to receive his wet flesh she'd been itching to sample. He didn't disappoint and tangled his with hers, bathing her in the scent of peppermint.

Heat smothered her skin. His tongue kept exploring hers, licking and tasting. She groaned. He wasn't the only one experiencing hunger — she too was being drawn into his erotic dance.

His one arm remained buried under her shoulder, but his hand resting on the small of her back palmed her ass cheek. Shock screamed down her spine. His fingers were electrifying excitement, fondling her into a trance. All she could do was follow his movement by lapping at his tongue, moan from his exploration of her buttock, and revel in his embrace that was warm and firm, telling her how much he desired her.

She drew her one knee higher and brushed his hard cock. The flutters in her belly intensified. Her clit was on fire, aching for his touch. She ran her hand down his abs, feathering the hard muscles constricting beneath the tips of her fingers. He groaned into her mouth, and his pleasure from her exploration increased the excitement rushing through her veins.

He used his arm behind her to draw her in closer, urging her to slide on top. She did. Their flesh melted as one. His cock was pushing on the mound of her pussy, and a hint of jizz wet her pubic hair. She couldn't help grinding against him while he continued to feast on her mouth.

His hands remained on her buttocks. He lavished her cheeks with slow strokes meant to torment, and he was. The pulsating between her legs was maddening. She deepened the kiss, furiously licking his tongue. As for his soft grunts, they were enough to drive her insane, telling her how bad he wanted her.

His mouth left hers and traveled along her jawline to her neck. He clamped down and suckled. She gasped. His cock kept pressing on her nest of pubic hair, now damp from his slick precum. She couldn't help grinding on his dick that pumped back and forth.

The low moan left her throat. There was so much heat going on, heat on her neck from his suckling, heat on her ass from his strokes, and heat on her pussy begging for his erection.

"Take me for a ride, driver," he whispered. His lips were still on her neck. With his tongue, he drew a sensual line across her skin.

To know she'd soon have him inside her raised the hairs on the back of Shannon's neck. Seamus unfastened the elastic binding her hair, and the waves fell around them.

"This is how I like seeing you." His murmurs steamed her neck. "Whenever it's up, I think of you hard at work. Having it down is very personal . . . personal to me." He rubbed his cock against the opening to her pussy. "I like it that you wear it down for me."

His hands glided up into her nightgown. He assisted her with shedding the flimsy material. The darkness didn't allow him to see her, so she shifted back to meet the head of his dick.

All she had to do was slide down a wee bit more and she'd trap him. Before she could consume him, he penetrated her, the tip slipping inside her flesh. Having him where she wanted him elicited the deepest sigh from her throat. She groaned and buried her face into his hair as he kept pushing, filling her with his girth and length.

He began pumping. She didn't even have to slide back and forth against his cock, not when it was thrusting in and out of her, awakening her to desire she hadn't felt in so long because of work.

Her body demanded she move in sync with him, and she met each of his thrusts. His lips found hers. He claimed her mouth, his tongue licking hers as she furiously returned the sensual licks with hungry ones of her own.

With it being almost forever since she'd last indulged in a night of fun, the pleasure was happening too soon. Her clit was rubbing on his length. The teasing his cock produced within her depths was maddening.

Shivers traveled down her spine. Her stomach had coiled tight. Every nerve was completely alive, ready to burst from the pleasure he was feeding her.

The delicious explosion was upon her, enveloping her in ecstasy. She cried out his name, and he joined her in the secret place where passion was taking her.

Séamus couldn't sleep, not when his wife was nestled in the pit of his arm, her hair draped across his chest and tickling his stomach. Her naked body was tormenting him, even though he'd had her a mere half hour ago, but she'd fallen deep asleep. The heavy breaths coming from her mouth were moistening the skin just below his neck.

He walked his fingers along her bare arm. How strange he'd had no inclination of marrying until Mom had tipped him off Friday morning. How could his life change so fast? Yet what he'd experienced with Shannon over these past three days was nothing he'd encountered before, even during his many vacations and exploration of the world.

Yes, he'd bedded his share of women, had his share of girl-friends, too. But marriage had never entered his mind. At twenty-nine, he'd thought of himself as too young.

Plus, marriage was what Father had wanted, so Séamus had avoided even thinking of proposing to anyone. Then there was the fact nobody had made him want to get on bended knee.

Was there more to asking Shannon for her hand other than his inheritance and job? He could admit she'd sure piqued his interest upon their first meeting. Naturally, he'd wanted to see what hid beneath her driver's uniform.

Still, after having her tonight, and experiencing her passionate response to his kisses and cock, the sex had been something else. So much that he was tempted to wake her and claim her as his own, instead of her on top, as he'd wanted her to be comfortable by taking the lead for their first time. Too bad he'd had the *gentleman* drilled into him.

There was no light present, since the drapes were always drawn at night. Just blackness. But with his adjusted sight to the dark, he could make out the silhouette of her profile. She had a beautiful nose—straight and slim. Her smacking lips, followed by a *mmm*, dared him to steal a kiss.

He gently claimed her mouth that puckered again with a *mmm*. She stiffened. Her lids flew open. For a moment, fear screeched in her eyes. Then she frowned, and her lashes fluttered. The light smile she graced him with released his own fear, because his lips were still glued to her mouth, her terror having frozen him in place.

"I didn't mean to frighten you."

"Sorry." Shannon's reply was softer than a feather. "At first, I wasn't sure where I was. And Keemooch wasn't on my feet. That's where he always sleeps."

"Yes, the cat." Séamus rose on his elbow and glanced around. In front of the window, where the chaise lounge was located, he made out the silhouette of the furry feline. "He's over there. On the chair."

"That's strange." Shannon also popped up. "He always sleeps with me."

"Maybe he's adjusting to his new room." *Please don't let her get the cat. Please.*

"Maybe it's you." She chuckled. "He must be unsure of what you're doing in his bedroom."

"His bedroom?" Séamus also couldn't help but laugh.

"He thinks wherever he sleeps, it's his spot." She glided

her short nails from one of his nipples to the other.

Was that an invitation? "Tonight, he can stay on the chair." He leaned in and slid his mouth over hers.

"Don't you mean this morning?" she asked while they were mid-pucker.

"Mmm . . . it's three. I'll be feeling the lack of sleep in the morning."

"It's already morning."

He tangled his fingers around her wrists and guided Shannon onto her back. From the smile she bestowed on him, she'd enjoyed this move. Or maybe she loved having his cock rubbing her pussy. He feasted on her parted lips, slipping his tongue inside to lick and taste hers. She squirmed beneath him, grinding back and forth against his dick.

He wasn't going to penetrate her yet. There was still much to explore on her lovely body. He broke the kiss. Her moan was one of protest. She was even trying to gather her legs around his hips.

He shook his head and murmured, "In due time, darling. All in good time."

Her breasts heaved, and he couldn't resist drawing a nipple between his lips. Her gasp of delight ramped up his horniness. He licked at the hard peak and suckled. The skin he tasted was as sweet as her. And her soft moans were driving him insane.

While he feasted on her nipple, she continued to writhe beneath him, her squirming telling him just how hot and bothered she was. His ego was about ready to burst because her excitement for his cock was stroking him in all the right places.

He tasted the skin of her flat stomach and didn't stop leaving a path of licks until he reached her warm mound of pubic hair.

The scent he inhaled was a mixture of fresh soap from her

shower and musky heat from her arousal. She raised her hips to meet his mouth. He kissed her pussy lips that were slightly parted, waiting for either his finger or tongue to slide between the warm flesh. Her wet skin was calling to him. He kissed her mound. The scent was heavenly, daring him to dive between her lips, and he did, flicking his tongue at the flesh around her clit.

His cock strained, demanding to fuck, but he ignored his own needs and explored her pussy with his tongue, lapping and tasting her cunt juices. Her thighs wrapping him tight were as smooth as the flesh he feasted on. She was nothing but satin, a temptation he never could've avoided. Even if he hadn't been pushed into marrying her, he had a good hunch eventually he would've tried his hardest to coax her into bed.

Her groans grew louder. She was ready for him to give her begging clit his undivided attention. How he was looking forward to suckling on her tasty nub. He clamped his lips down and drew the tiny tip into his mouth. Her squeals of delight stroked his throbbing cock, and she ceased writhing beneath him. Her thighs squeezed hard as she bounced her hips up and down while slathering his face with her pussy juice.

He furiously licked while she continued to pant and gasp. Her fingers claimed his hair, tugging on his short strands. He winced but never stopped sampling the hard nub under his tongue. Her wetness was all over his lips and chin.

The ripe scent of her orgasm was coating him in its heady aroma. Her bouncing and bucking had him fighting to hold on, but the perspiration on his palms that held her hips was making it difficult. He didn't want to lose momentum during such a pleasurable time for her.

"Séamus . . . Séamus . . ." she cried out.

Heady pleasure tingled down his spine to hear his name on her lips when she'd started out so politely and formally with *sir* and *mister*.

"Tell me how much you want me." He also panted. His words floated over her pussy where his mouth remained.

"Now. Please now."

Her begging was complete satisfaction to his ego. He shifted to his knees and gazed down at her, her eyes closed and breasts still heaving. She ran her tongue along her lower lip, as if still tasting the pleasure he'd given.

He lay over top of her, burying his hands in the sheets to give him leverage. His cock was pressing on the opening to her pussy, and he slid inside her tight, wet flesh that was fully open to him. He plunged deeply into her depths while she again clamped her legs around him. Her arms also draped his shoulders. He was drawn downward, his chest meeting her breasts.

"More . . ." She squealed. "More." She raised her hips and started fucking.

He joined her fast and furious pumps. His cock was locked in tight by her pussy that had claimed him, just as he claimed her.

He pounded her with all his strength, gasping and groaning from the pleasure her wetness and her moans were arousing in him.

The explosion came fast and hard. Tomorrow was going to seem like a forty-eight-hour day after being up all night with his bride.

CHAPTER FOURTEEN: EVERY DAY IS A WINDING ROAD

The knocking woke Shannon. She peeled open one eye to the maid, Ellen, done up in her black-and-white uniform, entering the sleeping area.

"Rise and shine, Mrs. Daugherty. Breakfast will be served soon." The maid scooted to the window and opened the heavy drapes to a sunny day.

The bright light blinded Shannon momentarily. She raised her hand to shield her eyes. "What time is it?"

"Ten o'clock. Your husband asked me to let you sleep late. He said you needed your rest." The maid moved from the window and plucked the nightgown and matching robe off the floor.

The nightwear must have fallen off the bed when Shannon had gotten busy with her husband. As for the maid prowling around the room, tidying up here and straightening up there, Shannon wasn't sure what to make of a stranger invading her personal space. There was such a lack of privacy with servants underfoot.

But her experience as a driver reminded her that *the help* didn't care about the personal lives of those they served. Naked beneath the sheets, Shannon kept the covers drawn up to shield her breasts.

Keemooch meandered from the bathroom, probably having used his litter box.

Ellen followed in the cat's wake, holding last night's outfit that had been in the hamper. "I will take these downstairs to the laundry room and will also feed your pet. Would you like me to run you a bath?"

"No." Shannon shook her head. "I planned on showering."

"Very good." Ellen marched for the door. "Mrs. Daugherty is expecting you in the sunroom. That's where she spends her mornings. Please let me know when you are dressed and I will escort you downstairs."

Escort? Shannon almost blinked. "How do I get a hold of you?"

The maid patted an intercom next to the door. "Simply buzz the kitchen. That's where I'll be."

"Okay." Shannon waited for the maid to leave, since she didn't have a bathrobe or anything else to wear.

Once Ellen vacated the room and closed the door, Shannon pushed aside the covers. She was running late. Although Séamus allowing her to sleep in was touching, she wished he'd have woken her when he'd risen. She wasn't a pampered princess who lounged about all day, not when she had to call Mom and tell her the news. Then there was the banking she had to see to and texting her friends regarding dinner so she could inform them about her marriage.

Her mind swirled. Maybe eating was the best thing to do. Her brain was growing foggy, and she was experiencing lightheadedness, whether from the lack of food or facing the day as Mrs. Shannon Daugherty.

"You devil. You ol' devil." Ethan lounged in the doorway of Séamus' office, cup of coffee moving back and forth. He swaggered inside. "Why didn't you tell me what you had up your sleeve? I bet he's pissed, isn't he?"

He plopped in the chair facing the desk. "You do know I was joking on Friday morning, right?"

Séamus swiveled in his high-backed leather chair. He was on his umpteenth cup of joe, having needed caffeine after rising at five-thirty, of all times, to sneak out the front door before Father started at him again. That was after he'd informed Ellen to let Shannon sleep in. Rollins had been forced to drive him to the office. Now he had to see about a new chauffeur.

"You're aware of my marriage?"

Ethan shook his head and threw out his palm. "I was joking. It was a joke. I didn't think you'd marry over the weekend. Your dad must've read you the riot act."

"Oh, he tried." Séamus waved his hand in a dismissing manner. "But there's not much he can do now, can he?" Yet, Father's threat if Shannon didn't measure up to Daugherty status lingered in the air like a bad odor.

"So when do we get to meet her?" Ethan crossed a leg over the other. He drummed his manicured fingers on the arm. "I'm assuming your mother is planning a party to introduce your new bride to everyone."

"I'm not sure. I left the house early. In fact, I need some sleep. I might nap on my lunch hour."

"I take it the honeymoon is still happening?" Ethan's usual elegant chuckle became a snorting cackle.

"Discussing a night with a lady is in poor taste. You know this," Séamus reminded his best friend. "This is my wife we're talking about."

"Understood. Beg your pardon." Ethan raised his free hand in a mock salute of defeat. "I shouldn't have gone there."

"Apology accepted. You know I'd forgive you of just about everything."

"Everything?" Ethan arched his brow and sipped from his cup.

"Just about everything. I do have my limits." Séamus rubbed his temple, where a headache was forming. He had to begin Shannon's business plan for her new endeavor and pay off her portion of the mortgage on the townhouse. But he'd best wait until she'd spoken to her friends.

"So . . . you even managed to escape Cillian? You know you can't hide from them. They'll confront you here if necessary," Ethan pointed out.

Séamus' headache grew to the size of a golf ball. If Ethan kept it up, Séamus could expect the size of a basketball. His phone buzzed. He reached over and picked up the receiver. "Yes?"

"Good morning, Mr. Daugherty. I have a message from your brother. He's reserved lunch at The Diner's Club. You are expected to be there at noon," Cillian's secretary said in her most strict voice.

"It's starting," Séamus mouthed to Ethan. He'd been summoned. How expected and unoriginal.

Shannon followed Ellen down the family staircase to meet her new mother-in-law. On their way to Mrs. Daugherty, they'd passed paintings hung on the walls, probably originals. The wainscotting was probably also original, refinished and buffed to maintain its opulence.

They reached the main hallway, where more paintings hung. Side tables, most likely antiques, held vases of flowers and other trinkets. The place wasn't a home, more like a museum specializing in nineteenth century Victorian era a historian would envy.

Shannon couldn't see a family like the Daughertys, who upheld traditions from over a hundred years ago, modernizing their house in what they'd view as tacky contemporary, much like her townhouse. They would keep everything original, with twenty-first century updates that complemented their estate.

She walked by closed doors, even those original and

apparently refinished, leading to rooms Shannon wasn't sure about. They never stopped until they reached the end of the hall and the back of the house.

The maid opened the door to a room that was welcoming and warm with its sunny yellow paint, white wicker furniture, two walls of windows, and the most breathtaking views of the many flowers in the gardens. Talk about a complete contrast from the rest of the home. The only displeasure was the stench of cigarette smoke.

Seated at a table covered in a white cloth was Séamus' mother. Her youthfulness almost took Shannon's breath away. The coolness in the woman's green eyes was the opposite of her youngest's son's that danced with the merriness of Ireland's legendary leprechaun. Mrs. Daugherty's painted mouth of sharp red lipstick was set in a straight, firm line. Hair the color of Séamus' chestnut thick locks was pinned off the woman's narrow, slim face.

A plate of untouched food sat in front of her that she chose to ignore, lifting a cup of china with the free hand not holding the cigarette instead.

"Will you require anything, Mrs. Daugherty?" Ellen asked.

"Breakfast for my new daughter-in-law. Coffee?" Mrs. Daugherty pinned her cold, assessing stare on Shannon.

"Yes. Thank you." Shannon took a seat in the adjacent chair Mrs. Daugherty motioned at with her long, thin fingers with just as long nails painted in a French manicure. Any other color, Shannon guessed, the woman considered tacky.

"It's good to meet you. I'm Roisin." Mrs. Daugherty took a drag off her cigarette. She had the courtesy to blow the smoke in the opposite direction. "You do know your name is traditional Irish, don't you?"

Shannon stiffened. "No. I didn't." Well, maybe she'd managed to check one prerequisite on the marriage list.

"Yes. It means wise river. The Irish spelling is S-i-o-n-a-i-n-n." Mrs. Daugherty had the same *droll* to her voice as Séamus, but hers was two octaves higher and full of boredom, not amusement. "Thank you for joining me. I thought it was best to acquaint myself with my son's new bride."

"It's good to meet you, too." If only Séamus had said more about his mother to Shannon.

"If you don't mind, I would like to give a party for you and my son."

The woman was taking the time to ask? Shannon stifled her sputter. "Thank you. A party would be nice."

"Wonderful. Once I set a date, I'll let you know. Planning does take time, but I have a hunch Séamus will want to introduce you to our extended family, friends, and of course, business associates, as soon as he can."

Oh great, Shannon could imagine what everyone would say about Séamus daring to not marry someone of Irish descent, let alone an Ojibway woman from the rez. "Sure."

"If this is also okay with you, I'd like to make reservations for this week at the Irish Tea Room so you can have a chance to meet Courtney. She's your sister-in-law. Cillian's wife."

Between parties, teas, and dinners, when was Shannon supposed to start her business? She nodded, but maybe it was time to speak up. "I do have a dinner date this evening. I'm taking out my roommates. Former roommates, that is."

"You won't be joining us?" Mrs. Daugherty arched her black brow just like Séamus did.

"No. Séamus is aware of this." *I feel like I'm asking for permission. It's my life. I don't need permission. I'm twenty-eight years old.*

Mrs. Daugherty pressed her lips together. She glanced to the wall of windows and back to Shannon. Her gaze remained unexpressive. "I do know my husband would like a chance to meet you formally. Will you be available for tomorrow night?" The lifting of only one brow this time meant Shannon had better be available.

"Sure. I can do that."

"Then I'll let my husband know."

Just then, thank goodness, Ellen returned carrying a plate and a platinum coffee carafe. She turned over the delicate cup in front of Shannon and poured.

The tiny portion the fine china allowed didn't hold enough caffeine to sustain Shannon for the morning. Back at the townhouse, she had an extra-large mug she gulped down before work and then purchased more java at a drive-thru.

Before her was a spread of melons and toast. As for the egg cup holding her soft-boiled egg, that must have also been expensive. She hated to tap her fork against the shell in fear of damaging what looked to be pure sterling silver.

"Is there anything else I can get for you?" Ellen asked.

More coffee. "I'll probably require a refill pretty quick."

"Yes. I'll return." Ellen left the room, taking the carafe Shannon desperately needed.

She must've been too busy staring at the vanishing coffee, because Mrs. Daugherty gave a dainty *ahem*. Shannon turned her head.

"Please, eat first." Mrs. Daugherty motioned at the plate.

The pattern was lovely. Flowers in dainty blue. Shannon could imagine how old the setting was. The lady of the house had probably inherited the fine china from Séamus' great-great-great-grandmother. "Very pretty." She patted the plate.

"Yes, it is. And old. It's been in the family for generations. It was Séamus' great-great-great-grandmother's first extravagant purchase when the business became a success." There was a hidden sigh in Mrs. Daugherty's reply, as if the wealth of the family bored her.

A smidgen of hope spread like a flame in Shannon's chest. Maybe her mother-in-law didn't fit the classic mold joked about on TV shows. There was something in Mrs. Daugherty's gaze that embodied quiet resignation, a woman who'd submitted herself to . . . Shannon wasn't sure of the *what*.

"It's nice the family has many heirlooms." Shannon tapped her spoon against the egg's shell.

"I guess it is," Mrs. Daugherty murmured. "Can you tell me a bit about you? I'm aware my husband contracted you to drive my son."

"Yes, he did. My boss . . . well, my former boss asked me if I'd like the position." Shannon set the eggshell on the provided plate. She dipped her spoon and spread a portion of the runny yoke and egg white across her toast.

"You wanted the position to drive my son?" Finally, warmth shone in Mrs. Daugherty's eyes.

This was strange for Shannon to find herself talking, when her preference was to keep silent or reply with perfunctory cheerful answers among the rich or famous. But she'd keep reminding herself she belonged here as much as anyone else in the household. "I've worked as a driver since I moved to Toronto. Taking on such a job is seen as an excellent opportunity."

"An opportunity for what, if you don't mind my asking." Mrs. Daugherty knitted her black brows.

A warning siren went off in Shannon's brain. If she divulged her career goal, Séamus' mother might get the wrong idea.

Yes, she'd married Séamus to achieve her own business, but Shannon wasn't a gold digger. He'd asked, even begged, and she'd relented. "As a working girl, I need to keep building my résumé. It allows for better paying positions, or even an increase in my wage."

"Understandable." Mrs. Daugherty plopped her cigarette butt into a device that resembled a thimble with a circular cut on top. The smoke vanished immediately. "I think it's wonderful you have a career. Will you keep working?"

Shannon couldn't disclose she was building her business

as of today. "We'll see. Séamus asked if I'd first acquaint my-self with the family."

Tonight, after she met Pashney and Ronnie, Shannon had to speak to Séamus. There were concerns she had, such as what his family would say when she started her own busi-ness.

Would they suspect why she'd married him? Would they hold it against her? Would they even believe Séamus was the one who'd dreamed up the scheme? Or would they think she'd taken advantage of their son when he'd been at his most vulnerable, needing to marry before a bride was handpicked for him?

Cold seeped down Shannon's spine. The portion of egg she'd eaten sat funny in her stomach. Now she'd have to force down the rest of her breakfast, when she ached to take her coffee and retire upstairs, far away from the formality and wealth suffocating her like a cloth placed over her nose and mouth.

CHAPTER FIFTEEN: FLAT TIRE

Séamus steered himself through the crowd in the lobby and breezed past the hostess straight to the table where Cillian sat.

After two hours of sleep, Séamus' weary body kept screaming for a nap. Instead, he drew back the heavy leather chair that harmonized with the rich interior of timber frame and plenty of wood decorating the restaurant, to meet his brother's flaring nostrils and red cheeks the color of the table-cloth.

"Really? Seriously? You'd do this to your own family?"

"Really? Seriously? Before I even sit?" Séamus parked his ass on the cushion meant to offer comfort but which failed, due to the company. "Where are your manners? I thought Ellen raised you better."

"You know exactly why I requested this lunch." Cillian leaned in. "I received an earful from Father after Judge Morson called. Father almost boarded a plane to read you the riot act. You should thank me and spare the attitude, because I asked Father to allow you the courtesy to explain yourself once you arrived home."

Thank Cillian? Hardly. Séamus also leaned in. "You both act as if I did the unforgivable. All I did was get married."

"To the wrong woman." Cillian huffed and pulled at his suit jacket, a habit he had never stopped performing when peeved. "You knew exactly what Father expected from you."

"Yes, to never break the mold of a Daugherty, no matter if I approve or not."

"It isn't that difficult to find a wife who meets four simple requirements." Cillian flicked his hand and sat back. He glanced about. "Waiter. We're ready."

"Meeting four simple requirements may have been easy for you, but it wasn't for me."

The waiter darted over, holding two large menus while the busboy filled their water glasses.

Cillian kept his lips sealed shut. Heaven forbid anyone overhear their disagreement. Appearances, appearances.

Séamus took the menu. He glanced over the entrées. "Just the soup of the day and a roast beef sandwich on rye. Hold the mayo."

Cillian kept his hard gaze pinned on the menu he held up.

The waiter took his cue and left.

Séamus rolled his ankle in a circle while waiting for his brother to pick an entrée. He glanced over the usual crowd smelling of wealth and power, outfitted in their designer clothes, all attempting to outdo each other with their credit cards, five-dollar words, and importance, some bemoaning how busy they were, or how they only had time for a quick lunch because they were due back at the office for a meeting. So busy, busy, busy. Nothing had changed.

Why he was taking note of the familiar custom playing out, he wasn't sure. Someone like Shannon had probably found the behavior of the rich and elite pretentious. She'd probably laughed outside with the other drivers, elbowing one another in the side, even smirking at the clients they drove.

He'd have to ask her about that.

He had a hunch in Shannon's world, the people flitting about the restaurant were seen with amusement. She certainly didn't take herself seriously, but she took her job seriously. He doubted she'd lament the demands to her fellow drivers in a voice of prominence. Hers would stem from desiring to be effective at her job.

Therein was the difference. Shannon viewed the job as important, not herself. While the people surrounding him in the restaurant perceived themselves as important, not the job.

Something good had come out of their hasty marriage he'd never expected to unearth — he was beginning to see the world through her lenses. And what he looked at, he wasn't sure he liked.

Shannon sat at the desk in her new bedroom suite. The laptop was fired up, waiting for her to video call Mom. At three-thirty, Mom would be home, since her shift at the restaurant started at seven and ended at three. Now that Shannon had gone to the bank, having sent the information Séamus required to his office, there was nothing to excuse her from calling the family.

Her fingers hovered over the keyboard.

Oh hell, just do it.

She moved the mouse arrow to Mom's name and double clicked. Maybe she should've ordered up something to drink first. Oh well, too late, because Mom was on the screen, staring back, perky as ever.

"This is a surprise. I never expected to hear from you this early in the afternoon." As always, Mom's voice was as cheerful as a glass of eggnog at Christmas. "How's my baby girl? And . . . how's your new client?"

Shannon shouldn't have shared her plans with Mom about why she so desperately wanted the Daugherty contract. She curled her toes. "It's going great."

"It must be, for you to be off at this time. Is he on a break? At work?"

"Yeah, at work. I . . . uh . . ."

Mom peered behind Shannon. "Is that your new room? I talked to Pashney this weekend. She said you went to Banff. How exciting. What was it like? Wait, let me get some tea."

She disappeared from the screen.

Shannon almost groaned. Great, Mom had probably called the townhouse looking for her since she hadn't dared to put her cell phone on roam during the flight and drive to Banff, or she'd have had to face massive charges, plus face her friends and family. Maybe she should've kept her phone on. All she'd done was put off telling everyone the truth.

Mom reappeared on the screen, holding her favorite mug with an eagle flying against a sky-blue background. "Well? I'm all ears."

Shannon dug for some courage. There wasn't a reason to be afraid, but Mom would be disappointed, and she loathed disappointing her parents. "I . . . I got married this weekend."

"Married?" Mom had moved the mug to her lips but quickly drew it away. In the process, her hand shook, and her eyes bulged. "Married? The girls . . . they told me you had to take your employer to Banff." Then her eyes narrowed. "Do you mean to tell me you went to Banff to get married?"

The flashing died in Mom's gaze, and her lips pinched. "Why? You just started your job. What did your employer say about you taking the time off? I thought this was your dream job? I can well imagine what your kokum will say."

Shannon swallowed. She opened her mouth to speak and defend herself, but Mom continued ranting.

"You didn't even tell me you were seeing anyone or how serious it became. Who is he?"

Shannon drew in a deep breath. "Séamus—"

"I don't recall you mentioning anybody named Séamus," Mom snapped. "And what kind of name is that? I never heard of the name Séamus before."

"Please, let me finish. Okay?"

Mom harumphed but nodded.

"The name's Irish. He's Irish Canadian. Séamus Daugherty."

"D-Daugherty? He's related to the Daugherty family?" Mom blinked.

"No, he's their youngest son. He's the one I'm driving. I told you this. Remember?"

"I can't keep track of everything you say . . ." Mom shook her head. "You married your employer's son?" She blanched, as if finally digesting everything.

Shannon nodded.

"B-but didn't you only meet him that morning?" Mom sputtered. "You told me you'd never met them."

This conversation was deteriorating fast. "We only met that morning." Shame burned hot on Shannon's cheeks, especially from the look of disbelief on Mom's face.

"Wh-what?" Mom's jaw slackened. "Wh-why? What on earth were you thinking?" She glanced away, frowning. "The first to graduate high school. The first to . . ." She stared back at the computer screen. The disappointment on her face almost blasted like a siren in the night. "You told me you had dreams. Why on earth would you marry a stranger?"

I'm beginning to ask myself the same thing. I'm wondering what I was thinking. I woke up this morning to a new world that feels like a dream, but it's real. Very real. Mom, I felt so bad for him. I couldn't help the connection I felt when I first shook his hand. It was . . . I can't explain. "I . . . he asked me to."

"He asked you?" Mom drew her fingers to her temples and massaged them. "I don't understand. What did he say exactly? Men like him don't marry women like us."

They don't marry women from the rez, you mean. Come right out and admit it. Fine, Shannon would give part of the truth. "He . . . his family . . . his father, I mean, he's a . . . he has complete control over Séamus' life. If he didn't marry, his dad . . . he would've disinherited Séamus and would've blacklisted him if he quit Daugherty Enterprises and tried to find another job."

"Blacklisted? Disinherited? What kind of father is this?"

Mom's mouth fell open. "Where are you now?"

"At their mansion. The family lives as one until they have a child. Then they—"

"Living there? I want you to get back to the townhouse right now. If that man finds out you married his son, he'll blacklist you, too." The shock had vanished in Mom's gaze and took on terror.

A wave of astonishment hit Shannon's backside. She'd never witnessed her mother looking so fearful before.

"See if you can get the marriage annulled . . ." Mom seemed to speak more to herself. Her mind was probably racing, and she was trying to figure out a way to yank Shannon from what Mom perceived as a horrible threat.

"I'm fine. Okay? I'm fine." Shannon did her best to speak in the most calming and soothing voice she could muster. "I met his mother. She was nice to me."

"It doesn't matter what his mother thinks." Mom almost spit the words. "He comes from a patriarchal line. You know exactly what patriarchal lines are responsible for."

Shannon cringed. Great, for the umpteenth time, she'd hear how the white patriarchal society had almost destroyed their own Indigenous world. "Mom, Séamus is different. Okay?"

"I'm not talking about that stranger you married. I'm talking about his father. His lineage. If a man disowns his son for wanting to pick a woman of his choosing to marry, he's a dictator who'll destroy anyone who gets in his way. And that means you, too." Mom dared to thrust her finger.

Okay, Mom wasn't all-out traditional and tended to point when she was serious, so Shannon wouldn't take offense. "Mom . . ."

"No. You pack your bags and get to your real house. I won't have that son of a bitch costing you your career—a career you worked hard for." Mom rose. In front of the camera, she huffed back and forth.

"I'm twenty-eight. I think I can—"

"I don't care how old you are." Mom bent and shoved her face into the camera. "You have no idea what you've gotten yourself in for. White men are about control. They want to control everything. The world. The land. The environment. Even what you say. Do you really think they want to hear what we have to say? Hell, no."

"Maybe if you met him . . ." Shannon weakly offered.

"Yes, I want to meet him. I want to meet a man who can't stand up to his own father."

Shannon's defensiveness rose like the mercury in a thermometer. "I think he can stand up to his father, but he has a lot to lose if he does. Would you want to be left penniless, your reputation smeared, unable to get a job in the field you worked hard to educate yourself in?"

Mom sank into the chair. She gaped at the camera and ran her fingers through her black hair. "I'd like if you visited during our holiday. We'll see what he thinks about the pow-wow."

National Indigenous Peoples Day was always a big celebration at the reserve. Shannon nodded. "I'll ask him. I still have to talk to Pashney and Ronnie."

"They don't know? They weren't in on this when I called them?" Mom's frustration and bite ceased. For once, she looked her fifty-three years, instead of a good fifteen years younger.

Shannon fisted her hand. She'd done this to her mother. And if Mom didn't approve, that meant Dad, her brother and sister, and Mishoomis and Kokum wouldn't either.

Séamus vacated the car and beelined for the side entrance the family used. He'd already spoken to Elite Limousines, and his new driver would arrive in the morning. His mood didn't match the sun shining but was more of a flat tire on the side of the road, with no spare in the trunk.

The worst part was, Shannon had already left for dinner and wouldn't be present to relax with him after a tough day. What he needed before facing the family was a hot bath.

Séamus shut the door to the side entrance. As he turned, Mom stood before him, which was very strange.

"How was your day?" Concern was in her question.

This was even stranger. Mom never spoke in the halls or engaged in idle chitchat unless she was in the sunroom or her receiving room.

"It went as expected. I had lunch with Cillian." Séamus clutched his briefcase. "Shannon's gone, isn't she??"

"Yes." Mom nodded. ""I don't know much about her. But from what I've experienced so far, she seems rather nice."

The tension at the back of Séamus' neck relaxed. Always, he could count on Mom to see his point of view. "Thanks. It means a lot to me. In a way, I'm glad she's not here for the . . . dinner."

"She'll be here tomorrow night, though. She does have to officially meet the family." Mom wet her lips. "I know she's extremely independent. She's going to work, isn't she?"

Working is why she married me. "Yes. She wants to start her own business, and I told her I'd help her."

"Her own business?" Mom squinted.

"Her own limo business. She wants to begin with one car."

"Like the Audi?"

"Plusher than the Audi. I have great contacts for her, and she needs to impress."

"The vehicles are very expensive." Mom frowned.

"I know. It's my wedding gift to my bride. Her own business. As for what Father and Cillian will have to say, I guess I'll hear their displeasure over dinner. She's going to work, whether they approve or not." Séamus lifted his chin.

"Then you'd best be prepared for tension, or even an argument. You know what your father and brother are like." The worry lines Botox couldn't erase appeared on Mom's forehead.

"I'm not sticking with tradition. Shannon's her own person." *I want her to be happy. Lolling about in bed until eight isn't what she's cut out for, and neither is shopping, charity work, and whatever else Father and Cillian expect from you two.*

Séamus was in for a fight, but this was one fight he wasn't backing down from. The gloves were off. Shannon had done so much for him, and he'd do everything possible to provide her with the support she needed.

CHAPTER SIXTEEN: COOL THE ENGINES

They were on the patio at one of their favorite dining spots. The place was packed with working professionals who had clocked out for the day. Being out for dinner meant Pashney might keep her yelling to a level three, instead of cranking the volume to eleven.

Already, they'd ordered. Unable to break her *no drinking* habit thanks to eight years of driving, Shannon had asked the waiter for an iced tea, which she could use a good gulp from, since her throat had dried.

Cars congested the streets, and the dining area was rather loud from horns honking, engines revving, and diners chattering.

Ronnie kept glancing at Shannon. "Okay. Out with it. You fucked your client, didn't you?" Mischievousness twinkled in her dark eyes.

For such a close guess, Shannon would say her dear friend was in pole position but still needed to win the race.

Her heated cheeks must have shown on her skin because Ronnie exclaimed, "You did do him, didn't you? So much for your *no fraternizing with the clients* rule." She leaned in and elbowed Shannon.

"Seriously?" Pashney paused mid-drink of her rum and cola and set down the glass. "C'mon, they're just a bunch of guys."

That was a typical and expected statement from Pashney, who was of the philosophy men were worthless. Probably because her father was a practicing alcoholic and had abandoned the family when she was eight, and she'd helped her mom raise her younger siblings.

"Fine . . . I did." *And I also married him.*

"I knew it. That's why he made up some vacation in Lake Louise. He wanted to get you alone." Ronnie giggled. Her pixie haircut gave her a sweet-as-an-elf-straight-from-Ireland appeal.

"He more than wanted to get me alone. He asked me to . . . marry him." Shannon hadn't meant to be blunt, but there wasn't any other way to ease her friends into the discussion.

"What the fuck?" Shock spread across Pashney's steel-hard features.

"Are you serious? Oh my God, he's stinking rich. Shit, he has, like, billions." Ronnie squealed. "What did you tell him? Frick, that's why you videoed us. Isn't it? You wanted to tell us about it. Geez, you should've instead of waiting for today."

"Why the hell would he wanna marry you?" The shock had vanished from Pashney's sharp words, and she was back to her sarcastic, realistic, dry self. "What's he want?"

Dammit, Pashney was too suspicious for her own good. Heaven help if anyone offered her something. The poor person would get an earful of questions. And Shannon was insulted that a man of Séamus' caliber wouldn't think twice about overlooking a gal from an Indian Reserve.

Wait, he'd only married her because she didn't fit his father's mold. She'd been used as spite and to keep an inheritance and job. She didn't mean to snap out, "Well, he did want to marry me." She withdrew her rings from her pocket, slipped them on her left ring finger, and held up her hand.

"Holy shit, those are real diamonds." Ronnie grabbed Shannon's hand and inspected the rings.

Pashney sucked in her cheeks. "You're nuts. Totally nuts. Why would you marry a stranger? What about the plan? What about your dream? All this for a useless man?"

"I'm not giving up my dream. Séamus is helping me buy my first town car." Shannon couldn't help her defensive tone.

"Oh, I see. Too scared to do it on your own, huh?" Pashney's sneer matched her buzzed haircut. "Had to get a man to help you."

"Maybe I'm helping him?" Shannon drew back her shoulders. "Maybe that's why I agreed, and the business is a bonus."

"Help? What would his rich ass need any help for?" Pashney fired back.

"It's private. Okay? Very private, but it has to do with his family. He needed to get married, and he convinced me to marry him." There wasn't any way Shannon could explain the connection she'd felt from the moment they'd met, or her friends would call her crazy.

"He convinced you by offering you your own business." Pashney's statement wasn't a question.

"I told you it was more than that. He needed my help," Shannon firmly replied.

"Typical man. Can't do anything on his own and has to enlist the assistance of a woman." Pashney snorted. "Boy, you sure married a guy with some major backbone and courage."

The accusation hit Shannon's stomach. She drew in a sharp breath. "You're talking about my husband."

"He's not your husband. That's insane. Can't you get a quickie divorce or something?" Pashney shook her head. "And what about the mortgage? Or is Mr. Rich and Spoiled paying it off for you?"

Shannon stiffened. "As I said, he needed my help, so I negotiated a deal. Yes, my portion of the mortgage is being paid off."

"What about our taxes? There's only two of us now." Pashney's natural low, direct growl grew louder. "And the maintenance fees?"

"I'll find another roommate." Shannon grit her teeth. "I thought everything over. Okay?"

"No, I don't think you thought anything—" Pashney clamped her mouth shut and glared at the people who gawked at their table. "Can't you see we're having a discussion? Go back to your meals. We'll speak quieter so we don't interrupt you." She then directed her glare to Shannon. "Way to go, girl. Is this why you dragged us out for dinner instead of eating in? Nice plan. You got about as much backbone as your rich husband."

Shannon returned Pashney's glare. "I wanted to find a way to explain myself, but no matter what I say, you're gonna be pissed. Aren't you?"

"You didn't need a man to start your own business." Pashney thumped the table, but in a quiet manner that didn't rattle the cutlery. She'd also lowered her voice. "Especially a rich man. You're out of his league, and he doesn't belong in your league. What's he gonna do at powwows, huh? Do you really think he's gonna fit in back home? Do you think he's gonna fit in with us? I'm not attending any of his fancy parties or stepping foot in his big mansion." She sniffed. "Your mom and kokum are gonna freak."

"They already know. I talked to Mom this afternoon."

"I betcha she wasn't too happy about what you told her." Pashney wouldn't stop with the retaliation of words and thunderstorm glare.

Ronnie sighed. "Shan, I know you want our support, and I am gonna do my best to support you, but you gotta admit, the marriage is a little fast. What if he hurts you? Isn't that how rich guys operate with women like us?"

Shannon bowed her head. True. There was a good reason why the missing and murdered Indigenous women were a big problem in Canada—because nobody cared about women who possessed red skin. "I think he's different. He's not—"

"How can you say that when you've only known him since Friday?" Pashney's jaw flexed.

"Can you at least support me by meeting him? I'll bring him to the townhouse. I already told Mom I'd find a weekend when I can take him to the rez."

"Yeah, what's he gonna do? Land his private jet on our gravel runway?" Pashney scoffed.

"If he must, he will. It's my home, and something he must accept. Don't think I'm going to be a doormat in this marriage. I already stood up for myself, and I'll keep standing up for myself."

"Oh . . . Shan . . . ." Pashney slumped in her chair just as a waiter passed by, carrying a platter of food.

Now that the forest fire was over, peace was close to settling, at least Shannon hoped so.

"We had it all planned out." Pashney dropped her arms and looked at the sky. "I can't see this working. Not in a million years."

"Will you at least meet him?"

"Yeah, let's meet him." Ronnie glanced to Pashney.

Pashney grumbled. "Fine. But don't expect me to like him. I already don't like him."

The dinner was silent enough to hurt Séamus' ears, as if pins were being pushed into them. Only the sound of spoons dipping into bowls and the tinkling of glasses being lifted broke the eerie quietness. He should be thankful Shannon wasn't present to witness the icy meal he endured night after night.

Mom occupied her same spot at the foot of the table with Father at the head. Cillian and Courtney were in their usual seats across from Séamus. One spot was empty in the family dining room used for informal dinners that still required suits and ties for the men and dresses for the ladies.

Father wiped his mouth. He set down his soup spoon. This was his cue for the servants to clear the table, no matter if everyone hadn't finished their clam chowder. Mom's bowl went untouched, Courtney's half full since she was always on a diet, competing with Mom to remain fashionably lean. As for Cillian, he'd learned how to eat at the same pace as Father.

Séamus had a few sips left of the delicious broth, but he set down his spoon and reached for his iced water.

"Tell your wife she's required to be present at dinner from now on." Father's order carried his usual sternness as he reached for his wine glass.

Séamus' chest constricted. "She's not a Daugherty. I think she's capable of deciding whether she chooses to dine with us or not. I told you already she had plans."

The usual straight line of Father's mouth deepened. "Will she be present tomorrow night?"

Séamus could almost see the unspoken words coming from Father's lips. *"Remember what I said, if she doesn't become a true Daugherty, the marriage is finished . . ."*

I'm not going to let you mold Shannon into another version of Mom. Courtney may embrace this life, but Mom is a bird stuck in a cage. He'd be damned if he'd let his father or brother stick Shannon in the same golden prison.

"Well, will she be here?" For cripe's sake, Father couldn't even hide the irritation in his question.

"I don't know. I'll ask her when she gets home." Séamus gripped the glass of his iced water.

The blanch on Father's face would've been comical under any other circumstance, but the threat from the previous night hovering around the table was stronger than the smell of the clam chowder the servants were clearing away.

If Seamus didn't—or should he say *they*—didn't bow down to a tyrant, he'd find himself out on the street with his wife. But how could he ask one more thing of Shannon, who'd already given up her freedom for him?

147

Having to speak to her once she arrived home left a film of dread on the back of his neck.

Séamus dragged himself upstairs after meeting with Father and Cillian for the last two hours in the study to go over paperwork and notes. He ambled to his new suite that was across from Cillian and Courtney's.

All was quiet. His brother and sister-in-law remained downstairs. Mom had excused herself early, feigning one of her many headaches. Father remained in his study, workaholic that he was.

The light under the door didn't mean Shannon was home, but hope still gathered in Séamus' chest, even though Ellen always readied his sleeping quarters for the night by switching on various table lamps, turning down his sheets, and closing the drapes.

He opened the door to Shannon curled up on the chaise lounge in the beautiful silk robe and sleeping gown he'd purchased for her in Banff. The attire molded to the contours of her hips and swell of her breasts. His sinking heart climbed back to his chest. He shut the door.

She glanced up from the e-reader she held. The tightness on her face indicated her dinner hadn't gone as planned, either. Still, he'd ask.

"How was your night?"

She set aside the e-reader and rose. He motioned for her to follow him to the walk-in closet so he could change from his suit and into his lounging outfit.

She padded after him. He stopped at his side of the closet and unbuttoned his shirt.

"They want to meet you." Apprehension was in her reply.

He had no problem sitting down for drinks or dinner with her friends. "Sure. Let me know when."

"My mom, well, my parents, also want to meet you. I . . . I

used to take my vacation time to be home for Indigenous Peoples Day. I'm not sure if you follow — "

"I'm aware of the holiday." Not that Séamus had toasted or acknowledged the celebration before, but he'd better start now.

"Our reserve holds a powwow that we attend." She coughed.

A powwow? He had no clue about Indigenous culture, but he'd learn. "You wish for me to accompany you?"

She nodded.

"I'd like to see where you were raised and used to live." He would, sincerely. He set his shirt in the laundry bag.

"It's isolated, so we'll have to fly in."

"That's not a problem. We can take the jet."

"It's a gravel runway."

"I'll ask the pilot if it's possible to land on one. I'm sure it won't be a problem. It sounds like planes land there all the time."

She coughed again. "How did your dinner go?"

Father's words kept spinning around in Séamus' brain like gerbils on a wheel. Asking one more thing from wasn't part of the deal when they'd married. He removed his pants and also set them in the hamper.

Her gaze sliding up his bare thighs and then feathering his chest was a stirring of embers in his crotch, but he had to keep them focused on their conversation, no matter how bad he yearned to take his new bride to bed and enjoy a replay of last night.

He reached for his robe on the hook and tied the belt around his waist. His stomach pinched as her lustful gaze turned to one of disappointment. *Trust me, I'd rather explore every inch of your body, too.* "We'll order up some tea."

He could admit one thing—the sexual attraction between them at least helped their marriage stand on one foot, but their differences and families might never allow them to balance using both feet.

"Sure. Tea." She left the walk-in closet.

Having already showered before dinner, Séamus simply had to wash his face and brush his teeth before retiring. That could wait. He'd join his wife in their sitting room and ask Ellen to bring them up a pot. Small talk might be the best way to get their discussion going in the right place.

When he entered the sitting room, Shannon was back on the chaise lounge, seated on the edge, not reclined as she had been earlier. He followed her lead and sat on the edge of the chair beside the lounger.

"Is there something you need to talk about?" Shannon peered at him.

"Yes. Dinner. Father was disappointed you weren't present."

"I already had plans." She shrugged.

"I know, but dinner is a rather formal event, and the family is expected to attend."

"I'll be there tomorrow."

"Dinners weren't formal at your house when you were growing up?" He kept his words light.

"We were expected to be home for dinner." She again shrugged. "Sometimes we weren't, like Saturdays because of the stock car races."

"Your parents didn't mind?"

She shook her head.

From the get-go, he'd known they were worlds apart. He'd best spell out Father's expectations and hope for the best she'd agree.

CHAPTER SEVENTEEN: ANOTHER HIT AND RUN

Wearing the new nightgown and transparent matching robe sure hadn't produced the effect Shannon had hoped for. She took the cup of tea Séamus handed her. Something was up, and instinct said she wouldn't like what he had to say.

She added two cubes of sugar but passed on the cream. A delicious herbal scent wafted from the fine china. She sipped the gentle brew meant to soothe away tension and induce sleep, which was a strange flavor to pick, considering he wanted to talk.

"Dinner . . . dinner would have gone better if you'd been present." Séamus moved to set down the sugar bowl and creamer.

"Oh? Did they need to speak to me about something?" Strange. Mrs. Daugherty hadn't said anything this morning over breakfast.

"No." Séamus returned to the chair. He leaned forward, elbow on his knee, and the other hand holding the cup and saucer.

"We have . . ." His gaze shifted upward toward the ceiling where the chandelier hung. "We have unspoken rules in the family. Dinner, for one, is very important. This is when the family gathers after a busy day to . . . speak . . . I guess."

He brushed at his hair. "Talk about the events or share any anecdotes. We don't discuss business. That's done in Father's study."

"I see . . ." Shannon's hand trembled. "I was expected this evening. Is that what you're saying?"

"It's my fault. I should've known better," Séamus quickly replied, his tone full of apology. "But I know how important seeing your friends was to you."

"Yeah, it was important." *And I sure got an earful.*

"I guess what I'm trying to say is, if you could please be present for dinner, I'd very much appreciate it." There was pleading in his eyes.

Why did she have a feeling he wasn't telling her every-thing? "Is there anything else you need to speak to me about?"

Each time the conversation turned serious, he was taking care of something for her, or required something else from her. This supposed deal they'd struck wasn't going according to her vision but his. "You said we had to start our marriage on an honest level, so please be honest with me."

Séamus glanced to the door and back again. His fingers tightened around the cup's delicate handle. "We are Daugh-ertys. My family has certain expectations from me. As my wife, they have the same expectations from you."

"Wait a minute. Are you saying . . . Tell me about your mother."

"What would you like to know?"

"How did she meet your father?"

"During her debut."

"Debut?"

"All young women who turn eighteen, some nineteen, have a debut. A debutante ball. Call it a coming out, a formal introduction as an adult into society." The *droll* had returned to Séamus' voice, the same bored, this-life-sucks *droll*. "Grandfather Daugherty and her father decided my parents would make an excellent match."

"Fine, their parents decided, but how did you mother and father feel about it?" Shannon already had her answer.

"My mother was opposed to it, but my father wasn't. He always does his duty." Séamus flicked his hand.

"If your mother opposed it, why'd she marry your father?" Again, she already had her answer. The poor woman had found herself in Séamus' predicament, the very reason why he'd married Shannon.

"I think you already know the answer," he whispered.

"What is it with these people?" Shannon's frustration came out in her question.

"Whatever do you mean?"

"Keeping with tradition. Obsessed with tradition. They're living by nineteenth-century standards."

"I told you before—your people weren't the only ones who encountered racism." Séamus set his elbows on his knees, still holding the cup. "When my great-great-great-grandfather built Daugherty Enterprises, he was tired of the racism and belittlement from the Protestants. He was out to prove an Irishman could succeed, and he did, but succeeding wasn't enough. We were considered *new money,* and new money was also looked down upon. You heard the saying you can put lipstick on a pig, but it's still a pig."

Shannon gasped.

Séamus' eyes were darker than the grass on an overcast day with a thunderstorm soon to invade. "Because of that, my great-great-great-grandfather had strict rules everyone had to follow, and this tradition has stayed in the family. In time, he did gain the respect he desired."

"We talked about this before—racism. The impact it has on generations afterward . . ."

"Haven't your parents done the same thing? Didn't your parents want you to succeed where they felt they failed?" He never blinked but stared.

He was right. Mom and Kokum had pushed her to get off the rez and explore the big world they'd never see, to dream big and reach for her dreams. Right now, Mom was freaking because Shannon hadn't attained her dream in the way Kokum and Mom had anticipated

Her stomach sank at the realization she and Séamus were both products of their upbringing and ancestors.

Shannon marched downstairs. Séamus had left for work already, again having let her sleep late without waking her. At nine-thirty, she still had much to do. First, she'd get a bite to eat.

When she entered the sunroom, Mrs. Daugherty was already seated, tablet in hand, her nail flicking along the screen.

"Good morning." Mrs. Daugherty set down the tablet. The gloom in her eyes brightened slightly. "I missed you at dinner last night but heard you had other plans. How did the meal with your friends go?"

Shannon sat adjacent from her mother-in-law, the only person who seemed to approve of her and didn't want to mold her into a proper Daugherty. "Good. I had to inform my friends about my marriage."

"Before he left for work, Séamus mentioned he's meeting them this weekend." Mrs. Daugherty picked up the cup.

"Yes, they . . ." Shannon cleared her throat. "They're looking forward to it."

"I understand." Wistfulness peppered Mrs. Daugherty's reply.

Shannon peeked at the woman and back to her place setting. "Do you have any plans for today?"

"Yes. I'm starting the list for your party. There's much to do . . ." From the almost roll of the woman's eyes, organizing a party seemed to be the last thing she wanted to do, but it was expected of her as a Daugherty wife.

Shannon wasn't going to become a Stepford wife. No way and no how.

Heels clicked on the floor. The scent of rich, spicy perfume invaded the room, overpowering the aroma of the fresh-cut flowers in vases.

"Good morning, Courtney." Mrs. Daugherty's greeting didn't match her congenial welcoming words. "You haven't met Shannon yet. Shannon, this is Courtney. Cillian's wife. Courtney, this is Shannon, Séamus' new bride.

"I was so hoping to take you both to the Irish Tea Room to become better acquainted . . . what can I say? It's been a busy week for us all."

Courtney's hair, the color of the sun first rising that flowed in thick loose curls, the same for her ivory skin and peach-tinted lips, was a becoming sight straight from a beauty pageant. Shannon's tongue was stuck somewhere in her mouth, and she couldn't form a simple hello.

Courtney nodded. She slid her tall, willowy figure gracefully into the chair adjacent from Mrs. Daugherty and opposite Shannon. "Forgive my tardiness. Cillian and I had a late discussion before retiring." She used her hand with the long fingers and French manicure to lift the silver bell from the table.

Shannon might have also been tall and slim, but her traditional dark Ojibway looks felt bland and ordinary compared to Courtney's sparkling, colorful loveliness. "It's good to meet you."

Courtney's icier-than-emerald-stone eyes focused on Shannon. "A pleasure to meet you, too. I wish we could have been properly introduced at dinner last night. That's when we make formal introductions, but you were not present . . ."

The spiteful remark stung Shannon's behind. "I already had a prior commitment before our flight touched down in Toronto." A lie, but she wasn't going to let someone tell her what she could and couldn't do. "We were discussing our plans for the day." She glanced to her mother-in-law.

"Yes ... plans ... hmm ..." Courtney steered her cold gaze to Ellen who'd entered. "Tea and toast. That will be all." She flicked her hand in a dismissing manner.

Ellen turned on her heel and left.

Shannon had to stop her mouth from falling open at the sharp order. Séamus must be the only one in the household who didn't treat servants like ... servants. She glanced to her mother-in-law.

"I told Shannon I'm planning the party for her and Séamus. I'm starting on the list and theme." Mrs. Daugherty patted her tablet.

"And what are you up to? The salon? Shopping? Deciding which car to drive?" There was a smirk in Courtney's words.

Oh, the witch thought of Shannon as a gold digger? She'd set her new sister-in-law straight. "No. I'm working."

"Working?" Courtney arched a microbladed mink brow.

"Yes. I've always worked." *And the sooner I get my business plan together and get working, the better to not have to sit down for breakfast with the likes of you.*

"True. Some people do have to work," Courtney replied in a tsking voice. "Such a pity."

"And some people enjoy working," Shannon added, her sweetness as fake as the crystal bowl of Splenda in the center of the table. "They don't like being dependent on anyone."

Instead of Courtney taking offense, the flinch came from Mrs. Daugherty.

Shannon was ready to smack herself across the face because she'd forgotten how the poor woman had come into the marriage to Mr. Daugherty. Dammit, she had to think before she spoke.

"I'm glad you have found your passion, Shannon." There was a shakiness to Mrs. Daugherty's compliment. "I think goals are wonderful."

"One must have goals to make them happy if they can't find fulfilment in their personal lives." The stinging barb came from Courtney.

"It's a bonus if you find fulfillment in both your personal and professional life." Shannon glanced to Mrs. Daugherty. "Your son is a wonderful husband."

"I guess a husband is wonderful if he can buy his wife whatever she desires." Courtney kept staring like a gunfighter who'd never lost a showdown.

"Quite true, considering the designer clothes you're wearing." Shannon forced another fake smile. "I'm sure Cillian makes you very happy."

Courtney frowned. "And what do you mean by that, exactly? I'll have you know I have money of my own. My family is well-off. Is yours?"

Never had Shannon traded barbs like this before, and her mind was growing weary from formulating new backhanded compliments. It was probably how Courtney spent her evenings, scribbling into a notebook of new insults to deliver to anyone who crossed her path. The woman was a true cheetah, unable to retract her claws.

"I think we are all fortunate." Mrs. Daugherty cleared her throat, but her interrupted statement didn't match the weariness in her voice. "Shannon, when is a good date for your party? Séamus mentioned to me earlier that he's accompanying you to your community during the summer solstice." The gentle lifting of her finger in Courtney's direction more than said Mrs. Daugherty wanted her other daughter-in-law to stay quiet.

"Any time, but not during the solstice. We'll be away."

"Excellent. It'll be sure to note that down." Mrs. Daugherty had such a beautiful tone to her voice, soothing and reassuring.

"Thank you. I really appreciate the party. I do." No,

Shannon didn't desire a fancy soiree, but telling her mother-in-law she approved elicited a sincere smile from the older woman, one that was in her enchanting gaze.

Meeting high society wasn't something Shannon had anticipated, but Séamus would get Shannon through the party, somehow. Well, he'd better, especially if the women shared Courtney's cattiness.

Dinner was at seven o'clock sharp. In five minutes, Shannon would meet the man who'd made her new husband's life a complete misery. The thought of sitting down to eat with such a man curled her stomach and soured her tongue.

"You look great." Séamus appeared in the mirror at Shannon's vanity table where she dusted the last of loose powder onto her face. The navy tie, crisp light-blue shirt, and tailored suit brightened his dark-brown hair. For a moment the breath left her. His handsomeness couldn't be denied. But was her sexual need for him enough to sustain a marriage of such differences? She'd soon find out once they ventured downstairs.

"So do you." She slid the brush into her makeup bag.

"It'll be fine." He set his hands on her bare shoulders.

"Do I look worried?"

He flashed his dimples. "A little. Come." He extended his hand.

She rose and fastened her fingers with his.

As he led them from the dressing room, her heart threatened to break through her chest. Each closing door reaffirmed she was on her way to the lion's den. When he steered them down the hall and to the family staircase, the lost breath that had returned earlier had vanished again.

Her ears were never so aware of sound. As she descended the stairs, a man's deep voice came from somewhere in the massive house.

Séamus motioned at what he'd referred to as the family

dining room, which couldn't be called informal. The interior was straight from a first-class Victorian painting. Everyone was already seated. Two chairs were unoccupied across from Courtney and Cillian. At the foot was Mrs. Daugherty, and at the head was Shannon's new father-in-law.

The men rose and nodded.

At least she'd gotten an acknowledgement.

Séamus pulled out a chair. Shannon found herself adjacent to Mrs. Daugherty and staring straight at Cillian, who'd followed her into a sitting position. His pale-pink lips moved into a half-smirk and half-smile. Great. Another one who probably classed her as a gold digger.

"We haven't been formally introduced. Cillian Daugherty. Welcome to the family." He was the striking resemblance of the elder Mr. Daugherty, with hair the color of a ripe carrot and a splatter of freckles dotting his round, pastel-colored face.

At least the two men who'd challenge Shannon's every move didn't appear as intimidating as their reputations. More like a cheery card from Ireland.

"Yes, welcome to the family, Shannon." Mr. Daugherty's scrutinizing stare was a dissection of an insect under a microscope. He flicked his attention toward Séamus. There was something enigmatic in the glance he cast his youngest son Shannon failed to decipher.

Ellen appeared, carrying a tray full of soup bowls. The scent was delicious. A combination of potatoes, carrots, and bacon.

"Our way of welcoming you into the family," Mr. Daugherty noted. "All the cuisine served tonight is what my great-great grandmother cooked."

Warmth melted the lining of ice around Shannon's heart. Maybe they did like her if they'd gone out of their way to share their tradition. "Thank you. I'm looking forward to this meal."

At least they wouldn't talk business. Séamus had assured her only polite conversation was allowed at the dinner table. That meant Courtney should keep her claws sheathed. As for Cillian and Mr. Daugherty, Shannon wasn't sure what to expect from them.

She set her napkin in her lap. Good manners and her own traditional upbringing hinted for her to follow the host's lead through dinner to avoid a faux pas and the classification as some chick from the rez who didn't know better. Kokum would expect Shannon to hold her head proud, and she wouldn't fail her grandmother.

Plus, she had Séamus by her side to keep his family in line.

CHAPTER EIGHTEEN: EXPRESSWAY TO YOUR HEART

Although Shannon had done fine at dinner, she'd frowned at the obligation of joining Mom and Courtney in the sitting room for a glass of sherry while Father had called Séamus and Cillian to the study.

Sure, she was excelling at accepting the changes in her life, but her tolerance level set off a firework of worry inside Séamus. Father, as usual, wanted to discuss business, however, he should've included Shannon, because Séamus planned on broaching her new venture.

He wasn't regretting marrying a woman who held no passion for an elite lifestyle, but if he displayed some enthusiasm, maybe Shannon might pick up on his keenness, and he wouldn't feel as if he was failing her. She knew how he felt about his wealth and prestige, so of course she'd be bored, too. He couldn't expect her to put forth an effort if his own grade bordered on a big fat F. She'd seen his true feelings from the first moment they'd met and had pointed out his lack of direction in his rich world.

"Did you hear me?" Father asked.

Séamus glanced up from his bourbon he'd been staring at ever since they'd entered the study.

"I guess the look on your face is my answer." Father sat back. He folded his hands across his stomach. "Perhaps you're reflecting on dinner and finally understand why I wanted you to marry a specific woman. Yes, she did fine, but this is not her life. It's in her eyes."

"Father's right. Maybe there's a way we can pay her off and—" Cillian began.

"She doesn't want your money, or my money, or any money," Séamus spit out. He set his glass on the table. "It's been a long day, and I've yet to recover from my weekend in Lake Louise. If you don't mind . . ."

Without waiting for an answer, Séamus strode from the study. He never stopped walking until he reached the sitting room, where he'd find Shannon.

When he entered his mother's domain, Courtney was running her mouth about her latest charity event she was planning.

Mom was listening politely.

Shannon was staring at a painting. The hollowness of her gaze more than told Séamus she was somewhere else.

"I hate to interrupt, but I am rather tired and wanted to ask my wife if she'd join me."

Shannon blinked. Her nodding was almost comical, as if screaming *get me the hell out of here*.

Séamus extended his hand. Shannon, very unladylike, scooted from the Chippendale sofa and barreled straight for him. She took his hand, bid Mom and Courtney goodnight, and dragged Séamus into the hallway.

"I'm sorry," he murmured as he led them to the family staircase.

"There's nothing to be sorry about." Shannon also kept her voice low. "I had a good hunch what I was setting myself up for when I said *yes*."

"Are there any regrets?" Séamus stopped and rested his hand on the polished railing of the staircase.

Shannon licked her lips. She gawked beyond his shoulder.

Her lack of answer and *I can't believe this* stare was a kick to his chest. She did regret marrying him. Perfect. Any other woman in his social circle would've jumped at the chance, but he stood with a bride who would've preferred to chauffeur him and live in the guest house.

The worst part was, he wanted to take her to bed and enjoy every inch of her flesh. All day she'd been on his mind while he'd worked out the mechanics for her business that he'd planned on reviewing with her after dinner. Maybe hearing about the strategy he'd developed might produce something in her other than a look of wanting to flee.

"You did great." He hoped his words stroked her the way his gaze couldn't stop caressing her bare arms.

"Thank you." She clasped her fingers.

"Come." He motioned at the stairs. "I'm sure you've had a long day. Or should I say long supper?"

She softly laughed.

The open wound in his chest sealed shut. Maybe she found the evening amusing in some strange way. "I know Courtney can only be tolerated for under five minutes, and you did wonderful."

"Do you think so?" She took his proffered arm as he guided them up the stairs.

"I know so. You did much better than I do."

"So is that the woman you would've been forced to marry?"

He stopped on the landing and glanced at her. "Not all within my social circle are as bad as Courtney, but yes, something close."

"There're nice women who won't look down at me at your exclusive country club?" Her smile was impish.

"As I said, not all are like Courtney. Some are quite down to earth."

"Then why didn't you date any of them?" There wasn't a hint of jealousy in her question, only mere curiousness.

"I've known them my whole life. I watched them debut. I

even escorted a couple of them to their balls, but . . ." *They're not you. Maybe I've been waiting for someone like you to come into my life.* "What about you? Any guys from the reserve pique your interest?"

"No." She blushed and ducked her head. "It's not to say I didn't date, but the couple of guys I did go out with, I knew they weren't *the one.* Plus, I was too focused on getting off the rez and to the city."

"Your dream meant that much to you, hey?" He steered them down the hallway. "Have you've known your friends your whole life?"

Shannon nodded.

They stopped at their suite and entered.

"So you decided to go to the city together?"

"Pashney's homelife wasn't the greatest. She helped her mom raise her brother and sisters. As soon as she could, she bolted. It made her pretty rough around the edges."

"Pashney. What an interesting name. Is it Ojibway?" He paused in their sitting room.

"It's Virginia. Her great-grandmother's name. But back in the day, nobody could pronounce Virginia, because the Ojibway language doesn't have the letters V and R, so whenever they said the name, it came out as Pashney, and we carry on that tradition by calling her Pashney."

"How interesting. What about your other friend?"

"Ronnie was raised by her dad and older sister. She lost her mom when she was eight."

"I'm sorry to hear that." Séamus couldn't imagine losing Mom at such a young age and being left with the tyrant. "Was her father good to her?"

"Very much so. He treated Ronnie and her sister like princesses. But he was away lots, guiding at a camp. He'd be gone from break-up to freeze-up."

"Break-up? Freeze-up?"

They beelined for the walk-in closet.

Shannon chuckled. "Sorry. Camps open in the spring after the ice melts on the lakes. They close when the lakes begin freezing."

"Ah, I see." Such an interesting regionalism. He rather liked the two terms. "What about your parents? Where do they work?"

"Mom's a waitress at the rez's one and only restaurant." She bent down to remove her shoes.

He couldn't help eyeing her legs as he discarded his jacket. She had a way of peeling off her clothes with the grace of a ballerina.

"Dad's head of maintenance."

Next came her dress. The shimmering black material slid off her gorgeous shoulders. Then she exposed her back. Finally, her hips and shapely buttocks were bared for his viewing pleasure. The skimpy black panties dared him to hitch his thumbs into the waistband and remove the silky treasure hiding her pussy he ached to taste.

He left his jacket on the bureau and came up behind her. The scent of her soap tickled his nostrils with its florally essence. She never sprayed on perfume, something he was thankful for. Always, she smelled simply fresh and clean, an intoxicating aroma as natural as her smooth, bronze skin.

She peeked over her shoulder. Maybe his gaze was saturated with the ripe heat searing his flesh, because her lips formed into an O. He never stopped until he closed the distance between them. His fingers automatically captured her wrists, and he nudged her against the stand of drawers located between her hanging dresses and shirts. She gasped.

The sensual hiss leaving her throat was his undoing. His cock pushed hard on his pants, as if trying to free itself on its own. He covered her mouth with his and tasted the delicate flavor of her tongue, a sensual combination of the mint and the lemon tea she'd drunk.

He used his knee to nudge her thighs apart. All that kept rolling through his mind was her black panties daring him to remove them. His kiss became hungrier the more his lust consumed him, skin too hot and sensitive. Her tongue matching his lick for lick was enough to tempt his cock into releasing the jizz responsible for the ache in his balls.

"All I could think about was taking you to bed during dinner," he fiercely whispered into her neck. He sucked the skin between his teeth, tasting her clean fragrance on his tongue.

She moaned. Her hands explored his hair, short nails gliding through the strands that left a deep need in his pants. His lips trailed her skin until he reached her breasts hidden from him by her matching bra. He pressed his face into her chest, taking in the aroma of the lace fabric pushing her breasts up high.

Her hands had shifted to his back, caressing his shirt. He reached around her and unsnapped the bra, freeing her breasts from the tight fabric. He claimed one with his mouth and sucked her hard nipple. Her heavy panting filled the closet, and the flesh of her tit in his mouth was alive with goosebumps.

"How wet are you?" he murmured.

"Oh, Séamus . . ." She sighed.

He licked a path to her naval, taking in the sweetness of her skin. The scent coming from her pussy was alive in his nose, a heavenly aroma of arousal. He slid his hands into the flimsy waistband and drew the panties down her hips, exposing her dark nest of pubic hair.

She pushed against his tongue, and he laid his lips on her mound. Her hips were gyrating, demanding he gorge himself of what lay between her thighs. He kissed the coarse hairs that were damp from her lust.

With his tongue, he parted her pussy lips and delved between the folds of skin to wetness and hot flesh. Her clit was hard and throbbing. He traced a path around the tiny nub, and she let out a loud moan, gripping his hair. Her hips thrust against his mouth as he licked and tasted her slippery folds of flesh.

He trailed his fingers down her leg while still lapping up her juices. Her heels remained on that she'd yet to slide off, and he caressed the smooth straps around her ankles.

"Séamus ... Séamus ..." Shannon's groans had become growls.

She kept thrusting her hips, grinding her pussy all over his face and slathering him with the heavenly fragrance of her cunt juice. He couldn't get over her response, her moans growing louder the more his tongue worked her into pure pleasure. Her thighs he was now caressing contracted, her slim muscles flexing beneath his palms.

Hearing her come while bouncing against his mouth stroked his hard cock. Oh, how he ached to plunge deep inside her.

He couldn't resist and sucked her clit between his teeth. She let out a low scream and wriggled. The chuckle building in his throat fought to release because he knew she was too sensitive right now to be touched, but darn if he couldn't help himself.

He slithered up her still writhing body and clasped her wiggling buttocks. With a heave, he lifted her off the floor. She was left with no choice but to wrap her legs around his hips. He smothered his mouth over hers and led them from the closet.

"How do you taste? Pretty good, hmm?" he murmured.

Her answer was a moan.

He steered them up the dais and laid her out on the bed. "Keep your legs spread. I can't get enough of looking at your pussy." It was a beautiful pussy, pink flesh shining beneath the light from her wetness and his saliva. Her slightly parted womanly lips gave him a wonderful view of her clit he'd just sucked.

As he unbuttoned his shirt, unbuckled his belt, and removed his pants, her gaze massaged every single ounce of skin he exposed. He reached down and cast aside his socks and shoes. Her legs remained open, her pussy waiting for his cock.

He moved toward the bed.

She shifted to her elbows. "Let me look at you."

The excitement in her eyes was almost his undoing, so he clenched his teeth. Her gaze lavished his cock with sensual strokes.

She curled her finger in a beckoning manner.

He rested his knees on the bed between her spread legs. "If you touch me, I'll come. You got me so hot and bothered, I can't wait to get in you."

"Then get in me," she beseeched him. "I want you. I want you so bad."

"Me, too." He slid on top of her. His cock feathered the wet opening to her pussy.

He claimed her mouth again and lavished her puckering lips with fierce kisses and slid his erection deep inside her. With her slippery flesh, she gripped him tight. Her hips came up and joined him in his slow thrusts. He squeezed his lids shut, savoring the feel of her pussy enclosed around his dick.

But she wasn't matching his leisurely rhythm. She was slamming against him, fucking his cock hard and fast. He had no choice but to join her, even though he wanted to try go slow and screw her into tomorrow. That wasn't possible. Her pussy was gliding up and down his dick, teasing him to the point of no return.

He braced his hands in the comforter for leverage and gave her what she wanted by humping her with all the strength he could muster. The quick and fast plunging was too much to bear. The release was upon him, toying with the head of his prick. He was left helpless as the build-up of jizz exploded from him and into her.

Right then, through his breaths and gasps while he savored being deep in her depths, he knew he had to find a way to make this marriage work. Only Shannon could bring him to such heights. Only Shannon understood him in a way that his friends and family couldn't. Only Shannon could almost make him see stars while he was fucking.

She was everything he needed.

CHAPTER NINETEEN: BACKSEAT DRIVERS

Séamus rode shotgun on his way to meet the two women who'd either give a *yay* or a *nay* to his marriage. During the drive, he'd let the stereo play a Gordon Lightfoot song that was a rather good tune. No, he might never embrace his wife's selection of music, but he could appreciate her preference.

"Ronnie's cooking. She's the one with the kitchen talent." Shannon stared straight ahead at the road, now in full chauffeur mode.

Séamus couldn't resist some teasing. "I know what your talent is."

Shannon tapped her nails on the steering wheel. "I was born to drive."

"Oh, I was thinking of something else. Like last night's bath . . ." Hmm, it'd been a wonderful way to retire after another of the dinners his wife had endured for him. To show how much he'd appreciated her effort, he'd soaped up her smooth skin and washed her hair.

Shannon steered them to a side street and parked. She switched off the car. "What talent is this that I possess, might I ask?"

Her teasing was music to his ears. Patience was a virtue he'd never appreciated until now. His once formal driver had truly unbound her hair from its tight braid. He leaned in and rested his hand on her seat. "What do you think?"

He stole a quick kiss.

"We'd better get inside. Pashney's a stickler for time. She's probably glaring out the window, wondering where we are."

"We're ten minutes early, thanks to your driving." Séamus

unbuckled his seatbelt. "I'll retrieve the wine." He'd brought a bottle from the cellar, a lovely chardonnay for their meal. Also, he'd made sure to bring two small gifts for Shannon's best friends. Nothing expensive, but something thoughtful after hearing a little about their life stories.

He retrieved the bags from the back and joined Shannon on the sidewalk. The sun was still up. Children played in the courtyard. They walked along the matching rows of houses.

"It's weird coming this way. I always enter through the back." Shannon had looped her arm through his.

"It's the same for me. When you were in the driveway for the first time, coming through the front door felt a bit odd." He couldn't resist giving her arm a little squeeze.

"And here I thought you appeared so natural strolling through your front door." She giggled.

"Did you like what you saw?" He couldn't help his laugh.

"I'll admit I did, but it went against my personal rule."

"Ah yes, your personal rule. How lucky I am that you broke it, hmm?"

"You do have a persuasive tongue." She glanced up at him, skin radiant.

He would've given anything to keep the bright smile and joyfulness on her face forever. "That's why I'm the director of marketing."

"This is it." Shannon used her chin to motion at the entrance.

They ascended the stairs.

"I guess I'd better knock since I don't live here anymore."

"Allow me." Séamus gave three quick raps on the door. He clutched the wine to his chest and regripped the handles on the two gift bags.

In seconds, the door opened to the meanest and most formidable woman he'd ever seen, with slashing black brows, a straight line of thin lips, narrow dark eyes, a face harder than leather, and hair buzzed to the scalp. He assumed this was Pashney, the tow truck driver.

After slowly assessing him up and down with the scrutiny of a serial killer deciding on their next victim, followed by a harumph, she shifted her tough stare to Shannon.

"Oh, get off it." Shannon flicked her hand. "Let us in." She sniffed. "It smells delish."

Pashney opened the door wider. A black-and-white cat scampered by, yowling.

"C'mon." Shannon curled her finger. "Ronnie's probably in the kitchen."

They were on the main level, having ascended the stoop.

"For you both." Séamus held out the wine and two gift bags.

Pashney folded her arms and cocked her brow. "What's up? Are you trying to buy us with all your millions?"

Séamus had expected as much from the brute-looking Pashney. "Of course not. It's only polite to bring the host something when invited to dinner."

"He has manners, too." Pashney glanced to Shannon.

"Of course he does. And where are mine?" Shannon chuckled. "Séamus, this is my bestie, Pashney Friday. Pash, this is my husband, Séamus Daugherty."

"Yeah, I heard you bought yourself a wife." Pashney snorted. "And now you're trying to buy us." She pointed at the gifts again.

"As I said, it's only polite to bring gifts for the hosts. Can we be friends?" He offered his most dazzling smile.

"Friends? I have enough friends already. I don't need any more." Pashney swiveled on her bare foot and tromped down the small hall.

Shannon shrugged. "Ignore her. She probably had to change someone's flat, and she detests changing flats, even though it's part of her job."

"Yes, I assumed her line of work required her to change flats." Séamus rubbed his chin.

"She thinks every woman should be self-sufficient and know how to change their own tire." Shannon motioned at him to follow.

He was led into an open kitchen, living room, and dining area. Music played from a small stereo next to the TV. A pop song he didn't recognize.

A tiny woman with hair cut into a pixie and as black as Shannon's pranced about in the kitchen. She glanced up from the chopping board. A big wide smile spread across her sharp elfish features that gave her a non-threatening demeanor and begged someone to lift her in the air and spin her around. "You must be Séamus. How nice to meet you."

She set down the knife—thank heavens the formidable Pashney wasn't holding the sharp object, or she would've used it to stab him, no doubt—and paraded over to the living room area. "I'm Veronica Wasaw. But you can call me Ronnie. All my friends do."

A bubbly electrician? Séamus hadn't expected to meet such a cheery person. "It's good to meet you, too. I'd shake, but currently both my hands are occupied."

"Let me get those." Ronnie took the wine and gift bags. "Oh wow, this stuff seems pretty 'spenive." Her giggle was a true giggle, not the low, husky chuckle Shannon gave. "Wow. I'm definitely downing a glass of this stuff. I hope you like roast."

"Roast is fine. Pork or beef?"

"Beef. With plenty of onions." Ronnie held the wine and shimmied to the kitchen. "Did you want this served during the meal?"

"Whatever decision you make is fine with me," Séamus assured her. A guest always acquiesced to the host.

He had scored a point, because Ronnie seemed to like him,

but he was back to zero, since Pashney more than made herself clear how she felt about him.

Séamus joined Shannon on the sectional. The foreboding Pashney sat across from them. She didn't say anything, other than staring him down with her hard gaze. This was going to be a fun dinner.

When Shannon set her hand on his knee, the apprehension tensing the back of his neck vanished. He had a great cheerleader in his wife. Maybe she wanted more to their marriage than a new business. Perhaps she was feeling the same as him.

Pashney said nothing. She simply cut him with her stare.

"How'd work go?" There was a stiffness to Shannon's voice Séamus hadn't heard before.

"I told you already." Pashney glared at Séamus. "I won't thank you for paying off her portion on our house."

"I didn't expect any acknowledgement." Séamus hoped someone would offer up a drink because he could use a shot of whiskey. He wasn't the only one sweating. Shannon's palm on his knee was damp.

"I wonder what we'll do about her portion of the property taxes she was paying, and the maintenance fees." Pashney continued to glare.

"I'm sure you'll find another suitable roommate." Seamus did his best not to grit his teeth. This woman never stopped.

"I hardly think so. We had a plan, but you reneged on your part, hey?" This time Pashney directed her frigid glare at Shannon

Séamus' defensive hackles rose. He leaned forward. "I can compensate—"

"This isn't about money, but you're rich, so of course you think everything is about money." Pashney had moved from sitting in the chair. She was on the edge, palms on knees and chin shoved in Séamus' direction.

If Pashney was trying to change Séamus' mind about

marriage, she was wrong. For her benefit, he set his free arm on the back of the sofa, right behind his wife. Yes, *his* wife. "No, I don't think everything is about money."

What a horrible hypocrite he was, because he'd married Shannon at first to keep his money and job. Not going unnoticed by him was his wife's stiffening presence. Perhaps she was sharing the same thought, too.

"Then why did you say you'd compensate us?" An almost smirk formed on Pashney's lips.

"Okay, no more picking on our guest. He brought us a nice bottle of wine," Ronnie called out from the kitchen where she stood mashing potatoes. "Zip it."

Pashney turned in her chair. "Don't you tell me to zip it. I have a right to—"

"Yeah, it's always about your rights and nobody else's." Ronnie giggled. She didn't gaze at them but remained focused on the pot of potatoes she attacked with a masher. "Be nice for once. I wanna enjoy our dinner."

Séamus almost sputtered. He hadn't expected the bubbly one to shut down Pashney's running mouth.

Shannon cast Pashney an *I told you so* look.

Rather amusing. Séamus peered at both women. Did Pashney and Shannon tend to argue, and Ronnie was the buffer? Time would tell with this dinner.

Shannon finished helping Pashney set the table in the dining area. Damned straight she'd dragged her bestie to aid her with the chore before Pashney could launch another attack. Ellen should be thanked for raising Séamus with such good manners. Anyone else would've thrown a tomahawk.

She set the last of the cutlery at its place setting.

The music was up louder, something Shannon was responsible for so Pashney couldn't speak over the volume, and for

Ronnie's benefit, who kept dancing in the kitchen, readying the last of the meal.

"Séamus," Shannon called out. The wine was already on the table.

Her husband rose from his spot on the sectional and strode to the dining area. He took the chair Shannon motioned at. There wasn't much she could do about keeping Pashney and Séamus apart, since there were only four chairs. She'd speak to Ronnie, plead with her other bestie to keep Pashney's angry mouth closed. Right now wasn't the time, because that would mean leaving Séamus alone with Pashney.

Shannon sat, and so did Pashney.

Ronnie brought over the meal of roast, mashed potatoes, glazed carrots, and some dinner rolls.

Séamus picked up the wine opener and manipulated the cork from the bottle. A loud pop sprang up over the music.

"How much did this cost?" Pashney asked.

"I don't know." Séamus began filling the glasses.

"Oh right, probably came from Daddy's cellar, huh?" Pashney picked up the platter of roast.

"Actually, it did." Séamus set down the bottle. He reached for his napkin.

"Kinda thought so. Tell me, did you ever do anything on your own in your life?" From the way Pashney's eyes went almost up and to the side, she was close to rolling them.

Shannon was on the verge of throwing down her cutlery. Why did everything always have to be a fight with her best friend?

"Yes, as a matter of fact, I did." Séamus focused on Pashney. "I earned my bachelor's degree on my own. My marketing degree on my own. Father couldn't grease someone's hand for me to acquire my driver's license, so I did that on my own, too."

"And I bet your dad paid for your schooling and provided

a car for you to get your driver's license, huh?" Pashney leaned in. The gleaming look she sent them said *gotcha!*

Shannon passed the carrots. "Can we please eat dinner in peace? I brought my husband here for you to meet him, not interrogate him. Enough already, or we're leaving."

"Leaving? Is that what you're threatening me with?" Pashney's gleam turned to a dark thundercloud. She tossed aside her napkin. "Then go ahead and leave. See if I give one freaking big deal." She shoved back her chair and stomped up the stairs.

If not for the music playing, an eerie silence would have followed.

Shannon rose at the same time as Ronnie. "Let me talk to her. You stay here with Séamus." She turned to her husband's red face, who stared at his place setting, jaw slack. "It's okay." She rubbed his shoulder. "It doesn't matter who you are. She would've treated whomever I brought home the same way."

She headed up the stairs to the top floor, where she'd find Pashney in her bedroom. "Hey." She knocked. "It's me."

"Go finish your nice dinner," Pashney muttered.

Shannon opened the door anyway to her best friend lying spread out, stomach down, on the bed, hugging a pillow. The cat, Marble, kneaded the pillow.

"How's he doing?" Shannon sat on the edge and petted the orange-and-white cat.

"How do you think? He misses Keemooch. You know he can't stand Puss N' Boots," Pashney said into the pillow.

"I wish you'd try and understand." The pleading in Shannon's heart came out through her mouth.

Pashney continued to face away. No doubt she'd felt abandoned again, the same as her father had abandoned her. Shannon reached over and rubbed her best friend's lower back. The muscles under her palm stiffened, and so did Pashney's shoulders.

"We had a deal." The words were almost spitting coming from Pashney's mouth.

"I know." Shannon's voice grew smaller. She really had let her best friends down. Ronnie wouldn't fuss or bitch, because that wasn't her style, but Pashney more than made her feelings known from the day they'd met on the road and played hopscotch at the age of five. "I wish you'd understand I'm married. I made my decision, and it'd mean everything to me if you'd give me . . . well, if you approved."

"Approve?" Pashney snorted. "Shan, he's not the guy for you. Can you really tell me you're happy living in his mansion, being fussed over by servants, and eating dinner dressed like a queen?"

No, Shannon wasn't happy about having her schedule almost dictated by the Daughertys' family tradition, but what could she do? "It'll take some getting used to, but I'm sure I can adjust."

"Why'd you marry him, anyway? C'mon, you're not telling everything. You said it was for some family thing. What happened that's so bad? You can't tell me this is just to have your own business. I know you." Pashney turned and sat up, cross-legged. She clutched the pillow. "You could've easily pulled off your own biz. You had it all set. Get the old bastard's stamp of approval for an awesome client list."

Shannon cringed. She couldn't share Séamus' secret. Pashney thought less of him already, and if she learned the truth, she'd be calling Séamus a spineless coward again. "Can you please trust me?"

Pashney shook her head. "Nope. Can't do it. I know you're not gonna be happy there. Or with him."

Séamus held his glass of wine. So much for dinner. Ronnie was smoking out on the balcony, and he'd felt confident accompanying the bubbly friend outside. "Will she be okay?"

They'd been discussing Pashney.

Ronnie puffed on the filter. She held the wine. "I dunno. It's hard to say. Pash is pricklier than a porcupine. You touch the wrong spot, and it's instant quills, y'know?"

"I do believe I've already sampled a few of her quills. Do you know of a good remedy to remove them?" He held out his hand. "Nasty things, they are."

Ronnie giggled. "I think you'll live."

"Yes, I'll live, but what about Pashney? It's not my intention to come between my wife and her friends."

Ronnie sighed and sank against the balcony railing. Her dark oval-shaped eyes, reminding him of an adorable elf, studied him. "You probably already heard this from Shan, but we had big plans when we came here."

"She spoke about you two to me," he quietly replied.

"Being on the rez . . . it's okay. But to make something of ourselves, we had to leave. Do you know how scary that is? Three girls from an isolated place coming to the big city?"

"I can imagine it was a culture shock."

"It was more than culture shock. We were blown away. We helped each other. I don't think any of us would've made it on our own. Our first place was a total dump. I was in school earning my trade license, and those two were working their butts off. Shan was lucky and managed to land a job driving for Elite, and Pashney started out as a dispatcher for the towing company and worked her way up."

Séamus nodded.

"It took a lot of hard work for us to buy this place. I mean tons of work." Ronnie motioned at the sliding door. "Our dreams were finally coming true . . ."

And I came along with my checkbook and ruined what the three of you were accomplishing. I took a match to your dreams . . .

He stifled his sigh. The universe wasn't aligning for him. If anything, fate was telling him to let Shannon go.

CHAPTER TWENTY: LIFE IN THE FAST LANE

For the next two weeks, life moved one hundred miles an hour for Shannon. Between working in the evenings with Séamus to get her business established and spending her days readying for this weekend's party to meet the family, friends, and business associates of her in-laws, she hadn't found time to see her friends and try again to convince them to accept her marriage.

As for Séamus, if not for the two hours they spent after dinner working on her business plan, she'd never see him, since he was always gone. It was like he was avoiding her.

Each time she gazed into his brooding eyes and asked if he was okay, his tight reply was the same *yes*. But he wasn't okay. He hadn't been ever since the disastrous dinner with Pashney and Ronnie.

She'd asked if her friends could attend the party, but Mrs. Daugherty had given a regretful *no*, not that Shannon's two besties would've shown up anyway. Mingling with the rich and famous wasn't their idea of a good time. Still, Shannon had bristled because she knew the order had come from Mr. Daugherty.

She left the bathroom, having dressed for the day. Keemooch was perched on the chaise lounge, his favorite sleeping spot.

"Are you ready for breakfast?"

Ellen had tried to intervene, stating it was her job to see to the cat, but Shannon had put her foot down.

Her cat. Her responsibility.

Keemooch hopped off to the floor.

"C'mon."

She scooped up the cat and carried him downstairs to the kitchen, where the cook was busy preparing breakfast. "Good morning, Ira."

"Good morning, Mrs. Daugherty." The cook was busy at the range top, where something bubbled in the stainless-steel pot.

As for the four ovens, a delicious spicy scent wafted from one.

"I have his breakfast on the island." Ira half-smiled. She'd made no bones about her feelings about to animals in the kitchen the first time Shannon had brought Keemooch down-stairs.

"Thanks." Although Shannon could've opened the can of tuna herself, she took the crystal bowl and headed for the sun-room, something Courtney despised, stating animals shouldn't be present while others ate.

Fair enough, but Courtney never dined until around nine-thirty or ten, so Shannon made sure to be out of the witch's hair before she arrived. The big white clock on the wall read eight.

Mrs. Daugherty was already seated, papers in front of her and the all too familiar tablet. "Good morning. I'm doing last-minute preparations for the party."

Shannon set down the bowl and Keemooch. "You said it'll be on the lawn?"

"Yes. The weather is supposed to be lovely on Saturday. But I have arranged for a tent just in case."

"Oh, a tent? Is it going to be a big party? Did it involve lots of planning?"

"Much planning. Flowers. Entertainment. Tables. Chairs.

Dishes. There was much to do." Mrs. Daugherty set aside her tablet. "How about you? Did your fitting go well?"

"Yes. They're delivering the dress today." At least Shannon didn't have to wear a big elaborate gown, but the dress was as formal as the one she'd chosen for her wedding.

"The makeup artist and hairdresser will be coming to us. Did Ellen inform you?"

"Yes." Shannon could admit having a personal hairdresser and makeup artist at the house while she dressed was an excellent idea. What woman wouldn't want to prepare in her own bedroom?

"I'm glad you don't mind. It's much easier than going to the salon," Mrs. Daugherty replied.

Ellen arrived then, holding the pot of coffee. "Good morning, Mrs. Daugherty. What shall you have? Today, cook is making omelets served with melons or a heartier dish of sausages, scrambled eggs, and toast."

"I'll go for number two, please." Shannon could use an extra-big meal.

"Excellent choice." Ellen beamed. "Your husband chose the same breakfast."

"Did he?" Séamus must have risen with the birds, because he'd been gone when Shannon's alarm had buzzed at seven.

He was purposely avoiding her. No doubt he was regretting marrying her. And now she'd have to play one half of a happily married couple on Saturday, when her groom didn't even want to be a part of . . . anything.

Today was the dreaded day when Shannon would meet everything Daugherty. She stepped from the shower. In her mind, the fan did the wrong job of eliminating the steam in the bathroom. At the townhouse, the mirror had always been a haze of fog. Not this morning. She could see her reflection of grim and gloom in Séamus' vanity that he'd already used.

Great.

Not even her own husband was here to help her on a stomach-knotted hour. She'd order up some toast and tea to calm her tightened nerves. Mom would say the super wealthy were merely people who put their panties and boxers on just like everyone else on planet earth.

That would be her mantra — panties and boxers — when she greeted each filthy-rich guest.

Once she'd fed Keemooch and had her tea and toast, the hairdresser and makeup artist arrived. For the rest of the morning her hair was swept into an updo and face painted to rival a movie star's. Just as she slid into her gown, Séamus came through the bedroom door.

Whereas his look had been indifferent ever since the disastrous dinner, this time he lit up. "You look . . . beautiful." The words he spoke reflected the awe in his voice. "The guests are already gathered outside. I came up to get you."

A light-gray suit hugged his athletic build. His dark-brown hair was gelled off his face, revealing how strong his features were that hid ever so slightly when he wore his hair in his usual style.

Heat spread across Shannon's cheeks. "Thank you." She didn't mean for her reply to be stiffer than her shoulders, but having him compliment her after experiencing disinterest left a heap of uncertainty nesting in her belly.

She took his proffered arm and followed him not to the family staircase, but to the main one that led to the grand hall. From the balcony overlooking the entryway, she spied the family gathered down below.

"You should've gotten me sooner," she whispered, not used to being late or keeping anyone waiting.

"We are the guests of honor. It's only natural we appear last." Séamus kept leading them forward.

This must be how a woman felt on death row. She was

being led to the guillotine, ready to have her head chopped off. They ascended the staircase to the men frowning, her sister-in-law grimacing, but her mother-in-law smiling.

Shannon's racing heart slowed at the sincerity radiating from Mrs. Daugherty. The woman truly wanted this party, truly wanted to introduce her as Séamus' wife to everyone. A smidgen of hope spread across Shannon's chest.

"You look lovely. Absolutely lovely." Mrs. Daugherty air-kissed Shannon's cheek.

As Shannon leaned in, she caught Courtney's frowning lips and narrowed brows. "Thank you. Séamus and I really appreciate what you've done for us."

"It was my pleasure." Mrs. Daugherty lightly touched Shannon's bare arm. "Wait here with Séamus while we do the introductions."

Shannon nodded and set her arm back through Séamus'.

Mr. Daugherty led his wife down the hall. Everyone followed, with Shannon and Séamus bringing up the rear. They were advancing to the back door that would lead out to the pool, flower gardens, and main lawn.

"You'll do fine." Séamus squeezed Shannon's arm.

She glanced at him. It was the first hint of affection he'd shown her after being such a true gentleman from the get-go. Maybe he was reconsidering? Or was this all an act because he was taking center stage in a matter of moments? Playing the happy husband who didn't regret making a deal with his wife in Lake Louise?

While the others were called out by the person Shannon presumed to be the master of ceremonies, she kept chanting her mantra of *panties and boxers*.

"Now please welcome Mr. and Mrs. Séamus Daugherty." The MC's amplified announcement boomed across the lawn. "A big round of applause."

Shannon stepped into the bright glare of the afternoon sun

beating down on them to a packed lawn full of expensively dressed people clapping and smiling. Whether the smiles were genuine she wasn't sure, because she kept her gaze pinned on the pool, where gentlemen sitting on white chairs played romantic music from their violins.

Mrs. Daugherty had outdone herself on the decorating. The back lawn was an extravagant display of white mixing with the flower gardens. White chairs. White tablecloths. White flowers. White ribbons streaming here and there. A massive white tent where those who wished could hide from the sunlight and seek shade.

She was led down the four steps by Séamus' guiding hand. Boy, talk about being a million miles from the rez. Never in her life had she experienced this kind of lavishness. For a half hour, she was introduced to everyone, her arm never leaving Séamus'. She met so many people, she couldn't remember their names, other than they were CEOs, presidents, and vice-presidents of this corporation and that corporation.

Some asked if she golfed, played tennis, and other kinds of sports. Women inquired which charities she belonged to. All Shannon could manage was a pasted-on frozen smile as she shook hand after hand and air-kissed every woman's cheek. If her besties could see her, they'd be rolling their eyes and telling her to get back to reality.

After many introductions, she was ready for a glass of champagne the waiters were making the rounds with on silver trays. She snatched one of the crystal flutes. Her tense body was demanding to sneak away and relax where she could greedily gulp the drink instead of sipping.

Séamus kept his hand on the small of Shannon's back. So much for a fast getaway. He probably had someone else he wanted to introduce her to. As if she hadn't met enough people already.

Nothing about this gala affair sat right in her stomach. This wasn't about her, and it wasn't about Séamus. This was about Mr. Daugherty, and everyone obediently played their roles to his puppeteering. Neither of them had been asked if they wanted a party—they'd been told. Even Mrs. Daugherty had been ordered to plan the event. As for Cillian and Courtney, they were the only ones who happily bowed to the patriarch's wishes.

She had to talk to her husband after. Wait, what was the point? Given the stiffness of Séamus' movements and his absence from her life as of late, he'd handed her what she had asked for—a business and nothing more.

Séamus refused to let his guard down. If anyone dared to insult his wife, he was putting aside gentlemanly manners and lacing up the gloves. He should be proud to be on the verge of giving up everything to come to Shannon's aid, but the fact was, Ronnie and Pashney had known Shannon their whole lives, and what they'd said continued to crowd his head.

If he'd married a woman from his peerage, she'd be moving from circle to circle like a gracious host, but Shannon stayed by Mom's side, sipping her glass of champagne, nodding with the same frozen smile plastered on her face to the Tillsdale family. She didn't wish to be here anymore than he did.

But setting her free with a business so she could reach her dreams was a knife being plunged into his chest. They'd known each other a whole month, yet he couldn't picture his world without her. It was as if life had started once she'd slid into the driver's seat of the town car, as if she was meant to drive him to where he truly belonged.

Was she guiding him to his fated destination? Showing him who he truly was?

Séamus pressed his lips together.

"Old boy, well done. Well done." Ethan patted him on the back. "I must say she is a beauty. A real beauty. Am I ever going to get my moment to officially meet your wife?"

"Of course." Séamus nodded. "Once she breaks from her conversation with the Tillsdales, I'll introduce you."

Ethan winked. "You did great." His leering stare moved up and down Shannon's form like she was a side of prime rib being purchased.

Séamus gave his friend a polite elbow. "That's my wife you're talking about."

"Understood. Understood. Come. Let's get my date. I don't think you've met the lovely Elizabeth Kennedy yet. She's a charming lady. Right this way." Ethan swaggered off.

Séamus had no choice but to follow. He threaded his way through the crowd of designer dresses and tailored black suits until Ethan stopped at a small group of beautiful women holding champagne flutes and laughing.

In the past, Séamus would've found himself intrigued, even interested in taking one to bed, but not anymore. They were a group of stunning redheads, brunettes, and blondes. No doubt the ladies were highly educated with great jobs . . . until they married.

Father's threat resurfaced. How would he feel about Shannon's new business venture and working full-time? Well, that was a moot question. He'd be furious, an affront to a Daugherty, insinuating he was unable to financially care for his wife.

Right then, Séamus could've kicked his great-great-great grandfather for starting this madness.

"Ladies, how are you?" Ethan's greeting was about as a coy as a wolf upon sheep.

Their blue, green, and brown eyes glittered.

"Well, well, well, it's about time you made an appearance." Imogene batted her mink lashes at Séamus. "I have half a mind to pour my glass over your head. Now how am I going to spend a much-needed getaway?"

Séamus' face burned hot, because he'd taken Imogene skiing with him in Whistler.

"Tell me, does she measure up?" Imogene winked.

Séamus quickly buried their weekend of passion at the back of his mind. No, there weren't any complaints on his part during their getaway, but Lake Louise and Shannon had been a far more stimulating weekend. "She's speaking to the Tillsdales right now with Mother. But once I get a chance, I'll introduce you." *Highly unlikely, because you will make it a point to let my wife know about our weekend.*

Although he was no Casanova compared to Ethan, Séamus was hardly a saint. He could count on one hand of women in the crowd he'd shared a night with between the sheets.

"Oh, enough of the manners." Imogene sauntered away, straight for where Shannon and Mom stood.

Sure enough, Imogene rudely cut into the conversation, looped her arm through Shannon's, and steered Séamus' wife straight back to the circle.

The same frozen smile was plastered on Shannon's face. Imogene whispered something into her ear. She kept whispering as they approached, Imogene's high, tinkling laugh about as appealing as an earworm.

Séamus clutched the stem of his champagne flute.

"I was telling your bride how much you enjoy skiing and asked if you were taking her to Whistler." Imogene patted Shannon's arm. "It's a lovely place. Be sure to stay in the Red Rose suite at the Whistler Inn. It's an enchanting hotel. Quite romantic."

The ladies all giggled.

Ethan frowned. He glanced to Imogene. "Come. I need a refill and someone to accompany me."

Before Imogene could reply, Ethan whisked her off into the crowd.

Shannon glanced at Séamus. The darkness in her black

irises said she wasn't amused.

Séamus placed his palm on her rigid back. "Excuse us for a moment." He quickly led Shannon away from his crowd of friends.

"Are these the people you golf with?" Shannon stiffly asked.

"Yes. Sometimes." He gritted his teeth. "Ignore her. Imogene has always —"

"Hoped to be the next Mrs. Séamus Daugherty?" Ice was warmer than Shannon's reply.

Again, Pashney and Ronnie's words pinched the back of Séamus' neck. He wanted Shannon to fit in, he wanted her to be at home in his life, but wishing didn't do anything. Wishing didn't count unless he was determined to make his dream come true. So what exactly was his dream now?

It certainly wasn't divorce or an annulment.

Chapter Twenty-one: Permanent Passengers

Inside the jet's interior, Séamus toyed with his tumbler of scotch. They were flying over lakes and forests. Below him was a sea of green and blue.

After the disastrous reception to celebrate his wedding, his marriage had grown colder with perfunctory conversation. He didn't need to worry about bolting every morning before Shannon rose, because she'd taken up jogging, vanishing at the break of day to run The Bridle Path. Before she returned, he had always gone to work.

Not only did he have to endure a flight with his silent wife, who typed away on her laptop, furiously developing her business plan, but he had to admit she was purposely ignoring him.

Thank goodness Ronnie and Pashney hadn't accompanied them. Both had wanted to return to the reserve for the celebration of Indigenous Peoples Day, but their work had demanded heavy schedules.

Just Keemooch offered him company. The cat padded around the jet, sniffing here and smelling there. The odd time he'd curl up on one of the seats.

It was more than missing sex. It was their talks Séamus yearned for, but Shannon had become his chauffeur again, full of short, quick replies to any of his questions.

They were staying at the one and only motel, though, so maybe they'd have some alone time. He'd breathed a sigh when Shannon had informed him two of her cousins were already bunking at her parents' home due to the housing shortage on the reserve. She'd explained her brother and his girlfriend lived at the five-plex and didn't have room since another cousin was crashing with them. As for her sister, she lived in Vancouver and couldn't make it home.

Shannon's grandparents were retrieving them. Why her parents weren't coming, Séamus wasn't sure. Shannon had mentioned something about grandbabies. Perhaps the mother was watching them?

Shannon hadn't told him what to expect, so he drummed his fingers on the armrest. He'd never been to an Indian Reserve. But he'd view the experience as simply visiting another small town and nothing more. A small town with their own culture and beliefs. He hoped he wouldn't make a faux pas, because he had no idea of the customs or etiquette.

Séamus had bypassed on having Tonya make the trip. Shannon's family might find their jaunt rather expensive to fly in a private jet, but Séamus was used to the procedure.

The pilot's voice came over the intercom, telling them they'd be landing in fifteen minutes.

He snapped on his seatbelt.

Shannon closed her laptop. She stored Keemooch away in his carrier, set him on a seat, and fastened him in.

"You take such good care of . . . our cat." Yes, *their* cat.

The deadness in her gaze ever since the party vanished. Her dark irises brightened. "We all have to be safe." She sat and fastened her seatbelt.

Yes, they did. It was as if her words had cuffed him upside the head. He did have a family. His own family. Shannon and Keemooch. He gripped the armrests tighter. No matter what Ronnie had said, and Pashney's disapproval, he was going to make this work. He was done with spending the last month moaning whether to let Shannon go so she could reach her dream on her own.

He wanted them to attain the dream together. All he could do was hope her family wouldn't share the same philosophy as Ronnie and Pashney.

"So this is the man you married?" Mrs. Wayash, Shannon's maternal grandmother, who Shannon had referred to as Ko-kum, slowly looked Séamus up and down. There was a hard scrutiny in her beady black eyes. Her arms remained folded as she stood outside the airport beside the rusted car.

Séamus held tight to the pet carrier.

The airport couldn't really be called an airport. A simple small building sending travelers away from the reserve, or God forbid, coming to the reserve. Black flies kept buzzing around his head. He shooed a few away. "A pleasure to meet you." He extended his hand to Shannon's grandfather.

Mr. Wayash simply nodded. He picked up their luggage and the litter box, rounded the car, and opened the trunk.

A man of few words? Séamus wasn't sure if his presence was responsible for Mr. Wayash's silence or if the grandfather had simply taken an instant dislike to him. He then extended his hand to the grandmother.

"No need to get all formal on me. My daughter's already told me lots about you." Mrs. Wayash opened the passenger door. "We'd best get going. The black flies will eat you two alive." She shook her head. "You know better than to forget bug spray."

Shannon shrugged. "I'll put some on when we get to the motel."

"Don't be expecting five-star lodgings." Mrs. Wayash slammed the door shut. She rolled up the window.

Séamus held open the back door for Shannon. She scooted inside, and he slipped in next to her.

A blanket was strewn across the seats. He set the pet carrier with the yowling Keemooch on the floor beside an empty bag of chips, a duffel bag, and a plastic bag of groceries.

The scent of something sparked his interest. Like leftover cooking. Perhaps fried. He sniffed some more. The cozy aroma was coming from the grandmother now that they were enclosed inside the vehicle.

"I hope you're hungry." Mrs. Wayash glanced over her shoulder. "I made lunch."

"Lunch sounds great." Shannon settled her gaze on Séamus. "Did you want to eat first?"

Séamus didn't have much of a choice, and good manners said to accept the food. "Of course."

They were off, spitting up dust under the tires as they traveled down the dirt road with no view but tons of trees and plenty of underbrush.

Mrs. Wayash asked Shannon about the wedding, parties, and where she was living, and if she liked the place.

Séamus sank in the seat and glanced at the homes they were coming upon, all box-shaped with some lawns mowed and others needing more help than a weed-eater could provide. A few of the front steps required repairs. As for the back doors, those were located on the sides of the homes. A couple of dogs trailed the car.

Children played in the ditches or on the dirt road, so Mr. Wayash had to drive slowly.

Séamus peered out the window at the kids' laughter and screams. One in particular, maybe under two years, ran about in his diaper, which was strange, but perhaps part of the life-style up here. A girl around six or seven grabbed the toddler's hand and steered him back to a driveway where a woman stood, yelling and beckoning. Maybe the young child had snuck off.

"Well?" Mrs. Wayash asked.

Shannon nudged him.

Séamus steered his gaze to the grandmother. "Excuse me. My apologies. I was looking out the window."

"I asked what that plane cost."

He almost drew in a sharp intake of breath but stopped himself. Maybe asking the price of something was the norm up here. "I'm not sure."

"Does your family own it?"

"The company does."

"What's the name of the company again?"

They were passing a playground in dire need of an upgrade. Children played on the seesaw that hopefully wouldn't break, scrambled up the rickety Jungle Gym, and ran about on the sand. They were older, maybe around seven to ten years. "Daugherty Enterprises."

The old man turned left at a small intersection. Here, trees were sparse, and buildings filled the area, some big and some small.

"That's the bingo hall." Shannon motioned at a red-brick building. "And over there's the band office."

"Band office?" Séamus peered at the two-story building the shade of prison gray.

"It's where the administration of the band happens."

"Band?"

"The reserve. I thought I told you *the band* is the members of the reserve."

No, she hadn't, but Séamus nodded. He assumed *tribe* was the proper word, but he'd been wrong. "What about where the powwow happens?"

"That's over at the Treaty Grounds. You'll see it tomorrow."

"Where're the Treaty Grounds?"

"Down at the lake. We're in the area known as Main. Kokum and Mishoomis live at what's called Central. It's the area in between River and Main. The rez is like any other town.

We have names for different areas."

"Are you from Main?"

She shook her head. "I grew up a few doors down from my grandparents over in Central."

"What about your paternal grandparents?" Her last name was Nadjiwon—well, previously was.

"They died when I was a baby. I never knew them."

They passed another building reminiscent of a recreation center. "What's that?"

"The community center. It also doubles as the rec center. That's where the feast will take place. We always feast the day before the powwow. It's potluck. Everyone brings a dish, and the men fry fish."

"Oh? What kind?" Séamus was partial to swordfish, but he doubted that'd be on the menu.

"Walleye."

He'd never sampled cold-water fish before, even though he should've, but the restaurants he patronized only served ocean species.

"There's the motel."

Séamus glanced at a place that could've been any other roadside stop he'd seen on the highways. But an abundance of pine trees, the boardwalk in front of the room doors, and a picnic table made the place rather quaint.

They passed more box-shaped houses on their way to this mysterious Central. The road was winding, but the thick brush was cut back to the ditches on either side. They encountered a steep hill they had to drive up. Once they reached the top, two houses appeared that pretty much matched the other abodes they'd previously passed.

Mr. Wayash turned into the driveway.

Two dogs, a mix of many breeds, sat on the front step. Tails wagging, they bounded to the car.

Just as Séamus opened his door, the bigger black dog stood

on its hind legs and set both paws on his chest. Anything with four legs that he'd encountered so far had been well trained. Not these two. The medium-sized one with white-and-black fur barked and pranced around him.

"Enough." Mrs. Wayash snapped her fingers. "Mind your manners."

The dogs, thank goodness, jumped and yipped around the old woman.

Séamus glanced to the car as Shannon slipped from the back seat, clutching Keemooch's pet carrier. From inside the cage, the cat hissed and spit.

Now he fully understood what his wife was experiencing being thrust into a world which she felt she shouldn't be a part of, because he sure as hell did not belong here. Not that he had anything against the Indian Reserve—he simply was clearly out of his element.

But he had to at least try put his best foot forward, the same way Shannon had for his lifestyle and family, or his marriage would sink further into the muck, where it already halfway sat.

"Grab the groceries." The old woman headed up the stairs creaking beneath her.

"I got them," Séamus offered, since Shannon's hands were already full. He reached inside the back and retrieved the bag he'd spied earlier.

"C'mon." Shannon used her chin to motion at him to follow.

Mr. Wayash rounded the house and disappeared.

Séamus followed Shannon inside the small home.

Mrs. Wayash was already banging pots and pans around in the kitchen that was just off the front door. They stood in the living room. Two doors, also in front of him, led to where he assumed bedrooms to be. A table and four chairs were set up in the middle of the kitchen.

"Have a seat." Shannon opened the pet carrier. Keemooch stuck his head out.

"I got the bannock done. I just need to fry the burgers." Mrs. Wayash gave him a view of her bony backside as she dug around inside the fridge.

So this was who Shannon had inherited her height and slim bone structure from. The older woman was very spry. A little on the gruff side, but she kept her salt-and-pepper hair tidy in a bun. There was a loaf of a half-cut, round-shaped type of bread on the counter.

"That's bannock. We bake it." Shannon plopped in the chair adjacent from him. "Or we fry it." She used her lips to point at what Mrs. Wayash was doing with the cast-iron pan.

"Sounds delicious." And it did. Homemade buns with burgers.

A pot of soup simmered on the stove, had probably been simmering since the grandparents had retrieved them from the airport.

"Where's Mishoomis?" Mrs. Wayash produced a big tub of lard. She scooped out a tablespoon full and plopped it in the cast-iron pan.

"He went out back. He's probably filleting fish for the feast tomorrow." Shannon stretched out her legs and folded her arms.

Séamus couldn't help staring. In the small kitchen, his wife was at home, going by the contentment in the light smile on her lips, and glowing skin. He'd taken this from her when they'd married. If he'd been here with her previously, his heart told him he'd never have struck the deal.

The most he could do was try adapting as she had. Finding middle ground was imperative, or they'd fail.

He reached over and took her hand in his. Her fingers stiffened and then relaxed. The questioning look she sent him knocked him in the gut, but he continued to hold her hand.

Mrs. Wayash swiveled on her heel. Her gaze lingered on their hands. The old woman's lips puckered, and she glanced to her granddaughter. She said something in a language Séamus didn't understand.

Shannon only used one word in that language to reply, but her voice had been soft, even reassuring.

Before Séamus could receive another scolding glare from the old woman, a door opened from the side of the house just off the kitchen. Mr. Wayash entered. The scent coming off him was strong enough to almost knock Séamus from his chair.

"Did you finish filleting the fish?" Shannon asked.

Nodding, Mr. Wayash shuffled to the sink and washed his hands. Once he was done, he stole one of the round bannocks Mrs. Wayash had set on a plate.

"What're you doing? That's for lunch." With an oven mitt, the old woman smacked her husband's hand.

Mr. Wayash shrugged and pulled out a kitchen chair. He sat, his mouth making exaggerated movements of eating. His crinkly eyes were focused on Séamus.

Séamus wasn't sure if he was supposed to say anything or if the old man was offended that he was holding his granddaughter's hand. Maybe PDA was frowned upon in their culture.

"Do you fish?"

The old man's question took Séamus by surprise. Not because Mr. Wayash had finally spoken, but because his soft voice didn't match his gruff exterior of hard features and leathered, bronzed skin.

"Yes, I do. In Jamaica."

"I mean cold-water fishing," Mr. Wayash replied.

"No."

"Would you like to fish?"

Séamus glanced at Shannon. Weren't they supposed to only be here until Monday morning? Tomorrow was the feast.

Sunday was the powwow. "Fishing sounds great."

"Tonight. The evening fish."

Séamus squirmed. He again stole a peek at Shannon. Well, she dined every morning with Mom and had to tolerate Courtney. It was time for Séamus to reciprocate. If he didn't, for sure their marriage would be over before they'd celebrated two months.

Chapter Twenty-two: Ride with Me

Even though Mr. Wayash hadn't spoken a word, Séamus gave himself a thumbs-up for at least packing his casual attire for the trip. His jeans and polo shirt were the perfect outfit for sitting in a small skiff, jigging for walleye.

There was peace out on the lake, the same peace he experienced while skiing down the mountain in Lake Louise or Whistler, floating on his surfboard in Maui, or hitting a perfect golf shot to the green.

A loon sang its sad song. Séamus shifted on the installed seat attached to the bench seat. He could make out the shadow of the bird before it ducked under the water.

The sun sat low in the purple-and-red sky, and the water reflected the hues of pink, orange, and violet. Although they were safe from the mosquitoes, he'd rubbed on repellent, since the old man had warned him to expect a relentless swarm hungry for blood once they reached shore.

When they'd arrived at their fishing spot, Mr. Wayash had simply handed Séamus a fishing rod and set out the tackle box. He hadn't told Séamus how to fish or even shown him, something Father and Grandfather had always done. Séamus was left to his own devices, so if he fished on a small yacht in the Caribbean, he could very well fish off a skiff on a lake.

Maybe they could build a house up here, a place to get away for the weekend where Shannon experienced safety and peace. "How much does property cost on the reserve?" Séamus kept jigging his line.

"Eh?" The old man frowned. "You don't buy land on an

Indian Reserve."

"You don't?"

Mr. Wayash shook his head.

"Then how do you build your houses?"

"The band does," came the simple reply.

Séamus would have to dig for answers. The old guy really was a man of one-word answers. Hmm, this reminded him of his wife when they'd first met. Maybe she took after her grandfather in this respect. "How does the band buy your houses?"

"Government funding."

"What kind of funding?"

"CMHC."

Through Daugherty Enterprises, Séamus was quite familiar with the Canada Mortgage and Housing Corporation. "So your reserve is under their umbrella?"

Mr. Wayash nodded. He opened a thermos and poured himself a cup of whatever was inside. "Want some?"

"What is it?"

"Tea."

"Sure." The water lapping ever so lightly against the hull was more soothing than being rocked by his mother as a small child.

Seamus propped his feet on the gunwale. "To build a house up here, you have to officially ask CMHC?"

"No. Chief and council."

"I ask chief and council?"

"No. Shannon would."

Maybe it had to do with membership. There went Séamus' surprise, since she'd have to inquire on his behalf. "And if they approve Shannon's request . . ."

"Apply for minister's guarantee."

"What's that, if you don't mind elaborating?"

"Minister guarantees if you default on the loan, the band

will make the payment."

"Oh . . . there'll be no loan. Cash."

The old man nodded. "Then you ask chief and council. If they say yes, talk to the housing coordinator. He'll take you through the rest."

That would be the perfect present for Séamus to give his wife. A home on the lake at her reserve. He would meet with this housing coordinator and unearth where the hydro lines ran, because he might have to pay for the cost of poles and power to their spot, which was nothing of concern. "Thank you."

"For what?" The old man squinted.

"For being who you are." *And not telling me what to do, how to do it, and the why of it all, or how dumb I'd be to build a house on an Indian Reserve that would have to go under Shannon's name, and the risk of losing my money to her and the house if anything happens. I could spend a week out here with you. Easily.*

Séamus couldn't believe it. He'd met a man older than him who wasn't telling him what to do or advising him of the implications of his decisions.

Maybe coming up to the reserve wasn't so bad after all. Maybe tomorrow's feast would go as smoothly as fishing with Mr. Wayash.

Having already unpacked their luggage and settled in Keemooch with his food, water, and litter box, Shannon had nothing to do in the small motel room but peek out the window now and then. Mishoomis was a man of few words, which was why she couldn't stop wondering how Séamus' fishing trip was unfolding. The sun had set over a half an hour ago. By now, Mishoomis would be on shore.

Since the room had two beds, Keemooch settled on the one nearest the window and kneaded the pillow. She sank down beside him and petted his soft fur.

The door opened. The scent of filleted fish hit her at full force. "You're back. You caught something?"

"Caught quite a few." Séamus grinned. "I had no idea you didn't require a fishing license. Your grandfather told me he only needs to carry something called a status card so he can fish off the lake."

"I take rez things for granted that everyone knows around here." Shannon shrugged and stood. Her worries had been for nothing. She hadn't been sure how Séamus would react coming up here, but from his big grin, he'd enjoyed himself. "You helped Mishoomis fillet them?"

"Yeah. He said to do it right away. He's putting our haul on ice for tomorrow's fish fry. He asked if I'd help."

"Help fry the fish?" Shannon squinted.

"Yep. He said it's what the men do, since the women prepare all the side dishes." His grin got even bigger, big enough to show his dimples. "I rather like the equal partnership of it all."

She didn't want Séamus to get the impression that life was perfect on the reserve. "We have our traditions, but we also have our share of problems, like any other community."

"Your grandfather told me." Séamus removed his hoodie and bared the polo shirt hugging his athletic upper body. "He said the reserve is dry because of the alcohol and drug problem."

Shannon swallowed. "Mishoomis told you?"

"He also informed me how housing works. When the treaty was signed. How everyone was self-sufficient and built their own homes from the trees before the welfare and housing acts came into effect in the sixties. He told me he'd take me to The Point tomorrow to show me where the original log cabins were constructed. He said he was born in one, and his parents had built their own."

Goodness, for Mishoomis to talk someone's ear off meant

he had taken a liking to Séamus. "Yes, that's part of our history."

Séamus swaggered forward. "He also told me the reserve lost its self-sufficiency because of those acts. He mentioned, most members, not all, rely on the band for everything."

"There are some of us who were taught to make our own way." But she'd been bought by Séamus, just as some of the members of the reserve had let the funding from the government buy them.

"There's nothing wrong with relying on the charity or help of others to get your start. Your grandpa told me that's how they built their house. He said when the housing act came into effect, they weren't given the house they live in. They paid for it. They paid the band back every penny. Any renovations they did, they applied for a loan through the band and paid that back, too."

"I guess help can be good, if it's used properly." Although Shannon was receiving help, she could pay back the money once her business began turning a profit. Maybe she hadn't been bought and paid for after all.

"Is everything okay?" Séamus tilted his head.

"Oh . . . uh . . . why do you ask?"

"You're glowing." His dimples remained on display. "It's the first time I've seen you glow . . . since the dinner at your friends' place."

If Séamus was trying to understand and accept the reserve's way of life, Shannon was determined to reciprocate. No more merely tolerating his family and the lifestyle. She'd make a darned good effort to embrace the traditions of the Daughertys.

"I should've . . ." Yes, she'd tell him the truth. "I owe you an apology. I must confess I haven't been very accepting of your family and their . . . way of living. I . . . seeing you trying to fit in up here . . . what can I say? I was wrong. I need to start trying to—"

"Hey, hey." He slid his finger beneath her chin. "We haven't even made two months yet. It's gonna take time for us to know each other, even trust each other. I'll admit after I talked to Ronnie, and the way Pashney reacted, I was having doubts."

Shannon stiffened. Her suspicions had been correct.

"No, it's not what you think." He grasped her biceps. His gaze studied her. "I thought I had no right to take you from all of . . . this." He glanced around at the motel room. "This is your life."

"You have your life, too." She wet her lips.

"Hey, we agreed to this marriage." His grasp on her arms firmed, but not enough to hurt her, only to reassure her. "I know my father's watching us. He told me . . ." His hands dropped from her arms. He turned to face the TV.

"What did he tell you?" She set her hands on his sunken shoulders.

"That if you're not the perfect Daugherty wife, he'd have the marriage annulled." His words were but a whisper laced with a hint of despair.

Rage unfurled in Shannon. She couldn't believe the nerve of that man. "Is he serious? He'll still take away your inheritance? Still blacklist you?"

Séamus nodded.

"Don't worry. We'll figure something out." Having come this far, she wasn't about to let some tyrant threaten her out of a business that meant everything to her. "I'm sure we'll find a way."

He glanced over his shoulder.

Being without him between her legs for what seemed a year, talking wasn't what she needed. Instead, she ached to hold tight to what they'd discovered together from the night they'd consummated their marriage. Her mouth claimed his.

Séamus' sigh of contentment said he'd missed her as much as she'd missed him.

He swiveled and drew her against his chest. She locked her arms around his shoulders and gladly licked his tongue that had slipped between her lips. The smell coming from him was pure pleasure — the outdoors.

His fingers worked on her shirt, tugging the hem from her jeans. She unbuttoned his pants and lowered his zipper to his cock almost bursting from the fabric. Precum seeped from the tip, and she fingered the creamy jizz.

He jerked and gasped into her mouth. Then she was scooped up, carried the three steps to the bed nearest the bathroom, and dropped on the mattress. As she gazed up at him, he drew his polo shirt over his head, exposing his bare chest. Her fingers begged to explore his firm muscles that dared her to caress. He lowered his jeans, revealing his cock she'd touched for a moment that stood proud and erect.

The intensity between her legs was pure heat. Her clit throbbed, aching for his mouth, his hands . . . anything. He leaned in and peeled off her jeans and panties. The air hitting her bare skin produced goosepimples. The shivers probably came from being under his scrutinizing stare stroking her breasts, kissing her stomach, and settling on her mound of pubic hair.

"Oh, I missed you . . ." He planted his palms in the comforter and claimed her mouth. "I missed you so much," he murmured.

She rested her palm on the nape of his neck and tangled her tongue with his. The licks and delicious exploration he lavished on her was heaven. She took his full weight, reveling in their warmth flesh becoming one.

He ground against her, slowly moving back and forth while continuing to paint deep kisses on her mouth. She kept her arms locked around him.

His hard cock was pushing on her pussy, as if trying to sneak its way inside her. She couldn't resist and draped her legs around his hips. He obeyed her silent, urgent request. The head of his cock breached her, followed by his full length. She was consumed by his erection that stretched and searched her.

He thrust, and she palmed his buttocks to feel him fucking her. With each pump, his ass muscles flexed. She clung tight to him, never wanting to let go.

Up here, she didn't have to carefully watch her words, and neither did he. They could be themselves, and she anticipated witnessing her husband in nature's environment.

The pleasure Séamus fed her took her far from the motel room, far from the biggest hurdle they had to jump, far from his father's threats. If only they could stay this way forever.

"Séamus," she cried out. Heat was building on her skin and between her legs. The sultry explosion was sneaking up her spine, ready to consume her.

His own cries joined hers as she was taken to the heights of pure pleasure.

Later, they settled under the covers with Keemooch on top of them.

The realization they were her new family smacked Shannon upside the head. She stroked Séamus' chest where her head was settled, vowing she wouldn't let a tyrant of a man take this from her.

CHAPTER TWENTY-THREE: FREEDOM'S ROAD

There was no doubt in Séamus' mind he was building Shannon a home up here, a place worthy of what she deserved. Maybe a timber style as rugged as this land with lots of wood, exposed beams, and a massive stone fireplace.

The laughter, chatter, and odd screams from the children filled the community center. Séamus was outside with the men frying the fish. He stood in front of a cast-iron frying pan. Coleman stoves were set up on tables. He manned the fourth one.

A young boy scooped up plates and hurried inside to set the hot bread-coated fillets on the buffet table where people helped themselves to the massive amounts of dishes.

Someone slapped Séamus on the back. He glanced over his shoulder at Shannon's brother, Desmond.

"My turn. Go on in and chow down, man," Desmond told him.

"Thanks. I much appreciate it." One thing Séamus had noticed since meeting Shannon, the formality in his speech and thoughts were fading away. He was becoming as casual as her.

The back door to the center was open, so Séamus used that entrance. The curious glances from earlier he'd received had vanished. A few of the kids had asked if they could fly on his private jet. He'd assured them they could when he returned for another visit. Because kids never forgot promises, he'd better text his secretary to remind him to keep the jet and pilot on hand.

"It's the rich man." A little girl squealed and pointed.

"It's the man with his own plane!" A little boy also pointed.

They were shushed by their mothers.

Séamus made his way through the throngs of people. Some stopped and also had to comment on his wealth. Rather embarrassing. Just as he reached the table where Shannon's family sat, she stood.

"Are you hungry? Did you want me to get you a plate?"

Séamus hadn't expected to be waited on. He thought he'd have to stand in the buffet line. "Sure, and thank you."

Shannon's mother studied him with the same pinched expression as when they'd been introduced. She was another one against the marriage, besides Pashney and Ronnie. How on earth was he supposed to win any of the three over?

"How's your food?" He made sure his question was full of congeniality.

"It's good." Her tone was flatter than the slab of fish on her plate.

"Will you be dancing at the powwow?"

With a plastic spoon, she shoved around her baked beans. "Yes." Her tight reply matched her downturned lips. "I'm a jingle dress dancer."

"Shannon told me she doesn't dance."

Mrs. Nadjiwon half snorted. "My daughter was too interested in racing. She preferred being at the stock car track."

Yes, Shannon had told him she'd driven in those races. "Where is it?"

"Over in the northern district. She went every weekend with her brother."

"She told me she used to work in the pit."

"I'm not surprised she ended up driving people." Mrs. Nadjiwon set down her spoon. Her stare was sharper than the knife beside her plate. "It was her dream. Owning a limo company." The words she probably wanted to say seemed to dangle between them in the air — *and you took that from her.*

Séamus straightened in the chair. He curled his fingers together and set them on the table. "She will own her own company."

"Why?" Mrs. Nadjiwon kept staring.

"Why?" Séamus knitted his brows.

"Why marry her? Why ask her? Why not marry . . ."

Marry someone from my own peerage? "She's special." And she was.

"Special?" There was a cluck from Mrs. Nadjiwon. "You mean different, 'cause she's an Indian."

"No. I mean special. You did a great job raising her." And he meant it.

Pride glittered in Mrs. Nadjiwon's dark eyes. "I wanted her to stand on her own two feet. I didn't want her to end up here in a going-nowhere job. I wanted her to do what I never got the chance to do. What her kokums never got to do. What any of her female ancestors never got to do."

"And she will," Séamus reassured her.

"But I wanted her to do it on her own. I don't want her handed anything on a platter. I'm sick of the government handouts." Mrs. Nadjiwon glanced down at her plate. The look she cast the scrumptious dinner was as if she stared at a pile of rancid garbage. "They've been giving us handouts ever since *they* came over here."

Séamus flinched. She might as well have said, *ever since your ancestors came over here.*

"We don't need handouts. We don't need their damned money. When we do demand it, it's for our rights. Such as land claims. Compensation for what my parents endured at the residential school. That sort of stuff." She sniffed.

"Trust me, nobody is handing Shannon anything—"

"You aren't?" The raising of her brow was as sniveling as her voice.

"Your daughter has already built a successful life for herself. And she would've without my help."

"Yes, she sure would've." Mrs. Nadjiwon continued to glare.

"And she still will. It's up to Shannon whether her business will succeed or fail."

"I'm proud she doesn't have children yet. She's over twenty-five and childless. I'm already a grandmother five times over. Don't make it a sixth." Mrs. Nadjiwon shoved away her plate and stood. "I need a smoke." She stalked off down the aisle Shannon was proceeding up. His wife held two plates of food.

Fear gripped Séamus by his spine. Birth control. Goodness, he'd been so caught up in the events transpiring over the past month and a half he hadn't thought of . . . he'd never thought to protect his wife.

Shannon stood in front of him. She plopped in the seat her mother had vacated. "Where's Mom going?"

"Outside for a cigarette." His words had come out stammered, and Séamus' almost cuffed his own face. The last thing he wanted to do was tip off Shannon about what was whirling around in his mind. If they had a child, Mrs. Nadjiwon would never approve of him.

"Is there something wrong?" Shannon peered while she handed over his plate.

"Thank you." He couldn't ask her when she'd last had her monthly time. "I hope . . . I didn't upset your mother."

"She'll be fine." Shannon shrugged.

When had he'd last noticed her using a tampon? The feminine products were in the cabinet beneath her vanity in the bathroom. With their en suite being so big, they had their own garbage cans, so he couldn't have noticed her disposing of anything, even dental floss.

"Are you sure there's nothing wrong?" Shannon had spooned up a helping of baked beans. "Don't worry about Mom. She'll get over it."

Séamus nodded. He glanced down at the meal he'd been anticipating, especially the wild rice someone had rationed for the feast. Well, best he eat. As for inquiring about when she'd last had her period, that could wait for later.

How did a husband ask his wife about her monthly time?

There wasn't a hint of a breeze present during the MC's speech. Six men sat around a big drum. One hit the skin with his stick, and then the others joined him. They tapped lightly at first and then increased their beating until it became heavy pounding. Their wails carried high. The banging on the drum was deep in Seamus' throat. Grand entry. He sat in the stands with Shannon and the family members who weren't participating in the powwow.

The arbor overhead kept the sun off them, but the heat still found a way to torture him. He couldn't imagine dancing around in the grassy circle all day, exposed to the light.

When they'd first arrived, he'd been overwhelmed by the colorful displays of regalia made up of feathers, ribbons, and deer hide or cloth. What he'd most enjoyed was the tinkles coming from the silver cones slapping together that were attached to the jingle dresses.

Witnessing these people in their natural environment and wearing traditional dress was breathtaking, because everyone was handsome in their attire, even the elders. There was freedom in the open blue sky. Freedom in the drumming. And freedom in the singing that made him feel as if he could soar like an eagle. The heavy beat had gone from deep in his throat to reverberating in his chest.

The MC stood in the booth where dancers waited below.

The drummers picked up speed, their wails growing even louder.

"You're going to have to explain this to me," Séamus whispered. He stood, along with everyone else in the stands.

"First will be the veterans, or what we call the head dancers," Shannon murmured. "They are very experienced. You will see them in different regalia, depending on their dance."

"There are different dance styles?"

"Yes. For both men and women."

How interesting. The first four dancers were men and had bustles of feathers tied to their back ends, plume-like feathers on their heads, and tons of fringes and beadwork going on. The men cocked and moved about like they were imitating animals. Their fancy footwork was incredible as they spun and preened to the beat of the drumming.

The remaining dancers followed the leaders inside the circle. Jingle dresses with the tinkling silver cones draped some women, shiny material with lots of ribbons wrapped the various bodies of other ladies. What stood out were the shawls moving in harmony with their dancing.

He leaned into Shannon. "What are they?"

"Fancy shawl dancers. They imitate the grace of the butterfly. Notice how one arm is always extended?"

One arm did lie open on each dancer, with the shawl acting as a wing.

"There are also men fancy dancers." She used her lips to point at one dancer. "There are different types, too. War dances. Feather dances."

One was waving a feather about while he pranced to the beat.

Never in a million years had Séamus believed he'd find himself at a powwow celebrating National Indigenous Peoples Day during the summer solstice. He owed his wife a lot for introducing him to lives that expanded far beyond his exclusive peerage.

He couldn't help reaching for her hand and entwining their fingers. Or was that taboo during grand entry? But Shannon never released their hands. In fact, she squeezed his fingers.

With the mood she was in, tonight would be the perfect moment to ask her about her monthly time.

The powwow continued and would go on until midnight. But after eating bannock burgers and fries for dinner, Séamus had asked if they could return to their motel room before the mosquitoes made their appearance. They'd left at nine-thirty, hitching a ride with Kokum and Mishoomis.

Shannon didn't mind. From the time the powwow commenced at ten in the morning, they'd spent all day at the Treaty Grounds.

It'd been wonderful to take in the day with Séamus by her side, who'd been quite curious. Everyone kept referring to them as *The Millionaire and His Wife*, playing on the nicknames owned by Mr. and Mrs. Howell from the *Gilligan's Island* TV show. Shannon had laughed off the jesting because teasing was a part of the lifestyle up here. Nobody was allowed to take themselves too seriously. Séamus had also laughed at the nickname.

Ever since she'd arrived at Daugherty Manor to chauffeur Séamus, her life had been moving at breakneck speed. Returning to the room early was a splendid idea, because the plane was coming for them tomorrow morning.

She flopped on the bed.

"Tired?" Séamus removed the pullover he'd donned, even though the night was warm.

"Very . . . I feel like I haven't stopped ever since I met you. Is this what jet-setting means? If it is, I'm awful at it."

"It's no different than the number of hours you used to put

in at work." Teasing lingered in his words.

"True. But there's something exhausting about . . ." How could she make herself clear? "I feel like I never have a moment to catch my breath. Dinners. Breakfasts. Parties. It never ends."

"And up here it's the same. Going from one place to the next." Amusement danced in his eyes.

"You forgot working on the business plan. Y'know, when I was driving, I had down time. I'd read and relax."

"Time. Time. Time. My, oh my. That word is creeping up plenty. Perhaps this is the best time to ask if you've had your . . ." His voice grew smaller. " . . . monthly time?"

Shannon froze. Her beating heart bordered on coming to a standstill. For crying out loud, she'd been so busy — and with Séamus on her mind before their trip here — she'd overlooked her period. Or the fact she was overdue for her . . .

She scrambled up and snatched her cell phone. The reminder she'd programmed must have gone off without her noticing, because she faithfully had it scheduled for her next injection.

The date blared at her. She'd been due for her injection the Monday following the Friday when she'd started working for the Daughertys. The very Monday when she'd been too busy meeting Mrs. Daugherty in the morning for breakfast.

"I . . ." How could she say she forgot?

"I take it you forgot to . . . Hmm . . . what are you on?"

"I get an injection every three months." Shannon swallowed.

"You are past due for your injection?" Séamus' voice was soothing, even soft.

"Way past due. I was supposed to get my injection the Monday after we returned from Lake Louise." Her face grew hot.

"Have you had a period?"

"Look, this is some potent birth control. When they gave me the rundown, they said women must stop taking it a year before they want to get pregnant. And if you miss an injection, they give you a pregnancy test thirteen weeks after your missed injection. I'd say we're safe."

The look on his face wasn't what she'd expected. His brows knitted. He pressed his lips together and glanced to the dresser. "Okay."

"I thought you'd be happy." Shannon sure was. She had a business to think about.

"If you're happy, then I'm happy." He did smile, but his brows sagged.

"I already got the warning from Mom that if I make her a grandmother . . ." Shannon giggled.

"I got the warning, too," Séamus quietly replied.

"Wh-what?" Shannon sputtered. "She actually warned you not to get me pregnant?"

He nodded.

Okay, Shannon had about enough of in-laws, friends, and her own family dictating their lives. She rose from the bed and stomped her foot on the floor.

Séamus blinked. "Are you . . ."

"I'm putting my foot down. Nobody has the right to tell us when we can and can't have a child. It's bad enough they . . . all of them, my family included." She paced the small space between the beds and the dresser.

Keemooch meowed.

When Séamus' arms came around her, she almost jumped—she hadn't expected his touch. She turned her head, gazing up at him. Hope was in his stare, as if he wanted her to say more.

"What is it?" she asked.

He pressed his lips together. Then he set his chin on her shoulder. "Before we talk to anyone, I think we ought to be on the same page."

"The same page?"

"Yes, what we want."

"Want?"

"What we want from our marriage."

Chapter Twenty-four: Driver's Seat

"What do you want?" Shannon's voice shook. She kept her hands over Séamus' hand that wrapped her waist.

"I want whatever you want," he murmured. He snuggled his arms tighter around her.

There was comfort in this position — her head tilted against his that continued to rest on her shoulder, the warmth their molded bodies produced, and their breaths mixing as one.

She wriggled around until she faced him. "I want us to be happy."

"I'm already happy."

"Are you? Really? With your father —"

"What about your parents?" He set his finger over her mouth. "They don't approve either."

"Your father doesn't approve of me."

"You know who he wished me to marry."

The formality was slipping back into his words. She tensed. "I know I want our marriage to work."

"So do I."

"There's only one way it can work — if *we* set the boundaries and rules. Not anyone else."

He rubbed his thumb down her cheek. "Once we get the business going, and if we have enough contacts, gain enough clients, we can make it successful. Once successful, we can . . . start over."

She gasped. "Start over? Do you know that means giving up your inheritance?"

He glanced away and back at her. "I have a life now. A life

with you. We can do this, Shannon."

"Does your father know what you have planned?"

The slow shake of Séamus' head carried an ominous warning, similar to an approaching storm.

"So he expects me to . . . still be some kind of wife who hosts charities?"

"It doesn't matter what he wants. We can do this."

"Okay." She shivered. If he had faith, she'd do her best to also have faith. Still, for him to give up everything for her . . .

Not a chance. Somehow, sans his knowledge, she'd find a way for them to succeed without her husband having to make two horrible sacrifices — his inheritance and job.

A week after returning to Toronto, they'd gone shopping for their first car. Shannon was now taking the luxury sedan to a safe place where anyone, especially the Daughertys, wouldn't find out what they were planning.

Dread shimmied down her spine over having to call her friends for a favor, but even chancing a paid parking spot to keep the car could tip someone off to the business. She wasn't about to risk Séamus' inheritance over one mistake.

Her caution might be moot, since Séamus constantly repeated that their business was his top priority, so he was already making contacts, and his marketing efforts could likely alert his father.

She couldn't get over their team effort when they'd held hands and gone to a prestigious dealership. When she'd spied the black car, she'd known the vehicle was perfect for the clientele they were after — those wanting absolute privacy and a place to work while being chauffeured around.

At six o'clock, the traffic was abuzz in her old neighborhood. Already, she'd informed Mrs. Daugherty about her dinner plans for the evening. Whether Mr. Daugherty approved, Shannon didn't care. As much as she didn't wish for Séamus to lose his inheritance or his job, she also had to set her foot firmly with the tyrant.

She pulled into a parking space on the street. Children ran to the voices of mothers calling out for them to come home. Some pedaled their bicycles. Others road skateboards. She got out of the car and beelined for the stoop of her former home.

At six o'clock, the girls should be present, so she knocked.

Pashney stood in the picture window, having shoved aside the curtain. At least she wasn't frowning. The door opened. "Hey, what's up?"

Shannon would confess the truth. She owed her friends that much. "I need to talk to you guys. Did you wanna order in pizza?"

"Sure. Ronnie just got home, so we haven't started cooking yet." Pashney tromped for the living area. She picked her cell phone off the coffee table.

Footsteps came from the staircase. Ronnie appeared. "Hey, what brings you by? How'd your visit go? I wish we coulda gone."

"But we can't. Remember, we don't have a rich husband like Shan does." Pashney sniffed. Her fingers danced across the cell phone, most likely using an app to order their food.

Shannon almost groaned. This was not how she wanted their conversation to start, and she'd set her best friend straight. "Wrong. He's going to lose it all."

Both stopped what they were doing. Ronnie's purse that she'd been digging through dropped to the counter, while Pashney's phone fell to the sectional.

"What do you mean *lose it all?*" Pashney stalked forward, hands on hips and head cocked.

"If you thought your dad treated you bad by pulling a disappearing act, you haven't met Séamus' father." Shannon sank to the sofa.

At the mention of her dad, Pashney's face contorted into a

malicious scowl. "What do you mean? He's rich. His ol' man—"

"Has been trying to *buy* Séamus from birth."

"What do you mean *buy*?" Pashney sat on the coffee table and faced Shannon.

"He's been threatening him with disinheritance." Shannon wrung her hands. "Please, keep this between us. It's something I didn't want to tell you guys, but I have no choice. If Séamus doesn't comply, his father digs up the same threat. In the past, Séamus always gave in. It's why we got married. So he wouldn't be blacklisted in his field . . ."

She glanced to Ronnie. "But not this time . . . He said this is *our* marriage and we're going to run it how we want to, without a say from anyone."

"He . . . he's doing all this for you?" Pashney rose off the coffee table, eyes rounder than saucers.

Shannon nodded. "I don't want him to lose everything. I mean, we'd have money from his savings, bonds, and whatever else he's invested in, but he has a right to his job and inheritance. He's given up so much for me. I won't let him give up what his dad owes him. Not after what he put Séamus through."

She pushed at her bangs. "You should've seen him at the rez. He did all he could to accept everyone, fit in, try and be part of us."

Pashney slapped her hand over her mouth. "Oh fuck. Oh shit. Dammit." She palmed Shannon's knee. "I'm sorry. So sorry."

Shannon's heart almost tumbled from her chest. Never had she'd heard her best friend apologize before.

Ronnie inched forward. "If that asshole throws you two out, you can live here. You already paid your part of the mortgage. You can even have the master bedroom."

Tears threatened to form in Shannon's eyes. Her friends

understood. They were truly giving their blessing of her marriage. She threw her arms around Pashney. Ronnie joined in and hugged them, just like they had in the past.

One awful hurdle was conquered. Her two best friends not only approved of her marriage, but they were willing to help.

The taxi dropped Shannon off, since the new limo for the business was hidden in the garage stall at the townhouse. She dashed up the side walkway that led to the family entrance.

At nine-thirty, she'd find Séamus in their suite, so she darted up the stairs and shimmied straight for their quarters. When she opened one of the double doors, Séamus was stretched out on the lounger, tablet in hand.

"What're you doing?" Shannon set her purse on the small table.

His gaze moved from the tablet to her. He cast a lazy smile. "Reading the news. How'd dinner go?" He'd changed from his suit and tie to casual pants and a t-shirt.

"It went excellent." She scampered forward and plopped on the chaise lounge beside him. "Very excellent." She planted a light kiss on his lips.

"Hmm . . . it must have gone beyond excellent to merit such a kiss."

"It did. I had to take a cab home because — "

"A cab? Why didn't you call Rollins?"

"He's your mother's driver, and he has so much work to do around here. It was easier to call a taxi. Anyway . . ." She traced his soft mouth. "The girls are keeping the car. It's in their garage."

Séamus' lips puckered. "They need that parking spot. You didn't have to — "

"But I did." She set her hand on his chest. "The less people who know, the better chance we'll have of — "

"I told you already." His voice was hushed and reassuring.

"I'm not afraid of losing my inheritance or my—"

"I know. But the fewer people who know, the better chance we'll have of acquiring clients before your father finds out."

"Sweetheart . . ." he murmured, which took her by surprise because that was the first time he'd called her by that name. "My father has his eyes and ears everywhere. Consider our marriage. He found out before the ink was dry on our license. I'm aware of what I'm doing."

"I know." She ran her finger down his chest. "It's just that . . ." Only one person could help her, and she'd talk to that person tomorrow.

Shannon didn't venture downstairs until nine the next morning, once she received word from Ellen that Courtney had left for the hairdresser's. What she had to say was private. Having her sister-in-law's wicked ears listening was a headache Shannon could do without.

As she breezed into the sunroom, the maid was present, taking Mrs. Daugherty's plate from the table. "Good morning, Mrs. Daugherty." She smiled at Shannon. "What can I get for you?"

"Just a grapefruit and some toast, please. And thank you." Shannon sat adjacent from Mrs. Daugherty.

"Has Keemooch already eaten?" Ellen asked on her way out the door.

"Yes, I just fed him."

"You're in a wonderful mood. I must say that's the first time I've seen you truly smile." Mrs. Daugherty intently studied Shannon's face.

Shannon averted her attention to the flowers on her teacup. "I'm sorry. It's taking me time to adjust."

"There's nothing to apologize for." Mrs. Daugherty waved her hand. "I had to make the same adjustments after I married Padraig."

The opening Shannon needed had pretty much hit her lap. But forcing the words from her throat was quite the task. "Could . . . could we t-talk for a minute?"

Nodding, Mrs. Daugherty lifted the silver bell.

Ellen appeared. "Yes?"

"Can you please ensure we're not interrupted?" Mrs. Daugherty set down the bell. "We're going to have a discussion. Please bring in a pot of tea. We won't need to be served."

"As you wish, Mrs. Daugherty." Ellen vanished.

Shannon wiped her palms on her thighs. "I'm going to be honest with you."

Mrs. Daugherty simply stared.

"There's a reason why Séamus took me to Lake Louise and why he asked me to marry him." Shannon held her breath.

"I assumed there was a bargain." Mrs. Daugherty lit a cigarette.

"He told me about the dinner he was supposed to attend the night we flew out. He said he'd be given an ultimatum. One that didn't sit well with him." Shannon stared beyond her mother-in-law's shoulder at the cheerful painting on the wall that didn't match the mood of the tense room. "That's when he asked me to marry him. I said no."

Mrs. Daugherty never batted an eye. "I knew you'd say no. You remind me of me in some ways. I take it he sweetened the deal?"

"Yes. He knows I want to own my own limo business. It's my dream. He offered to buy me my first luxury sedan if I said yes. He also made a lot of other promises."

"Such as . . ." Mrs. Daugherty kept staring and puffing on her cigarette.

An ache surfaced in Shannon's lower back. "I told him I'd moved to Toronto with my two best friends because we each had dreams. My mom . . . she's a waitress at the restaurant on the rez. My grandmothers had the same lives. They wanted more for me. They wanted me to make my dream come true, something they couldn't do."

"I see."

Spellbound, Shannon had to keep her mouth from falling open. Her mother-in-law never stopped to assess the situation or have a true comment. "Because I kept saying no, Séamus offered to pay off my share of the mortgage on the townhouse. He made sure my friends would be okay once I moved out. And they are." Especially after last night. "It was supposed to be an agreement so Séamus could keep his inheritance and not be blacklisted by . . . well, Mr. Daugherty."

Again, Mrs. Daugherty nodded.

"But . . ." Shannon gripped her knees. "It became more than that. We're both trying. We're committed to the marriage now."

Finally, Mrs. Daugherty allowed an expression by the raising of her eyebrows, lips turning up at the corners, and a rosy hue appeared beneath her smooth skin. "You two are in love?"

Love? The word hadn't entered Shannon's mind, probably because she'd never been in love before. From what Séamus had shared, he hadn't either. After closing in on two months of marriage, love couldn't exist between them. Love usually took a good one or two years to happen, as least from what she assumed.

"Well . . . um . . . I don't know." Shannon's face heated. "I do know we care about each other," she quickly added before she insulted her mother-in-law. "He . . . he wants to give up his inheritance so we can start over."

Mrs. Daugherty set her cigarette in the snuffer and leaned in. "Séamus said that?"

Shannon stiffened. "I don't want him to. He's done so much for me. He's . . . Your son is the most kind, caring, and considerate man I've ever met. I can't ask him to give up . . .

whatever he's set to receive from you and Mr. Daugherty."

"He won't, because I won't allow it." Mrs. Daugherty's reply was crisp and quick. "Why does he think he has to give up his birthright?"

"Because . . . because of my business. He knows I don't want to . . ." *End up like you and Courtney.* "He knows how strongly I feel about establishing my own career. And he wants to help. We bought . . . we bought our first limo last week. It's . . . it's at the townhouse. Inside the garage."

"Shannon . . ." Mrs. Daugherty tapped her nail on the table. "Nobody's asking you to give up your career."

"But isn't that what your husband wants? I know Séamus doesn't have . . . uh . . . the greatest relationship with his father. I know that's why he lost his license. He lives recklessly out of the office and away from home. At least that's what I was led to believe, but I haven't witnessed his wild side yet."

"And you probably never will now that he has you . . ." Mrs. Daugherty murmured to herself. "Their relationship is quite strained. I'm sure you noticed." She lit another cigarette.

"I know you feel you can't be you." *Please don't let me hit too close to home and upset her.* "I . . . I do enjoy when you are you."

"Thank you." The warmness in Mrs. Daugherty's reply matched her gaze. "As a young girl, my nurse and governess set me straight on strong emotions, and this carried over into my marriage. Padraig . . . he doesn't like vocal displays."

How sad. Shannon bowed her head.

"I do know you're making an effort—"

"My effort could be better." Shannon raised her head and steeled her jawline. "Séamus made a great effort when we visited the reserve. He fits in . . . anywhere."

"I'm glad to hear that. I refused to let Padraig raise Séamus the way he'd reared Cillian." Mrs. Daugherty pressed her glossy lips together. "Firstborn. Even currently, my husband is adamant about tradition. Séamus became mine."

Shannon squirmed. "See? I know Séamus doesn't want our child raised as Cillian was. He wants—"

" . . . the tiny bit of freedom he was allowed," Mrs. Daugherty finished. "I say tiny, because Séamus has to follow tradition."

"He wants us to have our own life, but to do that, he has to give up . . . everything. He's excited about the business. He's been working on it ever since we married. I know it's only a matter of time before Mr. Daugherty finds out."

Mrs. Daugherty nodded. "And you are asking me to speak to my husband?"

"If you could. Please." Shannon couldn't help her begging.

"My husband has always done as he pleased. He . . ." Mrs. Daugherty glanced away.

You've never stood up to him in your life, have you? Maybe Shannon was asking too much.

"I'll speak to him." Mrs. Daugherty squared her shoulders and lifted her chin. Determination smoldered in her fierce stare.

CHAPTER TWENTY-FIVE: LEFT TURN ON A RED LIGHT

Shannon had to speak to Séamus after he arrived home from work. Questions swirled in her mind. Would he become angry because she'd failed to consult him first? He wasn't anything like his father, even in personality. Maybe he'd understand and listen, as his mother had.

She paced the floor in their sitting room.

One of the double doors opened. Séamus entered, carrying his briefcase. He bared his dimples. "How lovely to find you waiting for me."

Give it ten minutes and he might not be smiling. "How was your day?" She stopped so suddenly, she almost stepped on Keemooch's tail, who'd been trailing her.

"Excellent. I secured us a few clients already." He set his briefcase on the small table. "Overseas. They arrive in July and wish to use our services."

He loosened his tie and sauntered to the dry bar where he kept his brandy on hand. "I must admit they were rather surprised by the new venture. But once I told them about you and what you formerly did for a living, they were happy to offer us a chance to prove how luxurious and discreet they'll find our services."

For some reason, Shannon's stomach churned. Even though Séamus wasn't driving, since he didn't have a license, he was overseeing the business, and was this type of operation beneath a man with such a fine education and breeding?

"You don't mind that your wife is chauffeuring around your . . . business acquaintances?"

"They were quite impressed by your ambition." Séamus poured his drink. He held up the glass. "As am I."

"I . . ." She wet her lips. Last night, she'd told him Ronnie and Pashney were mum on the venture and had given their blessing, which had pleased him. "I'm your average working girl."

"So will I be. Not girl, though." He chortled.

"I . . ." She wrung her hands. "I care about you too much for you to throw it all away — "

"What makes you think I'm *throwing it all away*?" His eyes lit. "Do you know the amount of freedom I'm experiencing? For twenty-nine years I carried a noose around my neck. It's gone now."

He snapped his fingers. "Just like that. I owe it all to you. Don't worry about finances, sweetheart. We'll be fine. If you wish, we can go over my bank statements. Do you really think I'd allow us to become paupers? I'll secure us a condo downtown first thing. We can look for one next week."

Shannon shivered. "I . . . I care for you so much . . ." She tossed back her hair that had brushed forward from behind her.

He squinted and closed the small distance between them.

"I spoke to your mother. She knows everything." Shannon held her breath.

Séamus shrugged. "I planned on telling her myself. You saved me a chitchat."

"I also told her why we got married. I told her I didn't want to see you lose your inheritance. She feels the same way. She's going to . . ." *Please don't let him hate me.* "She's going to speak to your father."

Séamus almost dropped the glass of brandy. He gaped at Shannon. "When's she going to speak to Father?"

"She's probably speaking to him right now. He arrived home an hour before you did."

"What?" He stamped down the disbelief threatening to leave his lips. Of all the times for his upbringing and breeding to show itself—but he wasn't about to let his emotions get the better of him, not after being schooled to always conduct himself with perfect decorum.

"You deserve your inheritance, and your mother also thinks so. I did this because . . ." She intently studied him.

Séamus' heart pounded. She truly cared. This woman cared deeply about him. Was this what love felt like?

He'd never fallen in love before. Not even close. But everything they fought against was steering them toward one tiny word that was bigger than the universe. Bigger than his inheritance. Bigger than Father's threat.

This was why he wished to give up the money. Why he wanted to build a life free from the rule of Father's iron fist.

He set aside his glass.

Fear consumed Shannon's searching stare.

"It's okay." He cupped her bare arms with his palms. "We knew we'd have to face this hurdle. And we'll face it together."

"Oh God . . ." She threw her arms around his shoulders. "Thank you. I wasn't sure how you'd react, but after talking to Ronnie and Pashney, after you tried so hard to accept my family, after all you've done, I had to do something for you."

He petted her smooth, shiny hair. "We'll be fine. Nothing Mom says to Father will change his mind. We're on our own. What we'll do is ask the servants to begin packing for us. We'll get a hotel suite and stay there until we secure a place of our own."

"Don't you want to hear what your father has to say first?"

"I already know what he'll say, no matter how much Mom pleads and begs," he murmured. But pain squeezed his heart. He'd never gain Father's approval. Ever. He was simply another pawn for Father to move around on his gigantic chessboard.

Even after Séamus had showered and dressed for dinner, he still hadn't been summoned to Father's study. With Shannon on his arm, he steered them into the family dining room to find everyone already seated. He took his usual spot, ensuring first to pull out his wife's chair.

While they ate, nothing set off Séamus' suspicion bells. Cillian asked Courtney about her day, and she prattled on about new dresses she'd bought for some party the two were attending on the weekend. As for Mother, she had the same distant look in her eyes while Father dug voraciously into his meal as if he was starving.

Yet something Séamus couldn't put his finger on said everyone was behaving too normally. He reached for his water glass and sipped. Attempting to swallow the hearty beef entrée — no matter how perfectly done and juicy — was a tad trying on his dry throat.

Mom raised her wine glass. The look she cast Father spooked Séamus' spine. He'd never witnessed his mother firing such a warning shot at the tyrant.

Séamus peeked at Shannon, but she kept eating her meal. Father knew the truth. He was waiting until they entered the study with Cillian before he said anything. Séamus gripped his fork. There was no way in hell he'd allow Shannon to be left out of the conversation. Their seceding from the family concerned her, too.

"Perhaps instead of our usual routine of retiring to the study after dinner, Shannon and I could speak to you and Mom alone." Séamus kept his suggestion light but did add a smidgen of gravity to his tone so Father understood the discussion was important.

Father wiped his mouth. "Is there a reason why you wish to break with tradition?"

Tradition—that was all that mattered. Séamus curled his fingers into a fist. "Yes. It's rather important."

"I have no doubt this not only impacts your mother and I, but the family." Father glanced at Cillian and Courtney.

Cillian quirked a brow and nodded.

Great. The frustration tightening Séamus' shoulders goaded him to almost toss his linen napkin on the table, because his brother also knew the truth. Father must've acted quickly after talking to Mom.

"We can retire to the sitting room." Father pierced some beef. "We'll speak after dinner."

The man never ceased with the control. For sure Séamus would move into his own condo with Shannon. As for Mom, he wasn't going to leave her here. She also had a chance to break free. He'd take her with him.

They sat in the sitting room where the women always gathered after dinner for their tea, and that was what Ellen served each family member. Séamus wasn't sure why Courtney was present. This was a private matter and should've only included Séamus, his wife, plus Mom and Father.

Father lit his cigar, something he never did other than in his study.

Séamus grasped Shannon's hand. Her palm was damp, so he squeezed her fingers.

"It's my understanding you've started a business." Father puffed on the cigar. He wore his steely stare—the one reserved for the boardroom whenever he addressed the staff and directors.

Séamus nodded just as Ellen poured his tea and handed

him the cup and saucer. The stolen glance the maid sent his way was reassuring, as if telling him not to back down.

Ellen straightened and left the room. She shut the two doors behind her, trapping Seamus within the four walls where there was no escape.

But there was escape. The threat didn't matter.

"A limousine business?" Father tapped his cigar against the crystal ashtray Ellen had brought in earlier.

Séamus nodded. He didn't move his gaze elsewhere but continued to site his father as if he was staring down the barrel of a gun.

"Your mother informed me this is a venture you and your wife wish to execute on your own, separate from Daugherty Enterprises."

"Yes." Séamus finally sipped the soothing orange flavor of the tea.

"How are you to perform your current duties if you are running a limousine business?"

"Honestly?" Séamus set the cup and saucer on his knee. "I didn't believe I'd have a job once you received notice of my new endeavor."

"I take it your wife is involved? She is a licensed driver."

"Before I asked Shannon to marry me, I was informed her goal was to own her own limousine business. I promised this to her."

"Is this why you married my son?" Father directed his cold stare at Shannon.

Séamus' defenses rose. He replaced his hand over hers.

"I married your son because he asked me to. He said if he did not marry, he'd lose his inheritance and job." Shannon's voice was calm and direct.

"Your mother informed me your inheritance is of no importance to you anymore." Father pursed his lips. "Is this true?"

Séamus shrugged. "Honestly? No."

"You do realize the work involved to start a business—"

"Father, I'm twenty-nine. I do believe after running the marketing division, I have a good idea how much work is involved to succeed. This is what Shannon and I wish to do."

Of course, no comment came from the peanut gallery, since Cillian was the good son and knew when to keep his mouth shut.

"You have no desire to work for me?"

"To reiterate, I didn't believe I'd have a job once you found out."

"You can't perform two duties at once." The man never cracked, ever. It always had to be about appearances—Father's mouth remained in a firm, straight line.

"So I am allowed to maintain my job?" Séamus wasn't expecting this answer.

Father nodded. "The business can be an extension of Daugherty Enterprises. I will hire—"

"The business is Shannon's. She will decide who to hire," Séamus replied with the same amount of emotion Father had used—none.

"If the business is to be an extension of Daugherty Enterprises, I will maintain control." This time Father firmed his voice.

"Then it won't be. This is my wife's business. She will run it how she sees fit."

"Séamus . . ." Shannon twisted her hand out from under his.

"No, sweetheart. I know what this means to you."

"You haven't conferred, either of you?" Father glanced to Shannon and then Séamus.

"Conferred about what?" Séamus asked.

"About what her desires are." Father again focused on Shannon. "Did he ask you what you desire?"

Shannon ran her palm along her thigh. "Your son is a good, kind, and caring man. He's done much for me, and I know when he asked me to marry him, it was to secure his inheritance and job. As I've come to know him, I want what's important to him, and I feel he deserves to keep his inheritance. That's why I spoke to your wife earlier this morning."

Father tapped his cigar against the ashtray. "I do believe you are sincere. You truly do love my son."

Shannon let out a tiny gasp.

"You do really desire what's best for him," Father continued on. "I must say, you chose wisely." He directed his narrow-eyed gaze at Séamus. "Very wisely. I will admit I had my doubts at first, but she is remarkable."

Courtney sputtered. "Father Daugherty, what about me? Haven't I lived up to your expectations?"

"Yes, you have." Father gave a slight nod her way. Then he steered his gaze of steel back to Séamus and Shannon. "Your wife may run the business, but as a Daugherty, she cannot drive. That would be beneath her."

Séamus' blood ran cold.

Shannon gaped. "Excuse me?"

"You cannot chauffeur clients. A Daugherty does not perform menial work."

"Menial?" Shannon's sharp intake of breath filled the room. "With all due respect, driving is what allowed me to secure a mortgage on a townhouse with my two friends and allowed me to buy a car."

"Yes, it did." Father never broke his stare. "And you did well for yourself. However, as a Daugherty, I cannot allow you to drive clients. I stand firm on this issue."

Séamus squeezed Shannon's knee to keep her from tromping over to Father and slapping him across the face. "This is something my wife and I will discuss alone."

"Then discuss it. We'll talk in the morning in my study."

Father stubbed out his cigar and stood. "Cillian, we need to meet about today's activities at the office. Séamus is excused, since he'll speak to his wife." With that, he left the room.

Cillian rose. He glared at Séamus. "Really? A limousine business? Your wife driving clients? What did you expect?" He huffed out after Father.

Courtney stood, casting Shannon the stink-eye, then flounced from the room.

Séamus turned to his mother, who blankly stared back.

CHAPTER TWENTY-SIX: KEEPS YOUR HANDS ON THE WHEEL

"I know how much you love driving." Séamus set aside the cup and saucer.

Shannon remained frozen in her seat. She couldn't believe Mr. Daugherty had the gall to tell her what she could and couldn't do with her own business.

"If you don't stand up for yourself now, you'll . . ." Mrs. Daugherty sighed. She also set aside her tea.

"It's been that bad, hasn't it?" Séamus stuffed his hands in his pants pockets.

"Your father and I talked. I told him how important this venture is for you and for Shannon." Mrs. Daugherty's voice took on the distant tone that matched her distant stare. "I'm glad you married Shannon. She's brought much-needed change to this house after well over a century of tradition."

But it wasn't Shannon's intention to change the family dynamics. She simply wanted to live her own life. "I don't want to cause any trouble—"

"I know you don't." Mrs. Daugherty's neck and jaw tightened. "However, if you wish to run the business the way you want . . . You know what your father's like. It's too ingrained in him to fully relent. He'll always have to have some control."

"Do you even love him?"

Hearing the sadness in his voice, Shannon bowed her head.

"In my own way I do," Mrs. Daugherty said softly . "Early

on in our marriage, I accepted it for what it is."

"But you were never happy, were you?"

Shannon kept staring at her lap.

"I'm happy because I have two sons who I love with all of my heart," Mrs. Daugherty replied. "My marriage to your father is between your father and me. Please, don't involve yourself. Not for my sake. I'd never interfere with your marriage to Shannon."

"I know you won't or wouldn't." Séamus let out a deep breath. "I just want you to be happy, Mom."

"As I said, I am in my own way."

"What did you say to Father?"

"I told him that if he disinherits you, I will bring scandal to the Daugherty name and leave." Firmness was etched in her words.

"You did what?" Séamus sputtered.

"My empty threat did not work. Sometimes we don't get the fairy-tale ending." Wistfulness dusted Mrs. Daugherty's declaration. "But for my sons, I want a happy ending. Don't worry about me. I'll be fine with your father. I want you to worry about yourself and Shannon. I want you to do what's best for the two of you."

"What happens if—"

"I think the two of you should talk. And your discussion doesn't involve me." Mrs. Daugherty stood. "Let us know in the morning what your answer is." She turned and departed the room.

Shannon held Séamus' hand as they walked The Bridle Path. All was quiet, not even a car driving by. "I understand if you think it's best we leave." She sure did, after what Mrs. Daugherty had said.

"It's about what we desire. You desire." His heels clicked slowly on the pavement. "And I don't think you want

Daugherty Enterprises swallowing your business, dictating how you wish to run it."

"True." She didn't wish any interference from Séamus' family.

"Please. I know you're thinking. Say what you're thinking aloud. This is important to me, that we communicate. I don't want either of us having regrets afterward. Just tell me what you desire."

The streetlamps gave too much light to get a view of the sky, something she was used to after moving to the city. Only at the rez could she gaze upward and see the millions of stars. "I want us to have our own life. One that isn't dictated by your family." She glanced at him. "I do like your family. And I hope you like mine, but we . . ."

"I know. And I want the same thing." He squeezed her fingers.

"Then . . . we made our decision?"

"Yes. We will run the business as we see fit. And we will run our lives as we see fit. No amount of money is worth it." Séamus shook his head and gazed out at one of the many gates lining the street that led to the homes tucked away on acres of property.

"Are you sure?" They were talking giving up more money than her own reserve would ever see.

"My great-great-great grandfather came over here with nothing." He stopped. They stood under one of the many trees lining the road. "He built something from hard work and the sweat off his back. Who says we can't do the same thing?"

Her heart warmed. "Yes, we can."

"Only it'll be different for us. Our children are going to freely choose what they wish to be. They're not going to experience the same problems I did. My great-great-great grandfather may have built an empire, but it came with bars on the windows. I don't want that for us.

"I understand why he was the way he was, and what drove him. I do. He suffered a lot of prejudice. But it's not like that for the Irish anymore. Your people, yes, they're still fighting racism, but we can't keep living our lives based on what your parents and grandparents experienced."

She nodded.

"I wanted to build you a home at your reserve." His smile was wistful. "Your grandfather told me how housing works. That won't happen now."

Shannon's spine almost jumped out of her skin. A house at her reserve? But her excitement drained away, because he was right. That wouldn't happen now. "It's okay. We can go back to visit and stay at the motel."

"We won't have our own jet." His gaze searched hers.

"I don't care. I never had a jet before. And I only rode in yours twice. I won't miss something I barely had." She touched his cheek.

"Then we'll meet with them in the morning and tell them of our decision." He drew her into his arms and claimed her lips.

She kissed him back, reveling in the warmth his kiss produced, the safety found in his firm muscles, and the reassurance found in his embrace.

Séamus finished dressing. There wasn't a need for a suit and tie, not when he'd be packing his bags and vacating the manor after his impending disastrous discussion with Father.

He shut the doors to the walk-in closet. Everything he looked upon would be gone in an hour. The bedroom. The suite. The sitting room he'd just entered.

Relief should consume him. Freedom. Finally. But at a terrible cost of losing his family.

Maybe pieces of the traditions Great-great-great Grandfather Daugherty had started threaded through Séamus' blood like the tapestry above the fireplace in the grand room downstairs Great-great-great Grandmother had been fond of creating. The handmade craft depicted a woman laboring in an old-style kitchen. He'd been told it was her former kitchen back in Ireland.

His great-great-great grandparents hadn't forgotten where they'd come from. Father hadn't wanted Séamus to forget either. He dialed back his first meeting with Shannon, how she'd questioned him about his family's history and the history of the Irish, and he hadn't cared. So why did he now?

"I'm ready." Shannon appeared in the sitting room. She was also casually but smartly dressed in white bell-bottom pants, a belt cinched around her slim waist, and a yellow blouse illuminating her bronzed skin.

"And we are off to the guillotine, Ms. Antoinette." Séamus took her hand. There couldn't be regrets. He was starting a new life, one they required if their marriage was to survive.

"Are we, King Louis?" Shannon's reply was half-joking and half serious.

"Yes, we are." He kissed her knuckles and steered them down the hall.

When they reached the bottom of the stairs, he glanced at her, but she stared straight ahead, chin lifted.

"It's show time." He led them into the breakfast room

Father and Mom were already seated. The ambiance inside wasn't cheerful like the sunroom but as formal as the rest of the house. Father's narrowed brows stated he didn't approve of their attire.

Although Mom and Father sat on opposite ends of the table, Séamus drew out a chair for Shannon so she'd be beside him.

Ellen scooted in carrying the teapot, Father's preferred

drink over breakfast.

Father continued to tackle his food, not seeming bothered about the forthcoming discussion, given the way he slid the eggs and bacon into his mouth. Mom, as usual, picked at her meal of melons and toast.

"What can I get you?" Ellen filled the cups.

"The tea is fine." Séamus doubted they'd last through the whole breakfast.

"Eat something." Father kept digging into his meal.

Séamus glanced at Shannon and then back to Ellen. "Toast and melons for me."

"Porridge and toast, please," Shannon said.

Ellen rubbed Séamus' shoulder and left. She closed the doors to the breakfast room.

At least they had a nice view of the lawn and the walkway that wrapped the side of the house.

Once their meals arrived, the light crunching and munching of food was an earworm Séamus couldn't shake, unless he hightailed it upstairs to the master bathroom and retrieved a cotton swab.

Finally, Father wiped his mouth and set his utensils on his plate. He lifted the bell.

Ellen entered. She refilled Father's teacup and removed his plate. "Can I get anyone anything else?"

Séamus motioned at his cup. The same for Shannon. At the same time, they both set their utensils on their plates.

Ellen refilled the cups, grabbed the other plates, and left the room, again closing the doors.

This was it. There was no use putting off their answer any longer.

Séamus cleared his throat. "We made our decision."

"Oh?" Father was in the middle of fixing his tea and never glanced up. No doubt he was *that* confident Séamus would again bow down.

"We intend on running the business ourselves. Not under Daugherty Enterprises." From Séamus' peripheral vision, he caught Shannon's jaw twitching. He reached beneath the table and clasped her hand.

"Don't be ridiculous." Father's tone was dismissive. He lifted his teacup. "Everything is under Daugherty Enterprises."

"This won't be. Shannon and I are running it." Séamus made sure to firm his voice.

Father made a *tsking* sound. He sat back in the chair, teacup in hand. He looked over Séamus and Shannon. Then he let his gaze linger on Mom. "This is a tradition your great-great-great grandfather started that we adhere to ever since he built the business. I can't allow—"

"Father. No." Finality was in Séamus' words.

Father drew in his cheeks. His steely stare cut into Shannon. "Is this why you agreed to marry my son? To obtain your own business?"

Séamus began to rise. "That's all we're saying before I allow myself to speak words I'll regret. If you wish for us to leave, we can leave."

"Then leave." Father flicked his hand. "Keep in mind you are on your own."

"I knew we'd be on our own. Heaven forbid anyone dare to defy you. That's all that matters, right? It's the only reason Cillian is your favorite. Because he listens to you. If he was like me, you wouldn't be singing his praises." Séamus fully stood.

"I guess I'll meet with the board and inform them you've vacated your position. And I assume I'll also have to meet with Dudley to rescind your inheritance." Father never looked at them. He kept holding his tea, staring at Mom.

"You go ahead and do that." Séamus held tight to Shannon and ushered her trembling body from the breakfast room.

He rushed them down the hall, straight for the family stair-case.

"I never wanted you to—" Shannon's voice cracked.

"It's okay," Séamus reassured her. "I won't stay under his conditions. Meeting you was the best thing that ever happened to me. I have no regrets."

"But . . ."

He stopped and faced her. "We can do this. If my great-great-great grandfather could build an empire, we can, too."

"I never wanted to build an empire. Just a business." For a tall, sleek woman, she was smaller than a leprechaun with her rounded shoulders and downcast head.

"It'll be more than a business—"

"I don't want you creating something to spite your dad. I want us to create something we'll love, enjoy, and allow us to have a roof over our heads." Pleading was in her gaze.

He stroked her hair. "And that we shall do." He led her down the rest of the hall and up the stairs.

Pain throbbed at the back of his neck. At least he had the benefit of knowing Cillian wasn't truly loved or favorite because of who he was—but because of what he'd allowed himself to become

The old man loved nobody, not even Mom.

Séamus' days of living a fake, dictatorial life were done.

CHAPTER TWENTY-SEVEN: SPEEDING

They were living in a suite at a downtown hotel until they found the perfect condo. Shannon wasn't in a rush. The suite allowed pets, so Keemooch was content in his new home. After three weeks of nonstop work and meetings with the bank and other agencies to get the business up and running, they were officially open.

Pure Luxury Limousines. The name was perfect. As well as their slogan. *Indulge yourself, because you deserve the very best.*

She switched on the laptop to speak to Mom. Her parents were flying down for the weekend to congratulate them. Mom remained a bit grumpy because Shannon hadn't created the business on her own, but Mom was also proud.

The same for Pashney and Ronnie, who wanted to chauffeur clients, and had obtained their licenses. Shannon had been shocked, because the girls made great money in their current positions, but they insisted on buying shares into Pure Luxury Limousines to help the business grow.

Séamus had also lined them up more clients. He was constantly on the phone in their suite, conducting business from the desk in the second bedroom.

Someone knocked on the door.

Worry was constantly shadowing her, especially since Séamus had booked them into five-star digs with one of the most immaculate rooms. But he'd reassured her his bank account was fine.

Ronnie and Pashney barged their way inside.

"Where's the uniforms? You said they came in today."

Hands on hips, Pashney sternly assessed the suite.

"They're in the bedroom. I was in the middle of unpacking them. Give me one sec." Shannon darted down the hall. "Help yourself to a coffee." Since they had a kitchenette, she'd bought groceries, something Séamus found amusing, probably because he hadn't cooked a day in his life. But ordering up coffee every single day was a waste of money, the same for muffins, toast, and other snacking items.

She grabbed the box and shimmied into the kitchenette where the girls readied their mugs.

"Is that them?" Ronnie clapped her hands together. "I wanna try mine on." She snatched the box from Shannon and rifled through it.

Ronnie gasped and held out the smart black jacket with the silver buttons. "Wow, it feels so . . ." She ran her palm over the garment.

"Smooth? Plush?" Shannon touched the fabric. "As drivers, we have to be comfortable but smart-looking. I gotta video Mom. Be right back."

She beelined for the living area, Séamus having stepped out for a morning breakfast to meet with a potential client.

Mom appeared on the screen, not quite frowning but not quite smiling either. "How're you doing?"

"Busy." Shannon plucked the coffee mug she'd left on the desk. "The uniforms came in."

Mom's gaze shifted to the left and then back at the screen. "I see." She heaved a breath. "If this is what you want, then you have my blessing. And your dad's, too."

Warmth filled Shannon. "Really?"

"It's why we're visiting, isn't it?" Mom finally smiled. "I won't lie. I wish you would've done this on your own, but I'm happy for you. And for Séamus. It took a lot of guts to do what he did. That's a lot of money he threw away."

"It was his decision to make."

"Y'know, as upset as I was about this quick marriage, I never would've, I mean, your father and I never would've . . ." Mom glanced down.

"It's okay." *I know you wouldn't have thrown me out and disinherited me like Séamus' father did to him.*

"But we're worried. Marriage is based on love. Does he love you?"

Shannon stiffened. "Mom . . ."

"No. You listen to me. A marriage can't last if there isn't love. Does he love you?"

"We only married three months ago. I don't think love can—"

"Yes, it can. Your dad and I married four months after we went out."

Yes, went out. Whenever Shannon had asked about how her parents had gotten together, they gave the same reply— *oh, you know how it is. She was around. I was around. Then we got married.* Nine months after the wedding, Shannon's older sister had entered the world, which meant Mom and Dad hadn't needed to get married. They'd probably conceived Michelle on their wedding night.

"I'll see you next weekend. I called to say I love you, and I support you. I just hope that . . ."

. . . I haven't made the biggest mistake of my life.

Mom's eyes misted. "I have to get to work."

"I love you, too. I'll be at the airport to get you." Shannon touched the screen.

Mom did the same and vanished.

"Well, what'd she say? Is she cool with everything?" Ronnie stood behind Shannon, her reflection in the bare laptop screen.

Shannon swiveled in the chair. She pushed aside Mom's talk and eyed her best friend looking quite smart in a black jacket, matching pants, a crisp, white shirt, and black hat.

Ronnie slid on the gloves. "Reporting for duty." She

saluted, giggling.

"I still can't believe you guys gave up great jobs to—" Shannon didn't know what to say.

"Are you kidding? Séamus has benefits. Pension. Everything my dumb employer doesn't offer." Pashney snorted.

The cell phone buzzed. Shannon reached over and picked it up. "Hello."

"Sweetheart, it's me. I'm going to be a tad longer than expected."

"Okay." Maybe her husband had another meeting lined up.

"Unfortunately, Cillian wants to chat over coffee. He says it's important."

"Cillian?" Shannon stiffened. The family'd had nothing to do with them after they'd left Daugherty Manor. "Did he say what he wants?"

"Only that we must talk and nothing more. I'll see you after coffee."

Shannon clutched the phone. "Be careful."

"I always am. Bye."

Hoping not to alarm her friends, Shannon forced a smile. "That was Séamus. He's running late and has another meeting. I'm sure he'll have great news."

Or bad news.

Being a regular, well, a former regular, since Father no doubt had used his power to demand the board revoke Séamus' membership, he bypassed the host and beelined straight for the table where his brother sat at their exclusive club in a high-backed leather chair.

Already on the polished table was a carafe of coffee, cups, saucers, and a tray of muffins.

While pouring himself a coffee, Séamus inquired, "What's this about?" It couldn't be good news because they hadn't spoken after he'd moved out.

"Where is she?" Cillian held the cup and saucer, brows and lips straight.

The constricting of Séamus' stomach muscles was comparable to a light punch. He stopped pouring and sat. "Where's who?"

"Don't play ignorant." Cillian's voice was flatter than his emotionless expression. "Where is she? This is all your fault—"

"Who the heck are you talking about?" Séamus was in no mood to play twenty questions.

"Mother."

Séamus was between half sitting and half standing. "Mom left?"

A flicker of a fire smoldered in Cillian's eyes. "She left last week."

Séamus' mouth dried. He finally sat. "Where is she?"

"If I knew that, I wouldn't have asked for this meeting, would I?" Bitterness caked Cillian's words. "Father's very upset—"

"Are you sure she isn't missing?" They were wealthy. What if someone had kidnapped her?

"Missing?" Cillian scoffed. "She packed up her clothes. There isn't a stitch left in the closet. We automatically assumed she went to you."

"No." Séamus was thankful he'd sat, because his knees would have given out on him. "I haven't talked to her since I left. She reassured me . . ." *She told me she was happy if I was happy, if Cillian was happy.* "Is she answering her cell?"

Cillian slowly shook his head.

Séamus whipped out his cell and speed-dialed Mom's number.

"Hello, son."

"Mom." Séamus gasped.

Cillian half came out of the chair.

Séamus held up his hand to stop his brother. "What's going on? I'm with Cillian. We're at the club. He told me you left. Why didn't you call me?"

"I didn't want to worry you." The sound of Mom taking a drag off a cigarette carried through the phone.

"But you told me . . ." He squeezed his cell. "You told me . . ."

"I'm sorry." Her voice was small. "If I would've confessed the truth that I planned to leave, you would have stayed. And . . ." She sniffled.

His jaw slackened. Mother never showed emotion. Ever.

"I want you . . ." Her swallowing pierced his ear. "I want you to be happy. And leaving made you happy, didn't it?"

"Yes, but not at—"

"I told you not to worry about me. I'll be fine." But the forced courage in her shaky voice didn't fool him.

"Mom, where are you?"

"Honestly, I need time alone. Time to think. I'm not up to seeing anyone right now."

"But are you in a safe place?" Worry was a handful of spiders dancing across the back of his neck.

"Yes, I'm safe. As I said, I need time to think." The mask had returned in Mom's voice and words. She'd probably squared her shoulders and straightened her back in true posture as she always did.

"I'll call you later. Cillian's worried, too."

"Tell him I'm sorry I didn't return his calls. I so wanted to speak to him, but if I had, he would've told your father." Regret smothered her reply. "We'll talk more tonight. Tell Cillian I'll call him, too."

"Okay." Séamus kept gripping the phone.

"I love you."

"I love you, too." He forced his finger to press the *end call* button.

Cillian crumpled the napkin he'd picked off the tray. "This is your fault," he hurled out through a whisper. "She left because—"

Séamus' defenses rose. "No, it isn't. Nor is it yours. The blame rests on Father's shoulders."

"Father's?" Cillian sputtered. "You have no right—"

"He didn't take any of Mom's feelings into consideration. Do you really think she's happy living the way she's living? She's a prized parrot in a cage."

"Prized parrot?" Outrage spread across Cillian's features. "He treats her like a queen. He gives her whatever she wants."

"Yes, possessions. Don't you think she needs more than that? She needs a life of her own. A purpose, other than playing the perfect wife and mother. She's a human being, for goodness sake. Can't you see it in her eyes? Haven't you noticed she's never been happy?" Séamus had heard enough. Cillian was as bad as Father.

"Keep lying to yourself." Cillian stood. "If you would've—"

" . . . kept living under his thumb?" Séamus guffawed. "Perhaps you're content letting him rule your life, but he's not ruling mine anymore. Did you ever wonder why I behaved the way I did? Did you ever think I was as tired as Mom with living a life dictated by him?"

Cillian threw back his shoulders and puffed his chest. "He isn't dictating anyone's life. He is carrying on the tradition, as everyone has, ever since Great-great-great Grandfather Daugherty started it."

" . . . well over one hundred years ago. And I'm done." Séamus drew a straight line with his hand. "And so is she."

"I see. So you support her abandoning Father." Cillian folded his arms. "You give no thought to how this has impacted Father."

251

"Is it his ego that's hurt, or his feelings?" Séamus stifled his snort.

"What's that supposed to mean?"

"His ego or feelings. Come. Having Mom leave must have kicked his ego. That's all that matters to him."

"He's shut up in his study." Cillian leaned in. "He won't speak to me or anyone. Who do you think is running Daugherty Enterprises in his absence? Me." He aimed his finger at his chest.

Dread broke out at the back of Séamus' neck. Locked up in his study? Abandoned Daugherty Enterprises? This meant Mom had hurt Father. But . . . Father only cared about himself, at least Séamus had assumed so.

The hotel door opening and closing startled Shannon. She turned in the desk chair to Séamus entering. "How'd it go with your brother?"

He set aside his briefcase. "Mom left Father."

Shock slapped Shannon across the face. "What?" She scrambled from the desk. "But you told me she was fine with everything. She said she was happy if you were happy."

"Merely empty words so I wouldn't hesitate about leaving. She planned on leaving if I left." He ran his fingers through his hair. "She's phoning tonight. How did your video call go?"

There wasn't a chance Shannon could tell him Mom was concerned about whether they loved each other. Suddenly, the painting on the wall, a natural landscape of spruce trees and foliage peppering a still-water lake, became interesting.

"Your mother still doesn't approve?"

"She does . . ." Shannon toyed with her fingers. "Look, they'll be here next weekend. Let's not worry about it until then. I want to talk about your mother. Why did she leave?"

"As I said, she planned on leaving if I left, only she failed to tell me. I guess Father's enclosed in his study and won't come out." Séamus stuffed his hands inside his pants pockets. "I'm not sure what to do."

"I'm sorry. I really am." Shannon touched his arm. This was all her fault for wanting her own business. The worst part was that the excitement after seeing her friends in their uniforms was a rush of euphoria no job had ever given her before.

"There's nothing to be sorry about. I always knew she was unhappy." Séamus studied the same painting that had caught Shannon's attention.

She kept hold of his arm. "What are we going to do?"

His shoulders sagged as he continued to stare at the painting. "There's nothing we can do. She's never been happy." He blinked. "Ever."

Shannon's stomach tightened. "I picked up on that when I first met her. She's . . ."

"Aloof? Standoffish?"

Shannon nodded.

"Unfortunately, she's been bred to be that way." Sadness was a wave of water washing over his confession. "It's in her upbringing, and then her marriage."

"Do you think she finally wants to be herself?"

"Perhaps." Séamus kept studying the painting. "However, I'm unsure if even she knows who her true self is. Maybe time away from the manor will help her unearth who she truly is, other than a Daugherty."

"She can join us for dinner when my parents come into town." Maybe, just maybe, Mom and Dad's visit could help Mrs. Daugherty forget her situation and enjoy life for one weekend.

Chapter Twenty-eight: Two Wheels

Shannon led her parents down the hall. Having Séamus insist they stay with them in their suite had come as a shock. "So yeah . . ." She continued, "we moved the desk in the living area to the other bedroom to double as our office. It's easier when I take phone calls, or Séamus does."

Dad said nothing, as always. He was as quiet as Mishoomis.

"It looks expensive." Mom glanced around at the carpeted hallway and rich wallpaper. "What's this costing you?" She used her thumb to motion at the bellboy behind them wheeling the luggage.

"Allow me." The bellboy scooted around them to open the double doors. "Please . . . enter."

Mom barged in first, gasping. "What the hell is this? A suite for the King and Queen of England?"

"There's no king. Just a queen. And no, this isn't for royalty."

"Then what the hell is the royal suite like?" Mom set her knuckles on her hips. "How much is this swanky palace costing you? The boy gave up his inheritance and is flat broke."

"I wouldn't say flat broke." Séamus stepped in from the hallway. "It's good to see you again, Mr. and Mrs. Nadjiwon."

Dad nodded, glancing around. His expression said he might as well be back on the reserve for all he was impressed with.

"I should hope you have some money tucked aside." Mom harumphed and continued to pick apart the suite with her scrutinizing stare. "This is too much."

"Mom, we're fine." Shannon had to stop from rolling her eyes.

"Which room?" the bellhop asked.

Shannon looked to the busboy. "The second one. And thank you."

"Right this way. I'll show you." Séamus led the bellhop from the living quarters.

"Is that a real fireplace?" Mom shoved her chin at the gas fireplace.

"No. It's gas, but it does throw warmth. We're not chopping wood or anything." Shannon motioned at the sofa. "Why don't you relax? I'm sure you're tired after plane-hopping."

"Relax? I haven't been here in ages. I want to go shopping." Mom moved away from the sofa. "I'll need to get a fancy dress or something, won't I? I don't think my new son-in-law eats at fast-food places. And I'm sure his mother will be decked out to the nines."

"No. His palate leans toward . . ." Heat claimed Shannon's face.

"Palate?" Mom harumphed again. "Never mind the fancy words. Let's go. Where's she staying anyway after she walked out on her ol' man?"

"At a nearby hotel." Shannon looped her arm through Mom's. "Dad, you coming?"

Dad stretched out on the sofa and grabbed the remote control. "You two go ahead. I'm sure your mother will find me something."

"Get him!" Mom guffawed. "We travel all the way to the city, and he wants to watch TV. He could do that at home. Where're the girls?"

"Driving. What else? I told you the business is up and running." Shannon steered her mother to the door before she badgered Séamus with a million questions. There'd be enough questions over dinner tonight.

Shannon's worries had been for naught. Over a five-course dinner, Mrs. Daugherty had smiled and laughed at Mom's antics. Maybe her mother-in-law had been looking for a down-to-earth person instead of the constant genteel politeness of her world.

Everyone was still laughing as they entered the hotel suite.

Mrs. Daugherty continued to softly chuckle as she sat in the armchair in the living area. Her evening attire was smart. A lovely green dress molded to her lithe figure, hair perfectly coiffed in a chignon, and nails with color instead of her usual French manicure.

Shannon had expected her mother-in-law to bolt after dinner, but when Mom had suggested coffee back at the suite, Mrs. Daugherty had been in full agreement.

"I never expected your mom to hit it off with my parents." Shannon readied the coffee in the kitchenette.

"Why not?" Séamus retrieved the cups and saucers from the cupboard. "Your parents regaled us with some lovely stories about the reserve. Mom enjoyed herself."

Shannon winked. Carrying the condiments, she headed into the laughter-filled living room. Mom was waving her hands about, telling another story to Mrs. Daugherty.

Séamus handed out the cups and saucers.

"I see you got him trained well." Mom snickered.

"Mom . . ." Shannon's tone carried warning.

"*Stahh.* He don't mind." Mom waved her hand. "It takes time to train them." She leaned into Mrs. Daugherty. "And I'm not being sexist. A good marriage takes training. Training each other. Right, babe?"

Dad smiled and took the cup and saucer from Séamus. "Yup. I got her trained."

Mom laughed so hard she slapped her thigh.

Mrs. Daugherty placed a hand over her mouth and let out an elegant giggle.

Séamus' eyes almost popped from their sockets.

"Is everything okay?" Shannon whispered.

"It's just weird seeing . . . my mother so happy," Séamus murmured.

"C'mon." Shannon took Séamus' hand and led him back to the kitchenette to retrieve the coffee that should be finished brewing since it was a fast-flow machine. Sure enough, the rich brew had perked.

While she poured the java into a carafe, Séamus slipped his arms around her waist. "You think we'll be as happy as your parents?"

"I think so." Shannon capped the carafe. She glanced over her shoulder to face Séamus. "They've been married for over thirty years."

"Quite a difference in those thirty years, hmm?" His mouth sank.

"What do you mean?"

"My parents have been married just as long. I think thirty-four years." He sighed. "They never acted like your parents did tonight."

"You have to remember we come from different social backgrounds." Shannon didn't want to admit his parents' marriage had been less than happy.

"Your parents have an equal partnership." He touched her hair. "Mine never did. The same way they raised their kids. Your parents let you decide what you wished to do. My father, he decided for us." He glanced to the cupboard. "I don't want a marriage like my parents'."

"It won't be," Shannon reassured him. "And it won't be like my folks' either. It'll be *our* marriage."

His lips broadened into a deep grin. "Yes, it will be, won't it?"

Shannon nodded.

"My parents went into their marriage not really knowing each other. During Mom's debut, she was told who she'd marry."

"Same with my parents."

"Err . . . what?" For once he broke his formal decorum.

Shannon chuckled. "Mom didn't have a debut. But she told me they married five months after knowing each other, seeing each other around, so she tells me. I guess she was dating someone else and always said she'd marry my dad, and she did, even though she barely knew him, since he's five years older."

Séamus' eyes crinkled. "That's interesting."

"Not really. Everyone knows everyone on the rez. Kinda like everyone knows everyone in your social circles."

"True." He nodded. "I guess, then, we fall into the same category as our parents, minus the knowing each other part before we married."

She couldn't resist swiveling to face him instead of having to keep craning her neck.

"Your parents made it because, well, as your mother said, they trained each other." He chortled.

Shannon couldn't help lightly laughing.

"And I agree, although I wouldn't call it training," he stressed. "What they did was find a way to understand one another, anticipate one another's needs. That's what I hope we'll do for each other."

"I think we already are." Shannon touched his cheek. "It's why I tried my best so you could keep your inheritance."

"It's why I said *no* to my inheritance. It was handcuffs around my wrists—stopping me from doing what I truly desired." He wet his lips. "I guess what I'm trying to say is if we care deeply about each other enough to sacrifice so much for one another's happiness, I guess that's what love is, isn't it?"

Her throat tightened. "I don't know. I've never been in love before."

"Neither have I." His lips brushed hers.

She wrapped her arms around his neck and returned his tender kiss full of warmth and caring.

He broke the kiss. Their mouths were a breath apart. "What I'm trying to say is — I love you, Shannon." Warmth coated his quiet declaration.

The reply easily slid from her lips. "I love you, too, Séamus." Goosepimples spread across her flesh. "Like you, I truly want our marriage to work." She couldn't stop gazing at him, shivering.

"Then I think we're starting off on the right path." He touched her cheek. His palm was full of reassuring tenderness. "I want us to sit in a room, laughing and telling our children how we met and how we got married — thirty-something years later just like your parents."

A lump grew in her throat. "So do I . . ."

He claimed her mouth again.

"Okay, you can rest easy. He loves me." Shannon sat out on the balcony with Mom. The weather was perfect for coffee and toast, a pretty blue sky and the sun spreading its rays of warmth everywhere.

Mom lit a cigarette. "Really?" She reached over and patted Shannon's leg. "I gotta admit I had my doubts. I really did. But this boy is proving to have quite the backbone after all."

"Backbone?" Shannon sputtered.

Mom shrugged. "I figured if a man couldn't stand up for himself, well . . ." She waved her hand. "Ah, never mind me. Honey, I'm darn proud of you. So darn proud. And his mom is a hoot. What a great gal she is. We're going out this afternoon. I hope you don't mind."

"You and Mrs. Daugherty?" Unbelievable.

"Yeah. Why not?" Mom looked offended. "You think Mrs. Rich and Prissy is too good for the likes of a gal from the rez?"

"No. She's far from a snob. It's just that she's so . . . well . . . you two are different."

"You mean I'm blunt and bold and she's a woman of taste and manners?" Mom snickered.

"I didn't mean it that way. But yeah, you two do come from different worlds."

"So do you and Séamus. I'd say that woman did a great job raising her son. She made sure he sees all people as equals. She's the same way, too." Mom eyed her.

"I'm grateful. Séamus told me before he was sent to boarding school—"

"She told me she had to attend boarding school, too." Mom sighed. "I guess I can't judge. Her parents did have a choice."

"They did." Shannon rubbed the handle of her mug. "It's funny how other generations affect us. What they experience and endure, it impacts their children, and their children's children."

"It sure does." Mom picked up her coffee. "But cycles can also be broken. I'd say you and Séamus pulled out some major courage neither of you thought you had."

Shannon set her mug on her lap. "I guess we did."

"It took a team effort to do what you two did. That's what marriage and love is, honey. Nothing more. Standing by and supporting one another. I think you two will do just fine." Mom set aside her coffee. "Now, I'm going to get showered and dressed. Séamus' mother's got a lot on her mind. Don't think it was easy for her to leave her husband."

"Does she really love him?" Shannon squinted.

"In her own way she does, but he's gotta uphold his end of the bargain. A marriage can't be one-sided. The same for a family. If your father dared to dictate our marriage and tell me how to raise my children, I woulda been packing you kids up and bolting."

"I don't blame her. She never wanted Séamus to go to boarding school. I think it really hurt her. I know it bothered him. In a way, he was glad to go because it meant he wouldn't have to put up with his father, but it also bothered him because he couldn't see his mother every day."

"I'll see what she has to say. She needs a friend, and I'm glad to give her a hand while I'm in the city." Mom stood. "A friend who won't judge her or tell other friends, if you get my drift."

Shannon understood. If Mrs. Daugherty dared to confess her feelings to her so-called acquaintances in her social circle, tongues would have wagged.

"I'm off." Mom grinned and scooted inside.

Just then the sliding door reopened. Séamus stepped outside casually dressed in khakis and a polo shirt.

"And what do you have planned for this Saturday morning?"

"I'm thinking that I should slip on my hat and start driving on Monday. I can't let Pashney and Ronnie do all the work." Shannon beamed up at her husband

"There's no rush. Your friends are handling everything just fine." Séamus sat in the chair Mom had previously occupied.

"Do you know our mothers are going out together?"

Séamus nodded. "I met your dad. He's on his way out, too. That means we have the suite to ourselves . . . finally." He quirked a brow and bared his dimples in a devilish way.

Shannon took his hand and led him back inside. "I've yet to shower. How does a bath sound?"

"Tempting. Very tempting. Considering I've just dressed, I think I can be persuaded to wash again." Seduction cloaked his coy reply.

She laced her fingers with his and drew him to their en suite in the master bedroom. He kept grinning, even as she shut the door. "I think you can wait a few before you wash my back."

"Oh? What did you have in mind?" He arched his brow.

She slid down the zipper on his pants and slipped her hand inside to a nest of warmth. His cock thickened and hardened in her palm. A drop of precum dampened her knuckle.

He kept smiling as she moved to her knees, kissing the head of his erection that was smooth and full of heat. His fingers glided through her hair she'd yet to wash.

"Is this what love is? Doing it when you're still icky?" She pecked the tip again.

"Hmm . . . it doesn't matter to me what you look like, Shan. You're always beautiful to me." He stroked her face with his finger.

Her clit throbbed, yearning for his touch as she drew him into her mouth. He thrust, giving her his full length. She slid her lips back and forth along his erection, his taste always clean and enticing, daring her to swallow every inch of him.

She kept sucking on his cock. The *oohs* and *aahs* easily escaped from her mouth as he groaned and pumped. God, she loved how he fucked, whether he was screwing her pussy or screwing her lips. His length and girth was deep in her, covered in saliva and hot to her swirling tongue.

"Oh geez." He gasped.

Her panties were demanding to be ripped from her. The wetness of her pussy toyed with her clit. She feasted on his erection until his gasps intensified. From his deep thrusts, she was learning after many times in the bedroom, he was close to coming.

When his jizz spilled into her mouth, she was ready to have him explore her with his tongue.

CHAPTER TWENTY-NINE: GET IN THE CAR

"What did your mother want, exactly?" Shannon sat at the vanity, applying the last of her makeup.

"She said to meet her at her hotel. Nothing more." Séamus wasn't sure what Mom had planned. At the manor, she'd never allowed anyone to invade her personal space, and the hotel room was Mom's new personal domain.

A week had passed after they'd dropped off Shannon's parents at the airport. The business was full steam ahead, his wife enjoying being tucked behind the driver's seat of the original car they'd bought, while Pashney and Ronnie drove the other two.

He couldn't believe they had three cars in their fleet already. Part of him wished to jump in the air and high-five someone. Too bad Ellen had groomed him to keep his feelings in check. Instead, he leaned in and pecked his wife's cheek.

"Someone is happy." Shannon's gaze sparkled in the mirror.

"Very happy." He settled his chin on her delicate shoulder. "Mmm . . . I think it's time I took a break from all these meetings, phone calls, and networking. We can't stay here forever. I say I speak to the realtor and begin searching for our new home."

"Home?" She set aside a fluffy makeup brush.

"Yes. A condo to start. We won't require a home until the children arrive." He couldn't resist brushing his cheek against hers. Hopefully she wouldn't become agitated and chastise him for smudging her blush.

"Children." She swiveled on the cushioned stool to face him. "I guess we haven't really spoken about when we plan on starting a family."

"It's up to you. A gentleman always lets the lady decide." His words were cooing.

Warmth filled her belly. "I'd like for us to spend the year getting to know each other better." She couldn't resist running her short nail along his cheek.

"Then that is what we shall do." He straightened and extended his hand. "Come. I'm sure Mom is waiting."

He led them from the suite and into the idling limo. Naturally, it was one of their limos, and Ronnie sat behind the wheel.

While Ronnie and Shannon talked, Séamus couldn't help admiring the plush confines of the car's interior, rich enough to impress any wealthy client. A pull-down business console to accommodate a tablet, laptop, and cell phone. Comfortable seats of leather with cooling and heating built in at the touch of a fingertip. The same for the automatic climate control buttons if a client preferred a different temperature from the front of the car. A storage spot for newspapers and other reading material. Even more impressive was the rear entertainment system available for perusing the TV or listening to music.

Too soon they arrived a block over from where Mom was staying.

"What time would you like me to retrieve you, Mr. and Mrs. Daugherty?" Jesting was in Ronnie's question as she gazed at them in the rearview mirror.

"We'll call," Shannon said. "Stay where you are. I don't need you opening the door." She stepped from the car.

Séamus got out and offered his wife his arm.

The night was warm, and Shannon didn't require a shawl.

But he'd offer his jacket after they departed if she became cold.

He steered them into the hotel toward the elevators. The bellboy had to assist them with accessing the floor of executive suites, since guests required a special card to enter.

When they reached their intended floor, they walked out to rich carpet and cherry wainscotting. The lighting gave a soft glow to Shannon's exposed bronzed arms that piqued his curiosity, releasing any tension in Séamus' shoulders.

"I'm starving. I shouldn't have skipped lunch today. I hope your mother doesn't mind me eating everything in sight." Shannon chuckled.

"There's nothing wrong with a healthy appetite." Séamus stopped in front of the room number Mom had given him. He knocked.

Seconds later the door opened. Mom was outfitted in a red dress that complemented her brunette coloring. Hesitation filled her gaze, and she opened the door wider. "I never wanted to surprise you, but if I informed you ahead of time, I wasn't sure you'd come."

Séamus glanced at Shannon. What a strange thing to say. "Why wouldn't I?" As he eased past Mom, he stopped cold.

Shannon gasped. Her short nails dug into the sleeve of his jacket.

Father rose off the sofa in the sitting room.

Séamus' arms fell to his sides, his spine stiffening. He whipped his attention to Mom. What the heck was going on? She'd never betray him. Not in a million years. He'd hear her out, since the pleading in her eyes begged for understanding.

Mom clasped her hands together. "Please. Have a seat." She motioned at the two chairs opposite the sofa.

Spine still stiff, Séamus put his foot forward, but Shannon didn't budge. He squeezed her fingers and ushered her toward the two leather chairs.

A tray with a teapot, four cups, and saucers was on hand. Since he'd guided Shannon to their spot as if she was a robot, he kept a hold of her hand and led them into a sitting position.

He wasn't sure if she was intimidated by Father's presence or outraged, but he opted for intimidated, because her palm had grown moist. Perhaps she expected Father to triumphantly declare he'd blacklisted their business. Séamus didn't believe that. If Father had, they wouldn't be in Mom's room, because she would've tossed him off the balcony. However, Shannon didn't know that.

"You look most stunned by my presence." Father held a tumbler of, no doubt, the finest scotch.

"When Mom asked me here, I can admit I didn't expect to see you." Séamus glanced at his mother.

Mom clicked her nails against the other. Missing was the colored paint, and she'd resumed a French manicure. She sat on the edge of the sofa beside Father. When she set her hand on his knee, a good helping of shock whacked Séamus upside the head.

"I know I should have informed you in advance of your father's presence, but I was unsure if you'd come." Red spread across Mom's flawless skin. She peeked at Shannon, who stared straight ahead, mouth slightly open.

"If this is about the business—" Séamus kept squeezing Shannon's fingers.

Mom held up her hand and shook her head. "No."

"I see." Automatically, Séamus' foot moved in a circular motion. "Then what are we conferring about?" He couldn't help the coolness in his tone.

"It's about your inheritance. Your father is reinstating it."

Mom's words were so soft, Séamus had to lean in to hear. Her gentle announcement was a punch to his gut.

A soft sort of strangled cry came from Shannon.

"Reinstating it?" He quickly shifted his focus on Father.

"Why?"

"This past week, your mother and I reconciled our differences." Father cleared his throat. "It's not her wish to continue with this estrangement . . . from all parties involved."

"I did not start the fire." Séamus couldn't help the accusation in his reply.

"No, you didn't." Father set aside the tumbler and moved forward to Mom's position. "I did. We had a small family meeting the other night."

"Family meeting?" Séamus stopped moving his foot. "And I wasn't asked to join? Oh wait, I'm not family."

"You are very much family." Regret, something Séamus had never heard before, filled Father's tired voice. "It was I who . . ." He patted Mom's hand that remained on his thigh. "It was I who sparked this . . . estrangement. An estrangement that has never occurred in our family before . . ."

If he prattled on about tradition or Great-great-great Grandfather, Séamus was up and out of here.

"But we are our own family, aren't we?" Father glanced to Mom. "Understand, your mother means everything to me."

Séamus couldn't help his mouth falling open. From his peripheral vision, he caught Shannon doing the same thing. Father was about to confess he was wrong? Seriously?

"Sometimes it can be hard to undo over a century of — "

"I know what you mean, Mr. Daugherty," Shannon interrupted. Understanding filled her words.

Father squinted and shifted his gaze to Shannon. "Please, call me Padraig. You are my daughter-in-law, after all."

Séamus almost coughed. Courtney had to address him as Father Daugherty. There were changes happening in the family.

Shannon gazed at Father. "Maybe we, or should I say *I*, should have been more understanding, since my own people faced, and are still facing, the same issue. I'm aware of the

267

prejudices the Irish suffered when they first came over and how it never stopped until sometime in the early twentieth century. Correct me if I'm wrong. I'm more than aware what motivated the man who started Daugherty Enterprises and why he was insistent on keeping tradition."

If Séamus received any more surprises, he'd fall off his chair. He couldn't believe the words coming from his wife's mouth that were slowly melting the ice around his heart. Years of resentment against the man sitting across from him was running off his suit like water on a rock.

"At my reserve, we call it healing," Shannon continued. "Healing against the injustices done to us as a People."

Father nodded, lips pursed, and he actually kept listening, of all things.

"Life isn't easy on the reserve. My mom and kokum felt it more than I did, since Kokum went to the residential school and my mom was directly affected by that. So they pushed me to get off the reserve and make something of myself. I can see why you wanted the same thing for Séamus. Tradition is hard to break. It really is. It gets in your bones and stays there. But there are good traditions, too."

Her last statement drew Father's lips a smidgen upward.

"I knew my son had chosen wisely when I first met you," Father replied. "He chose the same way I did." He glanced at Mom. "She let me get away with too much for many years, but don't think our relationship is one-sided. Unbeknownst to my children, she had her fair say many times, however, I was too stubborn to listen."

Séamus cleared his throat. "I thought Grandfather Daugherty arranged the marriage?"

"He arranged the marriage based on who I chose." Father again glanced at Mom. "I was fortunate she met the *former* traditional requirements."

"Former?" Séamus dropped his hand from Shannon's.

"Yes, former. As a family, we get to vote on which ones to keep and which ones to expunge." Father's gaze again drifted to Shannon. "As for your new business . . . congratulations. I know it will be successful under your management."

His gaze then drifted back to Séamus. "Your position remains open. And I know your wife wishes to continue achieving her goal."

"You mean the business remains hers?" Unbelievable.

Father nodded. "It's up to Shannon whether she wishes for her business to fall under the umbrella of Daugherty Enterprises." He pursed his lips. "Understand, startup costs and overhead can cut deeply into the profits of a new business venture. And my son is an excellent marketer . . . But that is up to you. The two of you."

Well, Father was right about the overhead of a new business and the startup, but what they'd developed together was Shannon's dream, so she'd have the final say on deciding whether to operate as a separate entity or part of Daughter Enterprises.

"How does Cillian feel?" No doubt big brother was livid about the changes after being a dutiful son.

"We talked. He's aware of what's transpiring," Father reassured Séamus.

"But does he approve?"

"You know how your brother is. It will take time, but rest assured, he will come around."

"He already is. We had tea this afternoon." Mom lifted her palm from Father's knee. "Never mind any issues Cillian has. Those are his to deal with, but trust me, he has missed you."

Séamus' heart warmed. He could admit he had also missed his brother, although they weren't close, but maybe they now had a chance to share more than blood. "I'll give him a ring and see if he wishes to meet at the club over tea and scones."

"I think he'd like that." The same warmth in Séamus' heart

was reflected in Mom's eyes. She leaned in and poured tea into the first cup. "I must say your understanding is a big relief. I wasn't sure what to expect when you arrived."

"Whatever do you mean?" Séamus took the cup from her outstretched hand and passed it on to Shannon.

Mom finished pouring the second cup and offered it up to Séamus. "You could've easily turned and left."

Séamus took the cup. That'd be the day he'd hurt his own mother. "You surprise me. Ellen would've hunted me down and boxed my ears if I'd ever walked out on my own mother."

"True." Mom placed the cup and saucer on her lap. "But I'd want you to stay of your own accord, not out of obligation."

"I did stay of my own accord."

"Thank you." The tension on Mom's face relaxed.

"When are you checking out?" Séamus glanced around the modern decorated suite of light green finishings and hardwood floors.

"We're going to stay one more night." Mom's skin continued to glow.

It was strange witnessing an aura of positive energy radiating from her instead of the customary quiet resignation.

Séamus wasn't about to ask Father when he'd started visiting Mom here. Their marriage was their business, not his. "Then I guess Shannon and I have a lot to discuss when we leave. We'll be sure to inform you of our decisions. How does breakfast sound? Tomorrow you'll be checking out. Perhaps we can stop by the house the following morning."

"Excellent. We await your decision." Father rested his hand over Mom's that was on her lap.

Séamus couldn't help the breath leaving his throat at the love shimmering between his parents, something he'd always yearned for, hoped for, and now it was happening. He took Shannon's hand. It was time to leave and talk to his wife.

Chapter Thirty: Carefree Highway

"What do you think?" Séamus propped himself on his elbow. The sheet slid away, revealing his tight abs and hard pecs.

His flexing muscles were an invitation for Shannon to trace with her nail, and she did, drawing a line down the center of his stomach. "I think your parents made a great proposition."

"You think so?" He quirked his brow. The familiar *droll* was back, something she adored.

"I'll admit they shocked the hell out of me." She giggled and cuddled in closer, stealing his pillow that smelled of his rich, sexy scent. "Not in a million years did I see that coming."

"And why so?" His teasing was warm breaths on the top of her head.

"You know why. You made out your father to be a tyrant."

"He is. Well, he was." He remained propped on his elbow, looking down at her through his black lashes. "I guess we'll have to wait and see."

"You don't trust him?" Shannon couldn't help her frown.

"I trust my mother, and if she believes he's sincere in changing a few of the traditions in the family, then I believe her. She wouldn't have reconciled with him if she had doubts. Remember, she's been married to him for over three decades. She knows him better than anyone else."

"You're right. Maybe in time I will know you the best, too." Shannon couldn't help joking.

"You know my body the best." His smile was warmer than the sun, and he impishly wiggled his nose.

"Maybe not. I think Ellen has me beat." Shannon couldn't resist joking. "She did bathe you and change your diapers."

"Oh my." He chortled. "That hardly counts. I was a mere infant." He reached out and brushed her hair. "Now, as much as I'm enjoying trading quips with you, we have a conversation to finish."

"Mmm . . . we do." She gazed up at him staring down at her. "I'd like to keep the business separate for now."

He nodded. "Not a problem."

She resumed tracing the lines of tight muscles on his abs. "And I do enjoy having our own place, even if it's a hotel."

"We can begin looking for a condo."

Goodness, he was so agreeable. "But I do think we should stay at your parents' place until we start a family. I know this would make your mom and dad happy. And it's only fair to do some giving. How do you feel?"

"As I said, whatever makes you happy." He kept smiling his warm smile that was as cozy as a cup of hot cocoa.

"Stop it." Her fingers connected with the hard muscles of his pecs. "You're making me feel like I'm all take and no give."

"But you have given. You've given very much." He pecked the top of her head. "You took a huge leap of faith by marrying me. You put your dream on the line for me. I would say that's more give than take."

He scuttled down under the blankets. "I will ask for one thing. My pillow."

Shannon laughed and sat up. He laid his head on the pillow and motioned for her to join him, and she cuddled in the pit of his arm. His fingers rested on her shoulder. He rubbed her bare skin. The warmth his caressing generated left her feeling as if she was being wrapped in a big warm blanket on a cold night, even though it was the middle of July and they had on the air-conditioning.

"So, children next year?" His voice was playful.

"Considering we're getting in lots of practice, I'd say next year sounds good. We can start trying then."

"And I'm confident you're ready to run our business. I'll still be on hand with marketing, but I also have another job."

"Director of Marketing for Daugherty Enterprises?" Shannon tilted her head slightly to gauge his reaction.

"Yes. I can admit I missed my job. But I will also add I enjoyed getting our business up and running. However, I am more than confident you, Pashney, and Ronnie will do a fabulous job."

"Is that it?" She continued to draw lines on his hard abs. "Is our serious discussion over?"

"Hmm . . . one more item on the agenda."

"The agenda." She giggled and ran her toe up and down his calf. "Always in business mode."

"Hardly." He chuckled. "Where would you like to live once we do move out of Daugherty Manor? The Bridle Path?"

"It is a nice area, and it'd be a great place to raise our children."

"They'll also enjoy their lake home at your reserve."

"A lake home?" She scrambled and sat up. "On the rez? We're going to do it?"

"Yes. Your grandfather said it'd have to be in your name. I was thinking a timber frame to go with the rugged style of the area. It'd be perfect."

"I'd love that. It'd be great for weekend getaways." She slipped back under the sheets and snuggled up against him.

Never in her wildest dreams had she imagined being the owner of two homes, let alone living on The Bridle Path when she'd first arrived in Toronto to chase a dream. Even crazier, she'd never expected to fall in love with her client. Or have him fall in love with her.

In a way, she should thank Séamus' father. If not for

Padraig, Séamus never would've propositioned her with an irresistible offer too tempting to decline.

It was easy to fall asleep in her husband's arms, knowing in the morning they'd be starting the first day of a dream come true.

You may also enjoy the following from eXtasy Books Inc:

REDEEMED
Maggie Blackbird
April 19, 2019

An eXtasy Books Editor's Choice Award.

A single woman battles to keep her foster child from his newly-paroled father — a dangerous man she used to love.

Bridget Matawapit is an Indigenous activist, daughter of a Catholic deacon, and foster mother to Kyle, the son of an Ojibway father — the ex-fiancé she kicked to the curb after he chose alcohol over her love. With Adam out on parole and back in Thunder Bay, she is determined to stop him from obtaining custody of Kyle.

Adam Guimond is a recovering alcoholic and ex-gang-banger newly-paroled. Through counseling, reconnecting with his Ojibway culture and twelve-step meetings while in prison, Adam now understands he's worthy of the love that frightened him enough to pick up the bottle he'd previously corked. He can't escape the damage he caused so many others, but he longs to rise like a true warrior in the pursuit of forgiveness and a second chance. There's nothing he isn't willing to do to win back his son–and Bridget.

When an old cell mate's daughter dies under mysterious circumstances in foster care, Adam begs Bridget to help him uncover the truth. Bound to the plight of the Indigenous children in care, Bridget agrees. But putting herself in contact with Adam threatens to resurrect her long-buried feelings for him, and even worse, she risks losing care of Kyle, by falling for a man who might destroy her faith in love completely this time.

Excerpt

When the truck pulled up at the halfway house, Adam's disgust threatened to spill over. No woman could slam on the brakes like Bridget. He threw off his seat belt. "I didn't mean to make you pissed."

"I'm not pissed." She stared straight ahead.

Adam cracked open the door. She was going to let him go? Damn her. Promising himself to use patience was a stupid idea. The woman was stubborn enough to wait out the next coming of Jesus.

The twelve-step program, the anger management classes, his one-on-one counseling all screamed at him to leave his desires in the hands of his higher power. Yeah right. Creator had forgotten He'd shaped and breathed life into a woman a pack of mules couldn't push.

Welp, he could be stubborn, too. Adam shut the door.

Bridget almost jumped in her seat. "What're you doing? I told you I have things to do."

"Cut it. It's only eight-thirty. You're going home to pout." Adam folded his arms and sat back.

"P-p-pout?"

Any second his beloved *kwe's* internal volcano should erupt. Time for the countdown. *Ten, nine, eight, seven, six, five . . .*

"Listen here. Don't you dare assume anything about me. Got it?" Bridget swiveled to face him, steam almost exploding from her flared nostrils and flaming-red ears.

"Got it." Keeping his cool was easier than expected. Maybe because Bridget's temper never unsettled Adam. Her spunk was the lighter to his wood. Any kind of wood. A certain kind of wood in his pants.

He shifted as much as he could in the seat. And these were big, comfy seats. He met Bridget's glittering eyes.

"*Kwe*, you've been pissed since you first looked at me. Let loose. I'm serious. Tell me what you really think of me." If cussing him out cleared the fog thickening between them, Adam could hack a slap or two.

Bridget's red lips flattened. "I have nothing to say because we have nothing between us but Kyle. That's it."

Adam's own temper grumbled at the back of his neck. His skin burned. This woman's words always cut a man's balls in half. No con in the pen knocked the wind from him like Bridget Maria Matawapit. He had one up on her, though. She'd never taken an anger management class or earned praises from the instructor.

This might secure him a smack or something else, but at least he'd know the score. "*Kwe*, did I ever tell you how beautiful you are when you're pissed?"

The flash in Bridget's eyes died. The flatness of her lips faded. The fiery red shade coating her ears ebbed. Her mouth formed into a delicate O. Fire flickered behind her dark irises.

Adam's heart rattled. He lifted his hand and ran his index finger across her narrow jawline.

The smoothness of her skin softened the rough edge of his fingertip. When Bridget's gaze continued to hold his, she locked Adam in a moment he'd dreamed about behind bars with nothing but his beloved *kwe*'s picture to keep him company.

The tight bones of Bridget's jawline diminished beneath his touch. She kept staring. Adam's heart kept rattling. He leaned in and brushed his lips against hers. As soon as his mouth met Bridget's, her yielding lips released an ache in his chest. An ache he'd carried for almost four years. He moved his mouth into a light pucker. Bridget's kiss matched his sweet movements, and his heart swelled.

Her scent invaded him. The familiar feminine fragrance

teased his muscles, stroked his skin, caressed his flesh. Her deep breaths fluttered against his ears. Their mouths moved in the same slow rhythm, a waltz of sensual heat full of longing and wanting.

His tongue yearned to taste her, claim her as his own again. He forced himself to draw back a breath from her. "*Kwe*," he whispered.

A puff of air from her lips skimmed Adam's skin. Bridget's smooth lids fluttered, along with her rich, thick lashes.

"I gotta go." Her voice was as drowsy as her eyes. Then her dreamy stare hardened. "I gotta go." This time her declaration matched the tension sharpening her jawline.

She shifted and stared straight ahead, delicate hands braced on the steering wheel.

Adam had given Bridget something to think about, and that was what he'd intended to do from the start. That was enough for him. "Goodnight, *kwe*."

Bridget kept staring straight ahead.

He slipped from the truck. With the passenger door barely closed, she drove off.

Adam slid the cigarettes from his shirt pocket and stuck one between his lips. He dug around in his pocket and withdrew the lighter.

Her delicate scent and the lushness of Bridget's lips continued to pound through his veins. He'd set out to unearth if she still possessed feelings for him, and she did.

Sleep wouldn't come easy tonight. Nope. Not at all. Her kiss had given him too much hope.

ABOUT THE AUTHOR

An Ojibway from Northwestern Ontario, Maggie resides in the country with her husband and their fur babies, two beautiful Alaskan Malamutes. When she's not writing, she can be found pulling weeds in the flower beds, mowing the huge lawn, walking the Mals deep in the bush, teeing up a ball at the golf course, fishing in the boat for walleye, or sitting on the deck at her sister's house, making more wonderful memories with the people she loves most.

Web Site: https://maggieblackbird.com/

Facebook Page: https://www.facebook.com/maggieblackbirdauthor/

Twitter: https://twitter.com/BlackbirdMaggie/

Goodreads: https://www.goodreads.com/maggieblackbird

BookbBub: https://www.bookbub.com/profile/maggieblackbird

Linked In: https://www.linkedin.com/in/maggie-blackbird-032798169/

Instagram: https://www.instagram.com/maggieblackbirdauthor/

Newsletter Sign-Up: eepurl.com/gJu2VL